A note from the original edition

*

This is a thoughtful and compassionate novel, set in a Glasgow working-class tenement. For a first book it shows a most remarkable degree not only of creative talent but of sheer technical skill. Its success, however, by no means depends on the usual sensationalism identified in literature with life in the slums. David Heylyn is the youngest of three motherless boys, and in the adventures and violence of his boyhood we see the origins of his later loves and hates. With an irresponsible, Micawberish gambler as a father, the brothers run the house in their own way, and David grows up with a deep affection for one of them and a blind hatred of the other. He is influenced by Mrs Ruthven, a midwife in the tenements, from whom he learns his first lesson in tolerance, and he becomes the confidant of her attractive daughter, who is only a few years older than himself and who in due course runs away to London with a married man. The brother he loves also goes to London, hoping to win fame and fortune as a camera-artist. The brother he hates comes back into his life after a long absence overseas. The change in the brothers' attitude to one another, and the rise and fall of David's esteem for Mary Ruthven, all have their place in his painful self-education.

D1323787

The Bank of Time

George Friel

Introduced by Gordon Jarvie

Polygon
EDINBURGH

First published by Hutchinson in 1959

This edition published by
Polygon
22 George Square
Edinburgh

Set in Perpetua by ROM-Data Corporation Ltd, Falmouth, Cornwall, and
printed and bound in Great Britain by
Short Run Press Ltd, Exeter

British Library Cataloguing in Publication Data

Friel, George, 1910–75
The Bank of Time
I.   Title
823.914 [F]

ISBN 0 7486 6153 0

The Publisher acknowledges subsidy from the Scottish Arts Council
towards the publication of this volume.

Contents

This novel plots the painful self-education of a young man. That theme is such a fictional stock-in-trade as to have given its name to a whole sub-genre: *Bildungsroman*. But in spite of the rather 'standard' theme of the book, *The Bank of Time* is an unusual novel in a number of ways. First, the social background is unusual. So many *Bildungsroman* heroes go to Oxford, or run away to London, or emigrate to America, and get a rather exotic education along the way. Publishers – many of whom seem to have done that sort of thing themselves – are used to that kind of storyline. But the protagonist of this novel grows up in a very unexotic, motherless, financially-impoverished and cultur-ally-deprived Glasgow tenement, and is still there at the end of the book. Superficially then, *The Bank of Time* is an unusual novel because of its setting, even if on the deeper or mythic level, it is handling several of the most basic of fictional archetypes, and is asking the reader to empathise with a young man who loses an eye (or half his 'vision'?), and to follow the processes of his domestic estrangement – the struggle of the son against the father. And in spite of the book's 'unpromising' setting, we watch enthralled and with sympathy as the hero develops and educates himself against all the odds, '. . . a provincial trying to acquire a shareholder's interest in English literature', as he puts it.

The (more or less) law-abiding north Glasgow tenements as opposed to the more sensational, gangland battlegrounds of the Gorbals – and of *No Mean City* – are a setting George Friel made peculiarly his own, and readers of his novels and short stories will be familiar with the landmarks of this environment: the backcourts, the ubiquitous neighbours, the Forth and Clyde canalbank and 'the oozing canal bridge', the Maryhill road (in which Friel himself grew up) – with its rows of little 'shops whose owners lived in better houses in another district', the new flats going up beyond, the papermill at Dawsholm, and the Botanic Gardens and Kelvingrove where this novel so memorably opens – 'a hunting ground . . . on the banks of the Kelvin' where the young protagonist and his gang 'roamed in timeless freedom'.

So much for the book's locus, very specific and beautifully realised: the working-class north side of Glasgow. The period in which *The Bank of Time* (first published in 1959) is set is slightly vaguer. The continuum of its genesis is probably the 1940s and 1950s, but there are no specific references in the book to actual historical events or circumstances to help us place the text more exactly. Adapting the book's title, we could perhaps say that the novel is set in that bank of time stretching from the mid-1940s (and a 10-year-old hero) to the late 1950s (and a 25-year-old hero).

Historical dates are less important to a proper appreciation of this novel. The key concerns of a good *Bildungsroman* far transcend the banks of mere historical time, and the problems of a serious young man of integrity growing up on his own are always and forever very much the same. David Heylyn, the protagonist, lived 'on books from the public library', we are told; he 'looked for company in books', and was a clear seeker after truth ('I tried to read books on ethics. I don't know why. I think I wanted to know how you distinguished right from wrong . . .'). From his early childhood, we see in David Heylyn 'the conflict of self-preservation and of duty', in the matter of the gangs in the park. Not for David the easy option, the course his two brothers would instinctively have taken. David is too morally honest, too straight for that course, and he is variously described as too much of a puritan, morose, sullen, straightlaced and uncivilised. But although he is fierce and uncompromising, and indeed given to physical combat in his youth, David Heylyn is a far cry from the stereotyped working-class Glasgow fictive hard man. This is not a Glasgow novel, whatever that may be; it is a universal and timeless novel that happens to have a Glasgow location.

A rather obvious feature of the book's universalism is the hero's name. As one of the characters says: 'Heylyn? That's an unusual name in these parts.' Quite so. What are readers to make of this name? Among other things, we probably have to note that it is a name totally without

2

sectarian overtones in this most tribal of cities. We cannot say if the Heylyns are Catholics or Protestants, because the novel doesn't examine such trivia. Not perhaps a ploy to endear the book to professional Glaswegians!

So much in *The Bank of Time* rings true because so much was based on the author's own experience of life. George Friel too grew up in the Maryhill road, fell out with his father and his brothers, and fought with the children in the street. He too managed – against the odds, and without paternal support – to stay on at school and educate himself. Of course, he went further than that later on, for he went to university and became a teacher among the self-same children he himself had played and rioted with. He never lost touch with his roots. But to say all this is not to say that *The Bank of Time* is an autobiographical novel. That would miss the point of the book. However, because of George Friel's deep understanding of his subject, because he is writing about the world he too grew up in, and because of the emotional sincerity and honesty of his writing, readers today will identify with the character of David Heylyn and find themselves drawn into a story which has dated remarkably little.

Readers interested in seeking out the 'sources' of *The Bank of Time* are advised to read Friel's 'Plottel' short stories, published in various small magazines in the 1930s and recently reissued in *A Friend of Humanity: Selected Short Stories of George Friel* (Polygon, 1992). All the key elements of the novel – the strangely un-Glaswegian surname, the quarrelsome brothers, the fecklessly inadequate father, the poverty and the tenements – were first presented to the world in these stories. The one significant difference was that the Plottel show was kept on the road by the single-handed sleight of hand of a larger-than-life mother, while the Heylyns were motherless. But in Anna Garshin and her mother, in Friel's very first published short story 'You Can See It For Yourself' (1934), we meet a clear precursor of Mary Ruthven and her mother in *The Bank of Time* a quarter of a century later.

And if the world of the Plottel tribe provides a fictive source for the Heylyn family, young David Heylyn is in turn an obvious forerunner of Percy Phinn, the hero with poetic ambitions in Friel's next published novel, *The Boy Who Wanted Peace* (1964).

If literature is social criticism, as critics like Roger Fowler would have it, the early fictions of George Friel offer a particularly fascinating social commentary. A fiction of working-class Glasgow, but without any production-line gangsters and headline-grabbing razor kings; a fiction in which the very Scottish preoccupations of self-improvement and self-education are central, yet without a shred of tartanry; here is no pander to the latter-day urban kailyard of a Jack House or Cliff Hanley; no orthodox Red Clydesider; no card-carrying nationalist; no laconic, bad-mouthing giro novel. Friel is not *like* any other Scottish writer, and fits no handy compartment. Yet he seems as quintessentially a Scottish writer, as much the product of his time and his Glasgow environment, as Neil Gunn was of the Highlands.

And as a bonus, there is the author's linguistic freshness, touching at times on the epigrammatic, which is a constant delight from the very beginning of this book – the *lonely* pavements, and the *tired* trams after their long *calvinist* journey from the other side of the city. Or this: 'Nobody loves his birthplace so much as a Scotsman or leaves it with such eagerness'; or 'Would any woman get married if she thought of the future?' or 'Women always say they never will and they always do'. There is quite a lot of this kind of writing to savour and winkle out from *The Bank of Time*, for it is the work of a linguistic craftsman, and that is probably the main reason why the book reads so well today. Ezra Pound said, 'Poetry is news that stays news.' One realises the truth of such an observation when reading a book like *The Bank of Time* some thirty years after its first publication: it is surely because the vision of its author was so essentially poetic that its news is still news.

George Friel bibliography

The Bank of Time (Hutchinson 1959, Polygon 1994)
The Boy Who Wanted Peace (Calder and Boyars 1964, Pan 1972, Polygon 1985)
Grace and Miss Partridge (Calder and Boyars 1969)
Mr Alfred, MA (Calder and Boyars 1972, Canongate 1987)

An Empty House (Calder and Boyars 1975)
A Friend of Humanity: Selected Short Stories (Polygon 1992)

Gordon Jarvie
EDINBURGH 1994

1

The Names of the Children

WHEN the moon came out in the gloaming it was time to go upstairs. The tall arc-lamp at the corner, rearing itself above the grocer's shop, blinked for a few moments and then looked brightly down on the lonely pavements, where the refuse of a summer's day that was dead littered the dry gutter. The trams came at longer intervals, crawling past the stop as if they were tired after their long calvinist journey from the other side of the city, swayed between the Barracks and the Stinkie Burn, clanged under the oozing canal bridge, and lurched into the depot at the end of the main road.

The Heylyn brothers, three quarrelsome urchins, ruled the back-court and the street outside, and went gloomily upstairs to the dark house when the rest of the herd were called home by parents who still exercised an erratic control. The interference of a bawling mother or a grim laconic father annoyed the Heylyns. They would gladly have protracted the evening's exploits to midnight. Under no authority themselves, since their father didn't come sauntering home till after one in the morning and their mother was dead, they were impatient of authority elsewhere.

Gregan, a weak reed of a boy, was genteely summoned to prayers and bed by the knocking of a toothbrush handle against the window-pane, for his widowed shrivelled mother thought it vulgar to raise the sash and shout to him. No such decorum restrained Mrs Hogg, a buxom dame who disliked the Heylyns only as much as they disliked her. Her sons William and Andrew were sly children, court-jesters and cynics. Sometimes they challenged the Heylyns, but Mark terrorized them by his bragging and his bunched fists. They lacked the ruthlessness to start a civil war and they became content to provide the comic relief for the gang, supplying outlandish oaths, fantastic curses, and ludicrous anecdotes of fornication. To their mother they were still babes, who she feared would be corrupted by the Heylyns, and she still addressed Andrew by the love-name of Bunty, given him when he was still in his pram.

'Bunty!' she bawled when the lamps were lit. 'Come up, you! If the Heylyns haven't a home to go to doesn't mean you haven't.'

Mark, Paul, and David Heylyn looked sullenly up at her, the gesture of their game arrested in a mute malevolence.

The tenement where the Heylyns lived wasn't a slum, though because of the vandalism of the large number of children there it was steadily deteriorating. It was a three-storeyed block with six 'closes', each close leading to an enclosed stairway with three tenants on each landing. The ground floor of the tenement was occupied by shops, whose owners lived in better houses in another district, and behind the tenement, at the rear of the closes, were the playing-grounds for the children – the back-courts. Originally each back-court was separated from its neighbours by a line of palings, and the children were as punctilious as coastguards about admitting strangers. But the Heylyns pulled down the wooden stakes between the two back-courts at their end of the block and ruled a united territory there. The other four back-courts were separated from them by tall spiked iron railings whose removal was beyond their talent for destruction. Since he couldn't boss the boys on the other side of the railings Mark despised them as lesser breeds without the law and looked elsewhere to expand his empire.

In the summer, when every day seemed to promise an eternal tomorrow, he led his gang across the main road and over the quarry to the banks of the Kelvin to claim a hunting-ground there. The sun melted the tar of the sidestreets under their feet, and when they deployed into the park they broke off branches from the trees, stripped off the bark, and carried them as staves. They wore their shirt-sleeves rolled to the elbow, a belt round the waist of their ragged trousers, and went barefooted. They crossed the bridge to the Botanic Gardens and roamed in timeless freedom under the summer sun. But when they came to the grassy slopes that Mark meant to claim they found a pack of smaller boys already there, scattered across the whole area, shouting and skirmishing in mimic warfare. Mark halted his troop and they fell into fighting formation, Paul on his right, David on his left, and the ruck of their warriors behind them. Mark watched the antics of the strangers for a few moments and then haughtily called a parley.

'This is our pitch,' he said.

'How?' asked the enemy chief, and spat at Mark's feet.

'Because it has always been ours,' said Mark.

'No, it hasn't,' the boy answered swiftly. 'We've been here every day this week.'

'No, you haven't,' said Mark. 'This is the first time we've seen you.'

'We were here yesterday,' the boy retorted, looking with calculating eyes at the forces against him.

Mark moved with an evil suddenness, pushed the speaker in the chest with both hands, knocked him flat on his back, and kicked him on the side.

He rose on one knee and glared up at Mark, his eyes glowing with resentment. His hands clutched the grass beside the path where he had fallen and it seemed as if he would have torn up the earth and hurled it at his conqueror. But he came slowly and silently to his feet and his followers spread out muttering on his flanks. Wheeling round to retreat they went backwards up the path while the Heylyn troopers fanned out and watched them go.

'We'll be back!' they shouted. 'You wait! We'll be back with our whole street!'

Mark stooped nonchalantly, picked up a stone, and sent it skidding along the ground to break before their feet and rise against their ankles.

'Get!' he yelled, the domineering ring that frightened his foes triumphant in his voice.

They retreated in good order, growling threats and oaths. When they disappeared round the bend of the path that descended then in a wide arc to the bridge the Heylyn force relaxed and wandered boisterously over the grassy slope they had conquered. They split into two parties, one to hold the crown of the highest hillock, the other to take it by force or stratagem. They manœuvred till they were tired crawling up and around the hill, exhausted attacking and defending it, and they sprawled panting on the grass. The sky was blue and unclouded, and the heat made them drowsy.

'I'm going for a drink,' said David suddenly.

He jumped to his feet, impelled by an overpowering thirst, and set off for the bridge, making for the fountain on the other side. He ran all the way, delighting in his own barefooted fleetness, his fingers grasping the reins of the swift black horse that carried him. At the left turn to the bridge he smote his right buttock and guided his steed across. His bare toes made little sound on the wooden planks and he supplied the clatter of hooves by exploding the sound rhythmically between his lips. Cantering to a winning finish he drew up at the squat well of cast-iron with the city's coat of arms embossed on it, and bent his sweating face to the spout, ignoring the metal cup that hung from the side of the well by a long clumsy chain.

The cold water washed his parched lips and ran down his chin. He bent lower, putting his mouth right under the spout to get every drop of the heavenly liquid, and some of it trickled down his chest inside his open shirt. When he had drunk his fill he kept the spout running and stood on one foot to waggle the other in the gush of water, washing the dust from between his toes. Looking up casually from his loitering ablutions he saw a ragged horde come down the path from the main gate. They were all armed with sticks and belts, twenty or thirty of them in all, a noisy undisciplined rabble, and behind the grim-faced stalwart leaders he recognized the boys Mark had evicted.

The aim of the expedition was alarmingly clear to him, and in a panic he bent his head to the spout again to hide his face as they passed. They marched on without a glance at him, and he straightened and stared after them with frightened eyes. They went over the bridge and on to the path by which he had come to the well, so barring his return by the same route. For a few moments he stood trembling. The instincts of self-preservation and of duty jostled each other within him. He thought of running away at once, out of the park altogether. No one would ever know he had seen the avengers come in, and his flight would never be known as a desertion. He had gone for a drink, and tired of playing he had gone on home. The simple story leapt fully created from his head, as perfect and wise and fully armoured as Minerva from the head of Jupiter. Who could question it? Who could even think of questioning it? And what else could he do? He could not race ahead of the avengers. Any attempt to outstrip them on the same path would only lead to his discovery and capture, all to no purpose.

But even as his nimble brain decided there was nothing he could do but run away and save his own skin, the contrary instinct of duty insisted on another course without condescending to argue its case. Driven unwittingly by it he hurried to the waterside and scrambled down the bank. Stepping gingerly into the cool water he cut across the stream in a long diagonal that would bring him to the other side at the point where his comrades lay. He paddled on with an encouraging feeling of safety, for when the enemy crossed the bridge they had to follow the path well inland before it came down again to the water's edge, and until then he was hidden from them by the shrubbery and trees on the high slope of the opposite bank before it dropped to the point he aimed to reach.

The water lapped round his ankles, and on the bed of the stream he saw egg-shaped pebbles, as smooth as a bald man's head, and large stones with slimy green stuff growing in the concave dip of their surface. He carefully avoided them in case he slipped and paddled on anxiously. The water came up to his knees, and with each step it came higher up his thighs. Without stopping he rolled his trousers up to his groin and clutched them there, stepping delicately ahead on tip-toe. The water questioned his knuckles inquisitively and he was frightened. He was tempted to turn and go back, before the crossing became any deeper, but he knew the only way to overcome his fear was to go on. The disappointed water fell away from his knuckles, lapped slowly down his thighs, and in another ten paces it was idling below his knees. He had won. His heart pounded violently with victory. Within a yard or so of his goal the water was no higher than his ankles. He stepped on to the gently sloping shelf of the bank and ran wildly towards the grassy slope, yelling at the pitch of his voice.

'Run for it! Run for it! Run, run, run!'

Mark rose from his siesta under a low untidy bush and stepped proudly out to meet him.

'What's the matter with you?' he demanded.

His chest heaving, David panted his warning in broken phrases. The troop flocked round him curiously.

'They're coming back, about fifty of them,' he managed to get out.

They looked to the path by which their foes must come, and seeing nobody visible as far as the brow of the hill they knew they need not wait for battle. There was time to retreat without disgrace. They turned and ran, scattering swiftly, each for himself, and left the park by the gate at the Botanic Gardens, scampering home by devious routes.

2

Mark's ambitions turned again to the boys who played on the other side of the railings and he planned to assert his power there too. His first raid was a failure. He found them far stronger and better united than he expected. They had become a disciplined fighting force under Black Carter, the coalman's son, a fighter with two hands and fewer words, a big fat neck and a broad bottom, an immovable mountain of a boy. Like Mark Heylyn he had completed the union of the back-courts on his side of the railings by pulling down the wooden stakes that separated them, abolishing in one short campaign all the old frontiers and making one unbroken land. More of a business man than Mark, he chopped the palings into little sticks, tied them in bundles, and sold them round the doors for firewood.

With nothing between them but the tall spiked railings the two gangs lived in niggling hostility. The Heylyns had once regarded the railings as the chief obstacle to their expansion, but as the power of Black Carter increased they came to look upon them as their best defence. Negotiations for a peace were started when Mark finally recognized the impossibility of beating Carter in single combat. He accepted without demur the conditions imposed on him by the ruthless son of the coalman. He not only abandoned all his claims to a right of entry to Carter's back-courts by any of the closes, obtaining no concession in return, but to secure an equal withdrawal by Carter of all entry-rights he solemnly promised to surrender a material symbol of power long coveted by the coalman's son.

This was an enormous stone, brought from the quarry in dateless years before the rise of the Heylyns, their most treasured inheritance and the proudest possession of their land. No one knew how many it had taken to carry it from the quarry or how they had managed to bring it so far. Six of them tried to move it once and could hardly raise it an inch from the ground. With a renewed respect for its weight they were content to let it remain where the prehistoric carriers had dumped it, in the furthest corner of the back-court. Moss grew in patches on its surface, and because of the length of time it had lain undisturbed it seemed embedded in the soil. As much for its size, weight, and antiquity it was valued for its shape. It resembled a throne, low-seated and low-backed but still unmistakably a throne. And this was the sacred monolith that Mark had wantonly promised to Carter.

The terms of the treaty caused dismay and discontent when they were known and Mark's position was weakened. David complained violently against the proposal to give up the visible embodiment of their tradition, and Mark derided his sentiment, wheedling the support of Paul, who thought the dispute unimportant since the stone was no use to anybody anyway. The Hoggs cared little for the stone as a symbol or as an object but they challenged Mark's right to dispose of it without their agreement. To silence the general grumbling and vindicate his leadership Mark organized another raid when Black Carter was known to be at the coal-ree. But the attack was a complete failure and instead of gaining prestige he lost the little left him. Angered out of all patience when he heard of the raid Black Carter demanded the immediate surrender of the stone, to be brought to his headquarters by the Heylyn brothers themselves.

He delivered his demand through the iron railings, flanked by his chief captains, his lesser warriors in loose formation behind him. On the other side of the barrier Mark jeered at his foe with fluent taunts and coarse nicknames. Carter remained where he was, quite unimpressed, and briefly repeated his demand for the stone to be brought to him within twenty-four hours. Mark denied he had broken a peace-treaty, denied he had ever made a peace-treaty, and talked himself into denying he had ever promised to give up the stone.

At the third unblushing denial the Carter gang stood motionless in an awed hush, staring at the brazen speaker with superstitious horror, as if they expected to see him drop dead before their eyes or shrivel suddenly in a bolt of fire or be whisked away by fiends from hell for so bold a lie. Nothing happened, except that a rain-cloud travelled across the sun for a few moments and the back-court was no longer bright and warm in the summer sunshine but over-shadowed and strangely chilled.

'Right!' said Carter abruptly and walked away without another word.

'If you want it, come and get it!' Mark shouted after him, though whether he meant it as an invitation or as a challenge was never known. Under either interpretation the remark was equally unnecessary. Carter needed neither invitation nor challenge. His intention was clear, written as clearly on his face as ever it could have been on paper. It was war.

There was silence for twenty-four hours, and after an unclouded afternoon the evening crawled serenely past tea-time and stretched itself lazily under a benevolent sky. The Heylyns and their troops stood to their posts, waiting for an attack they hoped would never come. Mark stationed himself in the close, a Scout's pole in his hand, and condescended to explain his plan of defence. If the enemy overcame his outer ring and broke into the close they would lose their freedom of movement there. He would then mow them down one by one, single-handed, as they filed into the bottle-neck. Paul made no comment, but circled round and round restlessly, never quite at his post and never quite away from it. David thought the plan was worthless and he criticized it angrily, but he had no other to put in its place and he was hampered by an unspoken fear that their position was in the last resort indefensible.

'We should go out and attack them,' he said sullenly, 'instead of sitting here waiting for them to come and attack us.'

'You haven't enough men to attack them,' Mark explained with supercilious patience.

'If we haven't enough for attack we haven't enough for defence,' David muttered.

'That shows how much you know,' Mark replied quickly. 'It always takes less men to hold a position than to attack it. We've got enough men to defend the close. And that's the only way they can get into the back-court to capture the stone – through the close from the front street.'

'Then why are you putting men in the back-court?' David demanded, sharp and quarrelsome.

'To watch Carter's back-courts,' Mark said patiently. 'To see what he's up to. They can't get through the railings.'

'That's what I'm saying,' David nagged him. 'They can't get through there, so you're wasting all those men. One would be enough if you only want a look-out.'

'I know what I'm doing,' Mark said, stepping nearer him with his fist clenched.

'It's a good job,' said David, and turned away. 'Because nobody else does.'

The brothers cut off their argument rather than foster defeatism by revealing their differences any further, and David went grudgingly to the post Mark had assigned him. He guarded the street at the close-mouth, bossing a squad there with an irritability that showed his misgivings, resenting the waste of Paul, who was placed in the back-court with another squad to guard the railings.

'He says nobody can get through the railings, then he puts Paul there to watch in case they do,' he muttered to Bunty Hogg.

'What did you say?' Bunty asked.

'Nothing,' he answered. 'Nothing at all.'

Within the close Mark sat royally at the foot of the stairs, waiting the signal that the enemy were moving, and out in the street David and his little force lounged against the baker's window. The calm of the summer evening seemed a far-flung promise that peace would reign till the sun went down.

'Do you think they'll come?' Gregan asked suddenly, noisily sniffing a bubble of mucus up his wet nose.

'Of course they'll come,' said David scowling at him.

He looked at the toy Bunty Hogg held in his hand, a lump of wood roughly fashioned to the shape of a revolver.

'What do you think that is?' he asked contemptuously.

'That? That's my gun,' said Bunty proudly.

He pointed it at him and said fiercely, 'Bang!'

'This is going to be a fight, not a game,' said David, shaking him. 'What good do you think that thing is?'

'I feel good with it,' Hogg answered. 'Gives you a great feeling, a gun in your hand.'

'Don't talk daft,' said David. 'This is a fight, I'm telling you. That thing's no use to you.'

Hogg tossed the wooden pistol in the air and caught it by the barrel as it came down.

'Well, I can use the butt on their head, can't I?' he said happily, miming the action against David's skull.

David put one foot behind him and pushed him backwards so that he tripped and fell on his back.

'If you let them come as near as that before you use it, you'll never use it,' he said.

'That wasn't fair,' Hogg whined.

'There's worse than that coming to you,' David retorted callously, prodding him in the ribs with his foot. 'Get up! You're supposed to be on guard.'

'I'm not playing,' said Hogg, rising slowly and pouting.

'There's nobody playing, Bunty,' said David with sarcastic affection. 'This is serious. That's what I'm trying to tell you.'

'They won't come, don't worry,' said Crabbe, squatting comfortably on the pavement, his back against the base of the baker's window, his grimy hands clasping his dirty knees and his bludgeon behind his heels.

'Why not give them the stone if they want it?' Hart asked carelessly, sitting at the close-mouth.

'Shut up, you!' David shouted, and brandished his pole at him.

Even as he spoke the war started. The elder Hogg came running through the close from the back-court, scampering past Mark and screaming as he ran.

'They're coming up from the end back! A whole crowd of them! They've got iron bars. They're coming, they're coming!'

At the same time another force came out of the lowest close down the street and advanced steadily along the pavement towards the paralysed defenders of the outer approach. David felt his warriors fall out of his hands like tumbled coins, rolling away beyond recovery. Hogg clutched him, trembling with fear, and slobbered wildly.

'They'll get through the railings, they've got iron bars! We'll never be able to stop them, there's too many!'

When he saw David was hardly listening to him he looked nervously about for someone else to appeal to, and only then did he see the force coming along the street.

'Look!' he shrieked, shaking David's arm frantically. 'They've got us on both sides!'

'I know, I can see,' David shouted him down. 'You get back to your post.'

He grabbed the wriggling boy by the collar of his jersey and tried to push him into the close. Hogg squirmed and kicked and cursed, wrenched himself free and ran across the street, round the corner, and out of sight. Gregan gaped after him, turned in a panic to the distraught Heylyn who was supposed to be his leader, and seeing only a helpless passion on that face he too ran away.

Black Carter's raiders filled the breadth of the pavement, six abreast and about as many deep. Some had a coil of rope slung over their shoulder and some had rope wound round their waist, and they were all armed. Between the first and second ranks there seemed to be a gap of a few feet, filled by a strange trundled object.

When they were still some yards away the six in front charged in unison, yelling with the lust of conquest. But instead of rushing headlong on the Heylynites they raced out into the road and round into their rear in a wide arc. The unexpectedness of the move and the alarming battle-cries confused Heylyn's forces. They didn't know if they should run out and forestall the six raiders on their flank or if they should remain where they were and await the full assault, and as they turned about and about in a pitiful indecision they saw what had been hidden by the front rank. It was an empty barrel, and the second rank sent it rolling forward with loud whoops of joy in the confidence of victory.

Its impact scattered the defenders and as they retreated in a rout some fell into the hands of the six raiders coming in behind and some were overtaken by the rest of the attackers. Bunty dropped his toy gun without a struggle and was immediately pinioned and roped. Fox and

Crabbe wielded their staves bravely but were quickly outnumbered, outfenced, and disarmed. Hart stood stock-still in the middle of the confusion of struggling bodies and held his hands above his head.

'I give in,' he panted, and kept on repeating the words like a patient in delirium even after his surrender was accepted and his arms tied.

David fled from the barrel into the close, hoping to defend it somehow against a complete breakthrough. There he ran into fresh forces of the enemy, rushing in pell-mell from the back-court. Mark was gone, and as he shouted for him he heard a door bang violently on the top flat and he knew where his brother had gone. He swung his pole viciously, but the close was too narrow to allow him to use it effectively. Somebody jumped on his back and strong arms came round his neck. He bent abruptly and bucked and the unknown assailant was hurtled over his head. But he fought in vain. He was crushed between the forces coming in at each end. His arms were held, his weapon twisted from his grasp, a clothes-rope passed round him with dexterous speed, and he was trussed and helpless. He trembled with impotent rage and cursed his brother as much for his useless strategy as for his desertion.

His captors shoved him through the close into the back-court, and there he saw his comrades sitting on the ground against the wash-house, heads hanging in shame at their own futility.

'Why didn't you fight?' David shouted across to Paul, and fought against the jostling of his captors as they urged him onwards.

Paul looked up and shrugged.

'Too many,' he said briefly.

David glared at him resentfully. But his humiliation was far from complete. They tied him to one of the stalwart wooden poles the housewives used for stretching their clothes-lines, and Black Carter stood before him, a looming figure of primeval justice.

'Where's your brother?' he asked curtly.

'How should I know?' David screamed. 'You let me go or it'll be worse for you! Let me go or I'll—'

He was near hysteria, pulling in a fit of passion against his bonds until the weals on his wrists burned hot.

'That won't get you anywhere,' said Carter, unmoved. 'Where's your brother?'

'I don't know. I told you, I don't know,' answered the boy. Then involuntarily he looked up at the tenement windows.

'It's not you I want,' said Carter, almost kindly. 'I've no fight with you. It's your brother I want. He's my age. You're only a kid.'

As he spoke he saw the direction of David's eyes and turned his head to look in the same direction. Three storeys above them a window was raised and Mark leaned out, his fingers splayed out from his nose.

'Yah, yah, black bum Carter!' he yelled.

Carter looked up with his fists clenched but gave no other sign of emotion. Mark waved to him mockingly, secure in his lofty retreat, the house to himself and the door locked.

'If it's me you want come and get me!' he shouted, and grinned.

Carter made no move and no answer. Provoked by that imperturbability Mark began to chant again.

'Yah, yah, black bum Carter!'

He put his fingers to his nose again and against the little finger he put the thumb of the other hand, all ten fingers extended. Carter unclenched his fists and his rock-like face cracked to a smile of stony amusement.

'The barber,' he said abruptly.

The obscure order was passed swiftly through the clustering gang and a lanky boy with large hands and an idiot's grin that showed a top incisor missing stepped forward happily. He grasped David by the hair of the head and laughed into his face. David stared in still wonder, shocked out of his hysteria, and the back-court and the wide evening sky, the tumult and the clamour around him, seemed to revolve and diminish and concentrate in a disembodied grin leering close to his face. The barber took a large pair of scissors from his back pocket and cut off the hair he had grasped in his left hand. Then he grasped another handful and cut it off too. He went on cutting, leaving the hair cut almost to the scalp in some places and raggedly long in others. Roars of laughter approved the artistry of his workmanship.

'You needed a haircut,' the barber jeered.

He put the scissors back in his pocket and slapped David once on the right cheek with the back of his hand and once on the left with his palm. David bared his teeth and jerked his head back. In the passage of the

21

blows from one side to the other the knuckles smacked against his nose and he felt his upper lip wet with a warm liquid and then the taste of salt as the blood dripped over his mouth.

'The barrow,' said Carter, his eyes fixed on the youngest Heylyn, who stared up at him in dumb bewilderment.

A runner went away and returned quickly wheeling a large metal barrow with a shallow trough. He guided it smartly towards the sacred monolith, reversed it, and looked to Carter.

'Get round,' said Carter, addressing no one in particular, his eyes looking from Heylyn to the stone and back again.

Six boys flocked round it and Carter stood by till they were in position.

'Bend,' he said.

They bent to the stone.

'Get set,' he said.

They found a grip.

'One, two, three, lift!' he chanted.

Together his warriors raised the stone and placed it on the barrow. It overlapped all the way round, resting on the rims of the trough, but the barrow took the strain. They steadied the stone with reverent hands while the trooper who brought the barrow grasped the shafts, laboured with a grunt, and then got the wheel turning. He went through the close, encouraged in his task by cheers and chants of victory, down the front street to the last close in the block and into the back-court there. Then the stone was eased off slowly, manoeuvred to its appointed place, and settled in its new site as the throne of Black Carter the Conqueror. The reign of the Heylyns was over.

When the conquering hordes had all departed David was released from his pillory by the fumbling hands of his red-faced allies, their clumsy tongues muttering vague comfort and empty pity, consoling his ridiculous hair, his bleeding nose, and his swollen wrists. The last knot was loosened and the coil of rope fell to his feet. He touched his wrists with fingers that trembled tenderly over the rawness of them and he felt a nerve quiver in the pit of his stomach. He broke down and wept openly, to the embarrassment of his friends, the delight of his enemies, and his own vexation.

3

Black Carter left school and passed beyond the rivalries of boyhood. His power descended to Menzies, a newcomer from the east-end who brought new customs and taught the worship of strange gods, modifying by his example the dress, speech, and morals of his court. He reduced the conquered Heylyns to nonentities by the absolutism of his rule and the ubiquity of his influence. Like Black Carter Mark too had left school and passed beyond the disputes of a childish empire, and Paul and David had to make what accommodation they could with the new regime.

David wandered alone round the margins of the reorganized land, sullenly observing the ritual of his successors and bitter at Paul's servile collaboration with them.

'Well, why keep things up?' Paul asked. 'Carter never harmed me, and Menzies is all right. You can't just mooch around by yourself.'

But David tried, and was derided by the conquerors whenever he came near them in his solitary moping. With the swift understanding of their years they saw that teasing him made him mad, and it amused them to put him in a temper. They soon stopped teasing Paul. He was cleverer than David and he smiled at their jokes, accepted their mockery smoothly, and in return he was accepted by them. The core of David's hatred meanwhile glowed steadily against Carter, whom he blamed for letting him be tied to a post and slapped and shorn. As he lounged one evening at the close-mouth the core of his hatred suddenly burst into flame, for he saw Black Carter coming along the street, grimy from the coal-ree.

'Hello,' said Carter, stopping beside him and looking him up and down with the glimmer of a smile on his dark face.

David doled him out a glare of implacable hostility and then looked the other way.

'Can you not take a beating?' Carter asked softly.

David looked at him again, awed by the whispering kindness in the low careless voice.

'Come on,' said Carter, his tone coaxing the younger boy to peace and forgiveness.

He put a hand on David's shoulder and shook it gently, almost teasingly, the teasing of a friend. David jerked instinctively to repel the alien touch and Carter put his arm round his shoulder and patted him lightly as he spoke.

'You're a rare fighter, but you've got a bad temper,' he murmured, still faintly smiling. 'That's daft. It doesn't get you anywhere.'

David felt his wretched boredom flow away from him and in its place a warmth pervaded his body. His head tingled round the crown as in his own way despite his heart he responded to Carter's words and touch.

'You don't need to keep it up,' said Carter. 'It wasn't you.'

He looked at David straightly a moment longer, and when he walked away the boy felt his useless hatred depart with him. The breadth and bulk of the heavy lumbering figure that had once offended his sight now seemed the upright strength of manliness, and he found quick and subtle arguments to suggest that the shedding of his blood had been against Carter's wishes. Certainly he had uttered no command. A shy admiration moved unwillingly within him and he meditated how he could find a place under Menzies and still save face. With Carter pardoned and absolved there was no longer any reason for him to stay outside the games organized by Carter's successor. He was tired of being alone. He wanted to be like Paul, easy-going, familiar, and accepted, everyone's friend.

He began to make up to Menzies, expecting to find a leader he could admire, but he found only a pagan whose coarseness was a constant offence to his growing sense of propriety. Unlike Black Carter the newcomer was ready and even fluent of speech, inventing words when he lacked them, with a wealth of obscenity that made the bawdy of the Hogg brothers sound like baby-talk. So the Hoggs worshipped him. Under his leadership the primitive games of battle were ousted by games of chase with the girls of the tenement as the prey.

Queenie Crawfurth was the first of these ripening girls to be singled out by Menzies from the corner of the back-court where she played with younger children. She was a backward big girl, but well developed physically – all body and no brain the housewives said of her and called her soft. Menzies lured her away from her little playmates by flattery, gifts, and chaffing, and enticed her into his licentious games. She was lined up with a handful of tomboys, intruders he had brought in from another district, and Menzies captained the band of boys who would chase them. The girls were released and given a few minutes grace to race as far afield as they could before the hounds set out in pursuit. But the range of the chase was limited by convention, and it was never long before she was caught. Her capture was always reserved for Menzies himself, and he brought her back to the prisoners' den and handled her familiarly.

His liberties increased when autumn came on and darkness fell before tea-time. If she half-heartedly objected the tomboys gathered round and maliciously coaxed her into submission. The situation amused them and they had a guiltless satisfaction in seeing her unwittingly excite a boy whose conceited confidence they criticized amongst themselves. Whenever he seemed on the point of going too far they burst into screeches of laughter and protected Queenie by jostling against Menzies till the danger was over, and then it was hard to say if Menzies or Queenie was the more embarrassed. But they weren't always present to restrain him. He had her alone in the corner of the back-court where the stone had once lain, and inflamed by his own freedom with the bewildered girl and by the darkness of the autumn night he blundered into an assault on her. She was as big as he was, and just as strong. Terror gave her extra strength. She wrestled obstinately when she found her frantic implorations were unheeded, and with a wild heave she managed to break his grip, escaped from the corner, and darted away in a panic.

She slipped swiftly through the railings that had been bent by crowbars the night Black Carter won the stone and raced for her own close at the other end of the block. She almost fell in her speed as she reached it and ran full tilt into Mary Ruthven, a bright-faced friendly girl not long out of school.

'Stop him, stop him,' she sobbed, clutching the elder girl and shaking hysterically.

Mary Ruthven stood still, letting Queenie embrace her, and patted her soothingly.

25

'It's all right,' she said calmly. 'You're all right. There's nothing to worry about.'

Menzies came slowly through the close and looked at the girls with a craftily apologetic smile.

'It was only a joke, Queenie,' he said. 'You don't have to make a song about it. Not if you're wise.'

'I know you,' Mary Ruthven said in a low fierce voice. 'I know you and what you are.'

'It was only a joke,' Menzies repeated pacifically. 'Anyway, it was your own idea, Queenie.'

He sidled past with a vague flourish.

'Only a joke!' Queenie wailed. 'He says it was only a joke!'

'Oh, stop it,' said Mary Ruthven crossly.

She gave her a handkerchief to dry her eyes, made her comb her hair, and with a glare at the frightened girl buttoned up the front of her frock for her. Queenie was snivelling to calm when Black Carter came through the close and stopped in confusion a few steps from them.

'Sorry,' he mumbled awkwardly, strange with two girls who seemed to have taken refuge in the close to solve some trouble.

Mary Ruthven stared hard at him and the blatant hostility in her eyes distressed Carter.

'I wish you would tell your friend he isn't in his east-end jungle now,' she said.

Carter was so plainly puzzled that she had to add some explanation.

'Menzies,' she said, saying the name as if she were lashing the owner.

Carter looked sadly at Queenie, but there was nothing he could say and he went silently upstairs. He never spoke to Menzies about it, for in a few weeks he moved with his parents to a villa in the new housing-scheme across the canal and he had no time for his successor.

Menzies left Queenie alone after that. He counted her flight as a victory for himself, and spoke of it as such to his awed cronies, leaving the details of his conquest to their inexperienced imagination.

But he worshipped Mammon too, and when the long evenings returned with the turning year he applied his unquestionable talents for organization towards promoting what he called a Mammoth Sports

Meeting. He held it across the canal bridge where a broad deserted road ran straight for several hundred yards between a paint-factory and a goods-siding. He wrote out a list of events on an exercise book he had stolen from school, putting each event on a separate page and arranging the competitors in heats. He appointed stewards, judges, and a starter, and made himself clerk of the course. From the competitors he exacted an entrance fee for each event, with the concession of entering them all for sixpence cash down.

He planned also a series of boxing matches. The final tie was to take place at the same time as his Mammoth Sports Meetings, and the fight for the championship was to be the culminating event of the evening. From an old professional boxer who lived across the street and spent his leisure time at a youths' boxing club in the Gallowgate he borrowed a set of six-ounce gloves.

'I'm going in for Menzies' boxing tournament,' David said to Paul, after brooding over it for a couple of days, thrilling to the thought of wearing real boxing gloves and showing he was a fighter.

Paul laughed at him.

'You're mad,' he said.

'Why? Are you going in for it?' David asked laughing. 'I'll meet you in the final then!'

'Me? Not likely!' Paul answered emphatically. 'And you won't either if you've any sense.'

But David was obstinate. He saw himself pledged to vindicate the family honour. Mark had simply abdicated after the battle of the stone. He had left school and gone to work, and he was too old to bother about these matters now. Paul was too pacific. So it was left to him. He was tired living on the fringe of events, there was no other way he could show Menzies the Heylyns were still important, even although he dimly recognized he could never fit into Menzies' world. Paul's easy-going surrender and the fawning of the Hoggs were equally distasteful to him. He would fight.

'You're mad,' Paul insisted. 'You don't think you've any chance, do you?'

'Why not?' David asked sulkily. 'I've fought most of them before with my bare fists and nobody ever beat me.'

'This is different,' Paul tried to explain, ill at ease with the brother so near to him, only a year younger, and yet so different. 'Do you really think Menzies will give you a chance?'

'He has taken my money,' said David.

'More fool you for giving him it,' said Paul impatiently. 'Menzies has it all fixed, if I know Menzies. Do you think he means to pay out prize money to the likes of you? He'll make sure his pals get it, and they'll take just whatever he cares to give them. Some wee thing from his auntie's shop. Something he has pinched. You're a mug.'

David remained obstinate. He fought four short bouts and became accustomed to the gloves on his hands. At first his fists felt odd inside so much padding and he couldn't judge very well with them. But he came to love the feel of them, came to imagine himself becoming a boxer, and although he saw Menzies wasn't an impartial referee he couldn't complain. He kept on winning, either on points or because his opponents withdrew after a couple of rounds. In one bout he knocked his opponent down, and the boy stayed down patiently till Menzies counted him out, very, very slowly. It was his wild ferocious style, or lack of a style, that made him victorious. He was completely ignorant of the science of boxing, and there was nobody to train him or advise him. But he barged in with such rash abandon that he intimidated his opponents. He was proud of himself, and boasted to Paul.

'Aye, all right,' Paul said ungraciously. 'But you've still the final to fight. And I still think you're making a mistake.'

'Fighting Stoorie?' David asked conceitedly. 'Who's afraid of him? He's only a skelf. He's got a bit of style, but he's got no weight and he's got no guts.'

'He's got style because old Drummond trains him,' said Paul. 'It was Drummond lent Menzies the gloves. And Drummond was a boxer for years. You won't find Stoorie so easy. I bet you he knows all the tricks. And he's a pal of Menzies.'

'I can still beat him,' said David.

'I expect he'll half kill you,' Paul answered callously.

Paul turned out to be right. David sailed in as he always did and the thin-made insolent-faced young boy nicknamed Stoorie tried to keep him boxing at a distance. But David, even in the course of the short tournament, had gathered there were some conventions in this sport of boxing, some points of technique and craft, some vague ways of scoring points. He feared that if he allowed Stoorie to go on boxing stylishly, keeping him out with elegant lefts and rights, then Stoorie would certainly win. All he could do was fight the bout in his own way and intimidate Stoorie with his whirlwind tactics as he had intimidated the others.

'All right, if that's how you want it, stupid,' Stoorie whispered in his ear as they clutched after a spell of close fighting.

From then on he jabbed viciously at David, easily penetrating his poor defence, and punching particularly at his left eye. When David persisted in coming in close Stoorie gave him some painful punches below the belt. Menzies must have seen them, and David appealed for a foul over and over again, but Menzies only smiled. In the third round Stoorie stuck the thumb of his glove in David's eye and the boy was blinded for a while. Stoorie taunted him quietly and tired him so skilfully that David began to hang on to him wearily and long for the end of the round. Every time Stoorie hit him in the eye the pain was an agony, and as often as not the thumb of the glove was jabbed in too.

The next round was worse. He became angry at the torture inflicted on him and rushed at Stoorie. He was close in and fighting beyond his strength when Stoorie did it again. David screamed involuntarily. It was the one thrust too many with the thumb. He covered his throbbing eye with both hands and stood helpless and trembling. Stoorie took the chance to knock him down and Menzies stopped the fight before David staggered up.

'You didn't count ten,' he protested furiously.

'Technical knock-out,' said Menzies. 'You're not fit to fight on.'

And indeed he wasn't. Menzies ignored him and lined up the runners for the final of the quarter-mile. The boxing final was meant to be the last event, but Menzies had brought it on earlier because Stoorie had to take the gloves into the Gallowgate Club before half past seven. David went away alone, down the broad street between the goods-siding and the paint-factory, over the canal bridge and on to the main street and home. He wanted to cry but his eyes seemed to need another relief than tears. He covered with his fist the eye that Stoorie had stuck his thumb into, and when he took his fist away all he could see was a vibrating mist in front of it. He was in a panic.

'I can't see,' he sobbed. 'I can't see with that eye!'

When he came to his own close he passed Mary Ruthven on her way to a tram for town. She stopped, came back to him, and took his hand away from his eye.

'What's the matter with you?' she asked anxiously, her heart gentle at the sight of the motherless, grimy urchin with tears rolling down his face and his body trembling. 'It isn't like you to be crying.'

'I can't see,' the boy repeated. 'I can't see. I can't see with my left eye.'

The young girl held his head by a tuft of hair and drew his head up and back and looked at the tortured eye.

'Oh!' she exclaimed, horrified, and her tone increased the boy's panic. 'You'll have to have that attended to.'

The eye was swollen, bruised, and bloodshot, and the pupil dead-looking.

'Here, you'd better come with me,' she said impulsively, and abandoning her appointment in town she took him to her mother. On the way upstairs she stopped and spoke again.

'Menzies?' she said softly.

The boy nodded mutely. He was past caring who it was. All he wanted was an end to the pain in his eye. The fame and glory he had set out to win seemed as insubstantial as smoke now they had eluded him, and his attempt to vindicate the honour of the Heylyns seemed a piece of unnecessary folly, a vanity that derided him.

Mrs Ruthven was playing patience at the kitchen table.

'Mother, look at this boy,' said her daughter. 'Just look at the state of him.'

Mrs Ruthven knocked the ash from a cigarette in a holder and rose silently. David retreated from her timidly. He had never spoken to her in his life before. He was slightly afraid of her. She went about in a strange uniform with a high starched collar, though indoors here in her own house she was dressed like any other woman, except that she looked cleaner than the tenement housewives, superior to them. She beckoned him back from his retreat, and obeying the summons of her finger and

30

the command in her eye he went slowly towards her. She held his head as her daughter had done, touched his eyelid gently with her other hand, and the boy winced. She emitted a series of angry clicks and bathed the eye and bandaged it and let him go with a sixpence.

'Davie Heylyn,' she said as she fastened the bandage. 'The last of the Heylyns, eh? You're not unlike your mother. She had fine eyes too.'

'I didn't know you knew my mother,' he said, feeling it surprisingly easy to talk to her.

'Oh, I knew your mother well,' said Mrs Ruthven.

She looked as if she was going to say more about that, and then changed her mind.

'If that eye still hurts you tomorrow,' she said, and he was soothed by the low unhurried warm speech, 'ask your teacher to send you to the clinic.'

He thanked her at the door as she let him out, and he went away gratefully clutching the sixpence. Her place in life puzzled him, for she had no man in the house yet she seemed to be better off than women who had. He had heard her called a midwife, which word he took to mean a woman who was on the way to becoming a wife, but since she was already Mrs that didn't make sense either.

He didn't have to ask his teacher to send him to the clinic. She spoke to him at once, curious and alarmed, and soon had the whole story out of him. She gave him a sealed note with the official card she had to fill in for the doctor, and he left the classroom gladly enough. The pain was dull and intermittent, and he was thrilled to be out of doors during school hours. A lady doctor read his teacher's note, examined his eye, and spoke in a grave whisper to a white-haired nurse who put drops in his eye and gave him a box of ointment. He was charmed to be the object of so much attention and thoroughly enjoyed his visit except for the strong smell of soap about the place. More pleasures were to come. He was summoned back to the clinic for another examination and then sent to the Eye Infirmary. He became used to going there, watching on his journey the hurry and press of the city and interested to understand that all this traffic and all these people were rushing about their business every morning while he sat in a classroom. He came to look on the specialist in the Eye Infirmary as an old friend and longed to speak to him at length, to listen to him, to learn about the infirmary and about eyes, about his own eye particularly, but all he was able to do was answer questions briefly and shyly.

'Well, you know, you've been a very foolish little boy,' said the specialist on his last visit. 'Boxing is a fine sport. I've nothing against it. I used to do a little boxing myself when I was a student. But what you walked into wasn't boxing.'

'No,' said David, half admitting it and half questioning it.

'No,' said the specialist, and the muscles of his severe mouth worked for a moment or two before he went on. 'No, you see the trouble is—'

He stopped again, and taking the boy between his knees as he sat sideways at his desk he grasped him by the elbows and spoke to him slowly.

'The optic nerve in your left eye has been very badly damaged. You can't see with that eye, now can you? Not really?'

'Not really,' David conceded.

'No,' said the specialist. 'I know. The trouble is, the sight is practically gone. And I'm afraid it won't get any better. Mind you, I don't think it will get any worse.'

'I won't be blind?' he asked timidly.

'Not any more than you are now,' the specialist answered. 'And it's only the left eye. Your right eye's perfectly good. But there's nothing more I can do for you. I'm sorry.'

So his outings stopped, and the specialist's information left him proud of his suffering. It made him different, and that was what he wanted. He had lost the fight but he had won a name. He was the boy who had lost the sight of an eye in Menzies' boxing tournament. His lonely fame kept him from being depressed, and he applied himself with a new industry to his lessons. There was no future for him as a fighter under Menzies. Menzies had nothing to offer him. He was done with the pursuits of his rivals.

He called on Mrs Ruthven to thank her for dressing his eye and advising him to go to the clinic. He called again by invitation to tell her what the specialist said. He liked going to see her, though usually he was embarrassed in the presence of grown-up people. She was so quiet, so rich in her voice, and precise in her movements that it pleased him to sit and look at her and listen, and he was fascinated to see a woman smoking and use a cigarette-holder.

'He says it won't get any worse,' he told her. 'So I'm not really blind in one eye. It's just that I don't see very well with it.'

'I don't think you see with it at all, Davie,' she said, and the diminutive of his name coming from a woman slightly annoyed him. It was the form used only by his brothers and by friends whose worth he had tested. From her it sounded soft. 'But don't brood about it. And don't let it depress you. You've still got one good eye, and that's more than some people have.'

'He says my right eye's perfect,' the boy told her.

She smiled, and sent him an errand. He became her errand-boy, more at home in her house than in his father's, and he became used to hearing Mary Ruthven talk to her mother – talk, talk, talk, telling her everything about her day's work, what was said and who said it and how they said it, so that he entered another world, a world where people he had never met were connected in a network of gossip. He marvelled that anyone could be so frank, for he thought it was always wiser to say as little as possible and confide in nobody. To confide in a person put you in his power, and sooner or later what you confided would be thrown back at you, twisted and torn, to make a fool of you. So he believed. But he couldn't imagine that happening between Mary Ruthven and her mother, and he came to see and understand a relationship foreign to his experience and alien to his nature.

Yet in spite of Mrs Ruthven's advice he couldn't help brooding once the novelty of being the unique victim of Menzies' treachery was gone. He stopped going out and sat alone in the front room, reading un-guidedly, his elbow on the table at the window and his left hand over his useless eye, a little Cyclops in his island.

4

Before another summer came Menzies was in disgrace through his own blunders. He had managed to get entry money for his sports meeting by promising valuable prizes to the winners, but he had seen no advantage in collecting cash only to spend it on prizes. He used the miscellaneous loot accumulated over a long series of thefts from the little shop kept by his aunt, where she sold newspapers, stationery, and fancy goods. She was a stout slatternly woman with no head for business, a face that always seemed to need a wash, and a bosom that flopped half-way down her torso. From the day she bought the shop out of her winnings in a football-pool she had allowed her nephew the run of it. His pilfering started from a natural acquisitiveness and went on until he had stolen so much that the concealment of his hoard became a nuisance. In awarding the stolen articles as prizes he killed two birds with the one stone. He diminished his loot to more manageable size and got money in its place. He had several dozen copies of comics and paper-backed novelettes, coloured pencils by the dozen, crayons, writing-pads, cheap fountain-pens, and a couple of hundred cigarettes. The prizes he gave out still left him with a fair amount on his hands, and later he raffled what he could. Finally he gave the remainder away.

He found his pleasure in the very act of pilfering, in the stealthy acquisition of attractive items, but he had little interest in them once they were safely hidden. The carelessness of his aunt, and the disposal of his original hoard, encouraged him to continue his thefts at a new and higher level. The money from the sports meeting appeared to him a form of wealth more satisfactory than the loot from the shop. It fascinated him by its exchange value, and its handiness freed him from the fetishism of his earlier commodity-worship. In hard cash he found the perfect form of power. He started raiding the till.

But the thefts that had been concealed by his aunt's slovenly book-keeping so long as they were confined to her disorderly stock were immediately apparent when they depleted the till. From cautious beginnings he advanced to indiscretions. He came under suspicion and a trap was laid. He was left alone at the counter selling the evening papers, and he thought his aunt was gossiping in the back-shop with his mother. He took a florin and a half-crown from the till and before he had time to pocket them he saw his aunt darken the doorway of the back-shop. Behind her loomed his mother, looking at him with big astonished eyes. He knew at once they had been spying on him, and just as quickly he knew why. He saw he would have to answer not only for the present theft but for all those that had gone before. He jumped over the counter and ran away.

'I told you it was him,' said Mrs Jackson, too stout to bother taking even a step in pursuit and calmly certain the culprit would be caught in good time.

'Oh no, not my boy!' her sister moaned.

'I'll put him the whole way too, you wait!' said Mrs Jackson with quiet venom. 'You see if I don't. I've lost pounds since I bought this shop. Pounds I should never have lost on a good-paying wee business. And it's been him. It's been him all along.'

'Oh no, not my boy!' Mrs Menzies wept. 'I can't believe it.'

'You're just after seeing it, aren't you?' said Mrs Jackson impatiently.

He was picked up two nights later as he lay sleeping in a timber yard on the canal bank. His aunt, true to her threat, made a police case of it, and Menzies accepted with an insolent smile his committal to an approved school for two years.

Paul brought the news to David as of something sensational, but David glowered at him. He had no interest in Menzies, not even enough to rejoice at his downfall. Young as he was, a neglected schoolboy, he was already oppressed by the impermanence of the world around him. Everything was changed and was changing, not least himself.

2

The Camera

1

MARK grew up tall, blond, and handsome, a well-built vigorous youth. Like all the Heylyns he was quick to learn, bright and obliging, a good penman at school, and with a good vocabulary, so that he was called a good scholar by his teachers. He left school at the earliest legal age and worked restlessly at odd jobs, a week here and a fortnight there. But he was ambitious and despised the dead-end work he drifted into. He felt it unworthy of his talents and longed for scope and opportunity. At sixteen he was working in a lawyer's office as a general utility office-boy after answering an advertisement and obtaining the post on the strength of his distinguished handwriting, for Mr Arbuthnot, Writer to the Signet, had an old-fashioned faith in the value of good writing. He believed it showed intellectual capacity. He interviewed Mark himself and was pleased with the boy's demeanour. There was a charm in Mark, a little smile, a judicious mixture of deference and self-reliance, and a candid countenance that attracted the old lawyer. But he wanted more than a bird of passage, an office-boy for a year, a lad who was merely filling in his time while looking for something better. He quizzed Mark gently about his purpose in applying for the job.

'Well, sir,' said Mark, 'I understand my father intends to make me an articled clerk to a solicitor if I find the work congenial.'

He paused and smiled, watching Mr Arbuthnot approvingly assimilate the last word, and then he added with an assumed shyness, 'And of course if he finds the firm suitable.'

Mr Arbuthnot smiled back at the idea of anyone finding anything unsuitable in the firm of Arbuthnot and Laing, Writers to the Signet.

'My boy,' he said, proud of the antiquarian lore common among Scots lawyers, 'Andrew Laing, the father of the founder of this firm, was a writer with Sir Walter Scott's father.'

Mark was lying when he mentioned his father, but he was accustomed to tell little lies for the sake of an immediate advantage, or to make a good impression, and he hardly thought he was lying. To him, such falsehoods were merely the oil required by social machinery if it were ever to operate to his service. He applied for the job without his father's knowledge, and he began work without his father knowing precisely where he worked or how much he was getting. He knew that in fact he would probably never become an articled clerk to a solicitor, he wasn't even sure what the phrase meant, but to work in a solicitor's office seemed to offer a certain status and he very much wanted to have some status. He was proud of himself, he was careful of his appearance, he liked to be clean and smart. A lawyer's office satisfied for the time being his vague ambition to get on. It would do till he found something else, or until Mr Arbuthnot found out there was little likelihood of his becoming an articled clerk – particularly if money were required, as Mark supposed it must be.

For Mr Heylyn, the widowed father of Mark, Paul, and David, had no money. He had nothing but a dapper appearance, a plausible tongue, and his job as a commercial traveller on a moderate basic wage plus commission. Mr Heylyn talked, ate, drank, and dreamt commission. He had only two vices, but either alone would have been enough to handicap a more prosperous man: he gambled and he took too much strong drink. Usually he drank only at the week-end, but every night in the week he went to a dingy club and played cards for money till after midnight. Irregularly he drank during the week too, so that his sons were never quite sure when to expect him or what to expect from him, and sometimes when he came home he was seized with fits of violence.

They grew up neglected, as heedless of their father as he was of them, but with the help of the woman next door they were fed somehow. She put soup into them every time she made it, she saw they had some sort of main meal every day, she mended the clothes that Mr Heylyn bought them when she nagged him into it, and with Mark as the boss and chef they saw to their own breakfast and supper, three aggressive boys who were proud of their male independence, of their toughness and hardness, and yet possessed of many of the skills in housewifery more commonly found in girls. They took it all for granted. It was the world they were born into, and therefore beyond questioning. The world could not be otherwise than it was. In so far as they noticed how other families lived they preferred their own way. They were left ungoverned, untrained, a law to themselves, and that suited the inherited wilfulness of their natures.

As Mark grew older he became more often and more openly opposed to his father. Mr Heylyn wanted more money from him, and the youth refused. At first he would claim he had spent it on essential provisions, exaggerating the price of them to be on the safe side.

'I had sausages to buy today,' he would say. 'And I've got some steak for tomorrow. I've only my tram-fare left.'

Soon, on the maxim that attack is the best defence, he learned to add, forestalling his father, 'You'll have to leave some money out for me.'

Then he became blunt and bold and told his father he was contributing no more than he was already: he needed the rest of his money for himself.

'And what would you be needing it for?' Mr Heylyn asked sarcastically. 'Are you saving up to get married?'

'I've got to look smart in my job,' Mark said firmly, ignoring the last question as merely silly.

He was saving hard for a new suit, so careful with his money that David called him mean. Too old now to fight outsiders in the back-court they fought each other in the privacy of their own house, and not with words only. David, a couple of years younger than Mark, came off worst. He was no match for Mark, who hit him with his open hand and kept him easily at arm's length. When he was bored of an evening Mark diverted himself by teasing David, provoking him to fight. Then when he had him knocked in a corner, glowering impotently with his one good eye, he would turn to Paul for approval of his tyranny.

'Isn't he a bad-tempered little brat?'

At such times Paul shrugged non-committally. He kept out of fights and he never took sides. So David brooded alone on the absence of justice in the disorderly world he lived in, and on the lack of law, and on the curse of fate that made him a whipping-boy for Mark. He had

41

never forgiven Mark for his desertion before the capture of the stone, and as they grew apart in adolescence he had little to say to him except when they were quarrelling. He found that although Mark had the heavier hand and the longer reach he himself had the sharper tongue. He learned how to wound with it, and he prepared his thrusts in advance, his solitude one long dream of revenge. The roles became reversed: Mark ceased to have enough interest in David to bother teasing him, and it was David who took every opportunity to taunt Mark, to belittle him and sneer at his style and dress, his polite voice, and his meanness, and he did it all the more boldly when he saw Mark had grown out of using violence against him. He watched him at the mirror one evening improving a wave in his hair, and he chanted softly.

'Mirror, mirror on the wall, who is the prettiest of them all?'

Mark went on combing his hair and patting it.

'Mark Heylyn with the big feet and the wave in his hair,' said David.

'Shut up or you'll be sorry,' said Mark.

But David was in a mood. He went on nagging and sneering until Mark strode over and upended him out of his chair.

'I hope you get your new suit,' David muttered, sprawling on the floor.

'If I get it, it'll be because I paid for it,' retorted Mark. 'You'd like everybody to be a tramp like yourself.'

He was angry with David for his continual pin-pricking. What David derided as vanity about his appearance was to Mark only the most elementary self-respect.

'Yes, I'll get a new suit,' he went on, warming to the topic. 'I can pay for it, and that's more than you could do, you wall-eyed little ape.'

There were several taunts in those few words calculated to insult David, who had his own brand of self-esteem, although being younger he lacked Mark's interest in being clean and smart. There was first the reference to his poverty: he could have left school at the same age as Mark and Paul, gone to work, and earned some money. But as the last of the Heylyns, a trio of classroom scholars and teachers' favourites, he had allowed his teacher to persuade him to stay on a little longer and prepare for examinations to the junior grades of the civil service. He had no particular interest in the respectable plans his teachers sketched for his encouragement, but he had come to like school, to like learning, to find peace and quiet in the classroom, after the damage to his eye had cut him off from the athletic pursuits that once interested him. About once a week Mark would remind him he was helping to keep him, and David took the reference to his inability to buy a suit as another reminder of his dependence. Secondly there was the reference to his blind eye, which seemed to him deliberately unjust since he had come by it in an attempt to vindicate the family honour that Mark had stained. Thirdly, he was convinced that in calling him an ape Mark was telling him what he already knew, that unlike his brothers he had no good looks, and the ugliness of his features was increased by the injury to his eye, which left his face with an odd, lopsided expression.

Impulsively, to hurt Mark for those ill-chosen words, he blurted out the secret he had been keeping for the better part of the week.

'You'd better make sure you can still afford to buy a suit,' he shouted, still sprawling where Mark had heaved him.

Mark stood over him, his arm raised and his fist clenched, his bright eyes sharp with anger, his handsome mouth tight. He took in the sense of David's jibe at once and his arm came slowly to his side. For a moment he stood trembling, looking down into David's eyes as if trying to see into his brain, and David stared sullenly back.

'You're telling lies,' said Mark, and David noticed with perverse delight that the lower lip was trembling as the words came out. 'You think you'll frighten me, don't you?'

'I don't think anything,' David answered woodenly. 'I can't afford a suit. You think you can, that's all. The difference is in the thinking. I know, and you think.'

'Oh, you little bastard!' screamed Mark, and David was shocked. They fought, they fought regularly; he was used to that. It was in the nature of the universe. But they seldom swore at each other, and it was the first time he had heard Mark use the word. It seemed to him, ignorant though he was of its primary meaning, to carry in its very utterance an overwhelming load of concentrated hatred. He rose slowly, picked up his library book, and sat down again in his shabby fireside chair. Mark ran through to the room where he slept, pulled up the sheets and bedding of his bed, and groped for the chamois-leather bag in which

43

he put his savings every week. The bag was there, but there was nothing in it.

He ran back to the kitchen, pulled David out of his chair and hit him wildly again and again. David was frightened now, and cowered, protecting his face and ears as well as he could with his arms crooked over them.

'You told him!' Mark shouted, and tears of vexation glistened in his eyes.

'I didn't,' David wailed. 'I didn't need to tell him anything. He knew. I didn't need to tell him.'

Mark pushed him away with quivering disgust, and sobbing miserably David picked up his book for the second time. His bitterness and frustration still strong in him, Mark snatched the volume from him, grasped the front board in his left hand and with his right hand viciously tore out one whole section, then another and another. When he had stripped the book he pitched the empty boards into his brother's face.

'There, read it now if you can!' he ranted. 'Try your good eye on that!'

He turned away, still shaking, and inwardly shocked at his own vandalism, for he was fond of books. Fiction and biography engrossed him. Their diversity of setting and character inspired him with a desire to improve his position, to move in a more exciting, more prosperous, and more rewarding world. In rare intervals of peace between himself and David they shared their reading, and David, who had more leisure, brought from the library such stories of travel, adventure, and espionage as he was sure would please Mark. And now he sat with a gutted book in his hands, weeping unrestrainedly.

'It's me that has to take that book back to the library,' he cried through his tears. 'You can go and tell them you tore it in bits, and you can pay for it.'

Alone in the front room Mark heard the anguished words but made no reply. He stood looking at the window, seeing nothing through it, and he quivered spasmodically.

Paul moved silently about the kitchen, washing the tea-cups, putting on a fire, sweeping the hearth. Then he began to whistle, not quite on a tune, as if nothing had happened. David grew quieter, and as he brooded a new question disturbed him. He saw quite clearly that it was his own words that had created trouble, and he found himself faced with the problem, posed to him as if by another person inside him, of how far he would be responsible for the additional trouble that would certainly come. He knew he needn't have spoken at all. He had seen his father take the money, but if he hadn't told Mark it was gone it would probably have been replaced at the end of the week, before Mark returned to the hiding-place to add to his hoard. But now it was certain Mark would challenge their father and for what happened after that David had a troubled feeling that he was ultimately responsible. He fretted over that feeling in distress, and rested on the conclusion that he had spoken and the damage was done. There was nothing that could amend it now. It didn't occur to him, he was too young, to tell Mark he was sorry he had spoken, he was sure their father meant to replace the money, there was no need to believe he would never be able to buy the suit he wanted. He was too full of the injury done to him by Mark's destruction of the book, and he closed the empty boards and opened them, closed them and opened them, nursing his own grievance.

Paul was the first to go to bed, calmly, methodically, preparing for his night's rest in the room where the three brothers slept, speaking impartially to Mark and David, not to reconcile them, but to insinuate there was nothing between them that concerned him. Mark sat up in the room that overlooked the main street and David sat up in the kitchen, patiently determined to stay up as long as Mark, to see what came of his impulsive words. But at half past one in the morning Mr Heylyn was still out, and when, sharp of hearing in the profound silence of the motherless house, David heard Mark go to bed he gave him just enough time to settle down and then he too undressed and crept into bed in darkness.

2

Mr Heylyn knew from Mark's manner that his theft had been discovered. He would have rejected the word theft if Mark had dared accuse him, for he was something of a sophist, accustomed in his daily canvassing to express things in the most favourable phrasing. The way he saw it there was no theft because he was only borrowing the money, and if it were argued that borrowing without permission was the same as stealing, he would have replied that he wasn't even borrowing the money since, as a father, he had full property rights over his son who was only a minor and who would never have been able to save so much money if he had done his duty and given it to him in the first place. To that extent it could be said his conscience was clear, if only it were clear he had a conscience. But like many simple men who live only for the day, so that there seems no depth to them, he was frequently seized by vague distresses and a passing melancholy, whose source he lacked the skill to probe. These clouds over the sunny shallows of his being gave him an erratic appearance of obscure depths. But it was impossible to chart them, for he fled from them himself, and never allowed anyone sufficient time or intimacy with him to find out what went on in his mind.

Perhaps he would have been a better father if his wife had lived, but she had worn herself out in the struggle with his elusiveness and he remained as she had known him; an essentially irresponsible man. It is hardly to be supposed that a man of his age, experience, and company, a man-about-town even in his daily work, a raconteur, drinker, and gambler, still didn't understand how the human species was propagated, but his understanding of it must have remained merely verbal, an abstract comprehension of something that had never come home to him with any personal application. He didn't actually disown his sons, but he seemed to look on them as accidents, relics of his dead wife, left in his house to be a nuisance to him. There was no doubt she was their mother; it was verifiable fact that he was her husband. Legally, therefore, he was their father; and nobody, seeing them, would have doubted the relationship. But it never seemed to have any emotional significance for him.

He watched Mark slyly, as a boarding-school master might watch a boy who was liable to be troublesome at any hour of the day or night. He had to put up with the boy because he was stuck with him. But he didn't have to take any cheek. He failed to see that, having been a poor disciplinarian for years, interrupting long periods of anarchy with brief spells of petty despotism, he was badly placed to assert his authority over an adolescent who was waiting the chance to challenge him. He

46

began to come home early in the evenings, trying to catch Mark staying out late so that he could intimidate him. He managed to get home first one night and when Mark arrived half an hour later he bawled at him angrily. Mark looked at him critically and saw a neat-made man with soft good looks behaving theatrically in an unimpressive temper.

'It isn't all that late, Dad,' he said calmly, always polite to his father, unlike Paul and David who were often insolent. 'Anyway, what brought you in so early? Surely you aren't short of a few bob for a hand of cards at the club.'

'If I were short, I wouldn't come to you,' said Mr Heylyn foolishly, so anxious to deny any accusation that he couldn't wait till it was made.

'No, but you might go behind my back,' answered Mark gently. His brothers never knew if the remark was impulsive or premeditated, and he never told them.

'What do you mean?' Mr Heylyn said, looking his son up and down with exaggerated contempt.

'You know what I mean,' said Mark, loud and bold.

His father turned away with a gesture of disgust to indicate he was unwilling to debase himself by arguing with a juvenile. Mark moved after him.

'You took my savings,' he said, and his voice quivered a little as it rose, showing he was worked up to a pitch where he was determined to have it out.

'I what?' demanded Mr Heylyn, turning to face Mark, his hand raised as if to strike Mark down in sheer horror at the absurdity of the charge.

'You took my savings,' Mark repeated. 'Every penny I had put by for a new suit. I do my best to get a decent job, I try to keep myself decently dressed, and you—'

He stopped, panting. Mr Heylyn grabbed him by the shoulders, shook him, and shoved him violently away.

'I took money that should have gone to the upkeep of the house,' he shouted. 'You hold back money you ought to be giving in, that's what you do. And then you complain when it's taken from you. You tell me a parcel of lies about you've no money, and all the time you're better off than any of us, you – you Ananias! It's a wonder God doesn't strike you dead for your deceit.'

Mark stood the length of the table from his father, staring at him with silent hatred. David rose from his book by the fire and stood trembling by, waiting the outcome. Paul mooned around from corner to corner and then drifted like a stray autumn leaf to the front room.

'You think everyone was born to minister to your comfort,' said Mark. His voice was lower but still venomous. 'All your life you've put yourself first. Nobody is to have anything till you're provided for.'

'I've to look smart in my job too, you know,' said Mr Heylyn.

'You're selfish through and through,' Mark swept on. 'You've no sense of duty or responsibility or kindness or a damn' thing. You're a selfish father and you were a selfish husband. You would kill your sons as you killed your wife if it suited your pleasure.'

'What are you talking about now?' Mr Heylyn shouted, his face red. He moved nearer Mark, and hit out at him, but Mark easily warded off the blow with his forearm, and in a state approaching hysteria he moved round the table and shouted across it at his father.

'You think I don't know! But I do! You killed my mother! You killed her! I know what a brute you are.'

Mr Heylyn stared at his eldest son and his eyes were glassy. His body swayed a little before he answered.

'That's a very unfair thing to say, a very unfair thing to say. You might as well say David killed her.'

'What's the difference?' Mark said, coldly, bitterly.

'Stop it, Mark! Stop it! You shouldn't say such things!' cried David, distressed and bewildered at the turn the quarrel had taken, and sensing in Mark's accusation a callous parade of knowledge of the kind he had often suffered from before, and dimly aware of a sexual knowledge in Mark he himself lacked.

'You don't know,' Mark said to him condescendingly. 'You're too young. You've a lot to learn yet!'

'God forbid he should learn it from you,' said Mr Heylyn mournfully. 'It's the grace of God your mother's not here to see what her eldest son has turned out to be.'

He put on his hat and coat, muttering to himself, 'Your mother, oh Davie, your mother!' And although it was nearly midnight he left the house.

'What do you mean, saying that about me and my mother?' David demanded. He knew that Mark remembered their mother well, that Paul remembered her vaguely, but he himself couldn't remember her at all, and it was one of the many grudges he had against Mark's seniority that there too his brother had an advantage over him.

'I'll tell you what I mean,' Mark answered with deliberate harshness, driven on as always by a demon to hurt his brother. 'I mean if you hadn't been born your mother wouldn't be dead.'

David looked at him, pleading silently that he should say no more. There it was again, the conceit of superior knowledge, the cruel taunting of his ignorance. And yet he wasn't ignorant. It was only that he didn't know he knew. He knew enough, and wished to hear no more. But Mark was started, and his demon had to have its say.

'I heard Mrs Ruthven,' he said. 'She didn't know I was there. She was talking at the close to Mrs Cluny, the woman that nursed you when you were a baby.'

He paused and looked at David harshly.

'Well, what did she say?' said David, calm and prepared before what he recognized was inevitable.

'She was talking about us because she saw Paul across the street,' said Mark. 'She didn't know I was there behind her, in the close.'

'What did she say?' David demanded, his voice raised.

'She said you should never have been born,' Mark answered. 'Mother was told she shouldn't have any more children. He was told too. He knew. But it didn't bother him. I'll tell you more she said. She said he wasn't to be found when you were born. Nobody knew where he was. His wife lay dying, and he was out enjoying himself.'

'Mrs Ruthven seems to know a lot about us,' said David coldly, looking Mark straight in the eye, trying to make him admit he was making it all up.

'She was the midwife,' said Mark. 'Or do you think they called in the royal physician just because you were being born?'

'I don't believe you,' said David, trying hard not to cry in front of Mark and strangely succeeding. He had indeed no illusions about his father. He knew he was selfish, irresponsible, and obtuse, but rather than condemn himself to accepting Mark's version he preferred to believe there was a lot more to it, and that his father was wronged by the way Mark told it.

'It don't worry me none if you believe it or not,' Mark answered flippantly. He moved to the kitchen door and shouted through to the front room:

'Paul! Paul! Come and make some supper, there's a good fellow!'

He was his usual breezy self again. His account of how their mother had died was allowed to lapse as if it had never been given, but there was a new hardness in his eye and mouth as he joked with Paul and ignored David, and the youngest boy brooded over his brother's words when they all went to bed.

In the morning they found their father had returned. He was asleep when they got up, and on the kitchen table was the money he had taken from Mark's little chamois-leather bag.

Mark put the money in his pocket, saying nothing and showing nothing. The recovery of his savings made no difference to his feelings towards his father, and his mind was made up. He was determined to leave the house and manage somehow by himself. He was turned eighteen and he felt a man. He waited an opportunity to speak to Mr Arbuthnot who he was sure would help him. Doing his work conscientiously and willing to do more than lay within the narrowest limits of his duty, he had made a strong impression on his employer and he knew it. He was conceited, but his conceit was always modified by a shrewd intelligence, by a careful observation of other people's reactions to him. He calculated that if he expressed himself with a judicious mixture of frankness and reserve he could play on Mr Arbuthnot's sense of decency and plead his case successfully.

The idea first came to him when he was alone in the office at lunch-time with his sandwiches while the others went out to eat. He snooped everywhere, adding in that way to the knowledge he had gained of Mr Arbuthnot's business by more conventional methods. He was careful in his spying never to tamper with any lockfast place, for though he was unscrupulous in his curiosity he saw it would be foolish to run the risk of betraying his lunch-time activities by leaving any evidence that he had been looking in drawers and files where he wasn't supposed to be looking. But he read all open correspondence and examined all accessible files, and he was surprised not only at the extent of Mr Arbuthnot's business but at the diversity of it. A chain of cinemas, a group of superior hotels, a score of property agents and tenement factors, well-to-do widows and retired professional men, people living on unearned income and people with plenty of money to leave, they were all there on the files as Mr Arbuthnot's clients. Many a solitary lunch-time he spent following through the file the beginnings of some business in a brief letter to its interesting conclusion in a legal document. It was a new world to him, an exciting, attractive world. Some of these people, he believed, somewhere, sooner or later, could provide him with a better job and better prospects than he had in Mr Arbuthnot's office. It was time to end the fiction that he intended to become an articled clerk to any solicitor.

He would have been content to bide his time and remain at home, but the scene with his father had embittered him even more deeply than he had shown, and he believed his only defence against the improvident claims of his father was to leave the house for good. To do that, he had to tackle immediately his long-prepared plan of asking Mr Arbuthnot to find him a place in one of the firms he looked after. He invented a jingle to give him the frivolous mood he always required before he felt the confidence to cope with anything serious.

'I'll solicit the solicitor,' he kept on saying to himself. 'I'll solicit the solicitor.'

If he allowed the serious side to oppress him, to the exclusion of all other aspects, he found his confidence was squeezed out of him and he muffed the situation. He had always to keep a lighter side in mind, or think of some private joke, and that gave him the self-assurance he needed. So he sibilated softly to himself when he was alone in the office, 'I'll solicit the solicitor.' The day he picked up the money his father left out for him he saw Mr Arbuthnot was having a quiet morning and looked even more benign than usual. Repeating his frivolous phrase behind his clenched teeth Mark took in some letters for signing and stood deferentially by.

Later he would say he never knew how he started speaking. He had long rehearsed the substance of it. The actual words he left to the mould of the moment to shape. Yet somehow, shyly and hesitantly, acting a

51

little but careful not to overact, he made his position clear to his boss. He admitted he had no prospects of ever becoming an articled clerk (without confessing he never had any), blamed it all on his father's intemperance, improvidence, and addiction to gambling, and generously explained those vices as due to the loss of a beloved wife, his own dear mother, who had had a little money in her own right but the sum put aside at her death for the education of her sons had been regrettably wasted by his father. He ended in a gallop by candidly asking Mr Arbuthnot to find him a better-paid job with one of his clients.

Mr Arbuthnot listened with critical astonishment. But he was kind and generous, he believed in giving a boy a chance, and it was only many years later that Mark regretted he had never looked at him as a human being, never tried to understand him, never even bothered to respect him, but looked on him solely as a means to an end, the instrument of his own liberation.

'Well, it's a great pity,' said Mr Arbuthnot, 'a great pity.'

He sketched some criss-cross lines thoughtfully on the large green blotter on his desk.

'I suppose it's only right you should get a chance somewhere else if you think you can't stay on here,' he said. 'You're quite determined to leave home?'

'It seems the wisest thing to do,' Mark answered. 'Don't you think so, sir?'

'Good heavens, boy, that's not for me to say!' Mr Arbuthnot said, shocked at the request for his free opinion on such a private matter. 'I think you should speak to your father first, I think you should speak to your brothers. You mustn't do anything hastily, and you mustn't do anything underhand.'

'No, sir,' said Mark.

Instead of being given as he had hoped a letter of introduction to one of Mr Arbuthnot's clients he was told to call on Mrs Arbuthnot two evenings later between seven o'clock and eight. Mr Arbuthnot had a great faith in his wife's judgement of character, and he would never have considered finding any other employment for Mark without hearing her opinion of the boy's reliability and veracity. Mark understood at once that he was being submitted for approval, and called on Mrs Arbuthnot at half past seven in the evening. His face was clean, his nails scrubbed, his boots polished. His hidden nervousness lessened for a time when a maid opened the door. She was small, dark, and pretty, and Mark was already responsive to women. Her gracious smile of welcome did him good and he entered the house with growing confidence, ready to face the lady who was waiting to inspect him. He was impressed by the size and furnishings of the hall, which seemed enormous compared with the tiny lobby behind the front door in his father's house. He was impressed by the wallpaper, by the carpets, by the substantiality and solidity of the furniture, and by the size of the room he was shown into. So this, he thought, is how the well-to-do live. And it seemed to him he knew exactly what he wanted. He wanted the space, comfort, and luxury he saw in Mr Arbuthnot's house. He was so awed by his surroundings that at first he had no reactions left for Mrs Arbuthnot. She was small, quiet-voiced, sedately dressed. She took his awed manner to mean he was shy with her. It pleased her he should have sufficient deference to be shy, and she treated him kindly.

The interview was entirely inconsequential in its course, as Mark had expected it would be. Mrs Arbuthnot simply wanted to see him, to hear him speak, and judge him by her womanly intuition. Like all the Heylyns Mark pleased elderly women by his good looks, his tempering of a juvenile modesty with a masculine forwardness, his air of attentiveness and admiration. A few days later Mr Arbuthnot himself raised the question of Mark's future. No mention was made of any of his clients, but he told Mark that Mrs Arbuthnot's brother was a shipping agent in Liverpool, and he could go there if he liked at a much higher salary. Arrangements would be made for him to live in a hostel, and perhaps he could manage to send a little money home every week. There was one condition: he must bring a letter from his father agreeing he should go to work in Liverpool.

Mark took the news home, not to his father and not to David but to Paul only. David heard enough to suspect what was going on, and saw Paul practise the writing of a letter purporting to be from their father.

'Of course I could forge it myself,' said Mark. 'But there might be something would give my hand away. Old Arbuthnot won't know your writing, so you needn't be all that careful.'

But Paul had the conscience of a craftsman, and he wanted to show off his skill with a pen. He was to some extent a vassal of Mark, getting a shilling or two from him irregularly. Enjoying the exercise assigned him, he fetched from the drawer where their father kept his business papers several examples of his handwriting and copied and re-copied them till he could do it fluently.

'Look,' said Mark impatiently, 'you don't need to go to all that bother. Arbuthnot won't know the old boy's handwriting. I just want a letter that obviously wasn't written by me.'

'It's got to be an adult's hand, hasn't it?' Paul replied calmly. 'And what better adult hand to copy than the one it's supposed to be? If a job's worth doing—'

Mark sighed away his impatience, and David squinted from his corner, trying to overhear their whispered conversation, and to understand just what Paul was doing writing and re-writing at the kitchen-table. When he felt sufficiently confident Paul transcribed a fair copy of a letter drafted by Mark, in which the writer declared he had no objection at all to Mark going to work away from home and thanked Mr Arbuthnot for his generous interest in his son's welfare.

'Paul the Penman, that's me!' Paul chuckled delightedly, looking admiringly at the sheet when he finished.

'It's a beauty!' cried Mark. 'You would swear the old boy had written it.'

'It's his writing all right, isn't it?' Paul said proudly.

'And his style too,' commented Mark. 'Isn't it a damn' good parody of him when he's laying it off! All the flowery phrases he loves to use, the old fraud. Sir, it is with a deep sense of obligation . . . It is my earnest and sincere desire to place on record . . . I have the honour to be your obedient servant. Bah! Humbuggery!'

'Isn't it just a bit overdone?' Paul asked critically.

'Not at all,' Mark insisted.

'An envelope!' cried Paul.

'Oh hell, yes! An envelope,' said Mark. 'I'd forgotten that.'

'There isn't one in the house,' David said quickly, maliciously pleased

54

to point out an obstruction to a scheme he had grasped in its essentials though not in detail.

'Who's talking to you?' Mark demanded crossly. 'You sit there and don't miss a thing. Mind your own business!'

He borrowed an envelope from the woman next door, and Paul addressed it with an old-world flourish.

In another week Mark was gone. He wrote to Paul, who by previous arrangement left the letter out so that his father could read it, and David too if he cared to. Mr Heylyn read it through silently:

Dear Paul,

I am sorry I couldn't let anyone know I was going away because it was all very indefinite up to the last minute, but it was too good a chance to miss and I felt I had to take it! I got the offer of a good job which meant I had to leave here. Mr Arbuthnot didn't mind my leaving him, and I don't suppose anyone else will. I shall write to you from time to time and let you know how I am getting on. I have no address to give you yet because I'm not sure where I shall be living, but I shall let you know as soon as I can and I hope you will write to me . . .

Mr Heylyn read on to the end of the letter and put it back on the kitchen dresser where Paul had left it, and the two boys saw he was weeping softly. They were embarrassed. They were used to him ranting in drink, used to him being melodramatic over trifles, used to him making a show of his trials and sorrows, but this unostentatious weeping surprised them. Mr Heylyn took his handkerchief from his top pocket and wiped his eyes furtively with his back to his sons. Before putting the handkerchief back in his pocket he rubbed it vigorously over his nose, mouth, and chin.

'I've tried to be a good father,' he said. 'We've all got faults. He didn't need to run away. He'll spend more on digs than he can afford, he'll be no better off.'

'Oh, he'll be all right,' Paul said vaguely. 'You see he says he may manage to send you something.'

'I don't want his money,' said Mr Heylyn, turning round and shouting.

Paul hovered a moment and then slipped away to the front room. David was ill at ease to be left alone with his father and silently made him a cup of tea. He felt he hardly mattered in the situation: he had never had much skill in handling his father, and he had nothing to say in this crisis. Paul was better at humouring him, but Paul had evaded the issue. Mark was the best of the three of them. In spite of the fact that he quarrelled oftenest with the father he seemed more in tune with him than his brothers, and he had a talent for never keeping up a quarrel, a talent David knew he himself lacked. His long hostility to Mark was increased by this new grudge, that Mark who was best able to cope with the troubles of their motherless house had walked out on the job, callously leaving it to others much less fit for it.

In the years that followed David accepted his hatred of Mark as a natural, inevitable, and self-justified sentiment. Its origin was forgotten, as prehistoric as the origin of those rocks whose formation occurred in remote aeons of geological time. Yet in spite of himself he often brooded about Mark. He persuaded himself Mark was cruel, selfish, and vain. Searching for the words he came to forget the reality they were meant to describe.

3

David was a regular visitor to Mrs Ruthven. Usually he was shy with people, anxious to break off conversation in case he detained them, for he was afraid of being a bore. But with Mrs Ruthven he felt at ease. Often he hung around after he had gone the errands that were now a routine for him, and even when she seemed to have no conversation for him he still felt quite happy loitering in her kitchen, saying nothing and expecting nothing. But most days she spoke to him freely, as to an equal, and he responded in the same way. Encouraged by his familiarity with her, and by her unembarrassed frankness on all topics, he prepared to ask her about his mother. He waited for the right opportunity, determined not to lose the chance of learning something from the only person he could trust to tell him the truth. Mark's gibe that he had caused his mother's death remained with him and remained with him and would not go away. He even dreamed about it, terrified by nightmares in which a strange woman, who loved him and whom he loved, who was neither identifiable with any woman he knew nor entirely unknown, a woman who was kind and understanding, suddenly paled and quailed before him, and he was cruelly assaulting her until at last she lay panting to death in the dark corner of a strange dim room and he himself panted and wept over her, triumphant and yet wretched that he had killed her. It was under the weight of that incubus that he determined to ask Mrs Ruthven, partly because Mark had quoted her and partly because he believed that she not only knew the truth but would tell him it.

The right occasion came one evening in the winter after Mark had gone away, when he sat with her in the kitchen after Mary had gone out to meet her current boy-friend. She seemed to have a new one every couple of months and her mother remained impartial. The fire was burning cosily, the little marble clock on the mantelpiece with a shepherd on one side of the face and a shepherdess on the other was ticking away placidly, and the table was clear and the room at peace. Mrs Ruthven was in reminiscent mood, speaking ramblingly of the degeneration of the tenements. Once there were respectable, hard-working families in every close in the block, and the closes were kept clean and the stairs well washed. But now the shiftless, the idle, and the dirty outnumbered the old inhabitants. She elaborated her recollections of particular families, now gone to their eternal rest or to the new housing-scheme across the canal, and when she paused in grave meditation he took his chance softly.

'You'll remember my mother then, Mrs Ruthven?' he said.

He carefully adjusted his tone to indicate a merely casual interest, though his heart quickened at the knowledge he was on the threshold of important discoveries.

'I remember your mother well,' Mrs Ruthven answered, knitting assiduously. She was always knitting, and it puzzled him that she kept the printed pattern on her lap but never seemed to need to look at it.

'Tell me,' he said brightly, lightly, 'what age was I when my mother died?'

She was surprised he didn't know, wary of what was to her a simple question but one that seemed to have for him implications she didn't see. She stalled. He started her again gently, insisting that strange though it appeared to her no one had ever told him or ever spoken much to him of his mother.

'I don't remember my mother,' he said. 'Well, I can imagine I do from her photograph. But I don't really believe I do.'

'Oh, I shouldn't think you could remember her,' she murmured, led to answer him by his innocent air. 'You were only about a year or eighteen months old at the time.'

'Then Mark was telling lies!' he cried impulsively.

She looked over her spectacles at him, spectacles she wore only when she was knitting or reading.

'Well, I don't know what Mark said,' she replied drily. 'How was he telling lies?'

'He said——' David began, and stopped in embarrassment.

Then he found his embarrassment was irrelevant. He could never have spoken about it to anyone else, but with Mrs Ruthven it became what it truly was, a commonplace of life, and he had no difficulty in going on.

'Mark said I killed my mother,' he said as if he personally weren't interested but were speaking on behalf of someone else. 'He said if I hadn't been born my mother wouldn't have died. But if I was more than a year old when she died . . .'

Mrs Ruthven went on knitting for a few moments before she answered.

'Well, Mark was right enough,' she said. 'In a way. Your mother wasn't very strong latterly. When you were born it was too much for her. She lived. But she was never the same. She was able to nurse you. But I suppose a doctor would say if she hadn't had you she would have lived for a long time.'

'Mark said Mrs Cluny nursed me,' said David.

'No, that's not true,' Mrs Ruthven answered, shaking her head. 'Mrs Cluny took you out in your pram. Your mother couldn't go out much. But she nursed you herself.'

'I see,' said David subdued to learn that after all Mark had been near enough the truth.

Mrs Ruthven held up her knitting and looked critically at the length and breadth of it.

'Give me a cigarette, Davie,' she said.

He took one from the packet she kept on the mantelpiece and struck a match for her.

'Look, Davie,' she said, so quietly that he had difficulty in hearing her, 'don't start brooding about your infancy, for goodness' sake. These things happen. Your mother was strong enough up to a point, but she didn't get over your birth. These things happen. You're old enough to understand. How was anyone to know beforehand? Doctors can be wrong. You mustn't go judging people or sharing out the blame. It's not your place to judge anybody, your father or your mother. It has nothing to do with you. Never judge people, Davie. Nobody knows enough to judge anybody. It was very wrong of Mark to say what he did. And it was very cruel. Just you forget it. It has nothing to do with you.'

He tried to obey her. He had become accustomed to obeying her. She was his judge and jury, the arbiter of his troubles, and he so much liked sitting with her that he wanted to do only what would please her, even although his failure to do so might never be known by her, so that with a clear conscience he could speak to her and listen to her speak to him.

There was peace in her house. There was some peace in his own house too, with Mark away, but it was liable to irregular interruptions by his father coming in drunk and incoherent, spasmodically violent, and rising the next morning in an ill humour that stayed with him for two or three days and kept Paul and himself on edge, not knowing where the lightning would strike next.

They worked well together, two brothers hardly into their teens, confronting an unpredictable father. They lived a life in which he had no part and of which he had no knowledge, for in the evenings when he was out and they sat in the house alone together they travelled in silence through the strange lands laid open before them in the books they borrowed from the library. David changed the books because he had more time to himself than Paul, who worked in a furrier's warehouse. And because he had more time than Paul he took over Mark's job as cook and did all the shopping. He became as shrewd as a housewife with a large family and a small income. He saved a few coppers here and there and unscrupulously put them in his pocket, trying hard to accumulate money. But it never came to anything.

The need to shop at the cheapest place made him swallow the dregs of his shyness with Black Carter, who had left off assisting his father at the coal-ree and gone into a little greengrocer's owned by his uncle down the street. He drove a small van for his uncle and delivered fruit and vegetables in the housing-schemes across the canal, where there were still no shops. He went to the fruit market early in the morning with his uncle, driving him there and back, and learnt how to buy wisely in the market. In between times he served in the shop. He had become a tall youth, not so heavy as he was as a boy, more brawn than puppy-fat on him, and yet deft and quick behind the counter, smart in serving and friendly with the customers. David had avoided going into the shop even before Carter began to serve there. The fact that it belonged to Carter's uncle was to him a sufficient reason for boycotting it. He was an extremist in his hates as in his affections, and when he disliked anyone he disliked anything connected with him. But the prices were too big a temptation and he yielded. He dimly remembered, too, that after the barbarous attack on him Carter had seemed to want to apologize. He couldn't remember clearly what had happened, for though it was only a few years back the events of his childhood seemed to belong to another world, even to another person. Some of them were forgotten altogether in their precise details. Only a hazy outline, an elusive atmosphere, surrounded them, making them resemble a dream that is entirely forgotten until some chance sensation recalls a fragment of it, and the fragment tantalizingly suggests rather than recalls the rest of it. Growing up, and living only in the worries of the present, griefs and grudges of his boyhood were like the furniture in a locked room that no one ever visited, dusty and decayed, and not his at all.

So it was with only a slight embarrassment that when he entered the greengrocer's shop for the first time he saw Black Carter was serving.

'Hello, young Davie Heylyn,' said Carter cheerily, a small sharp knife in his large hand as he stood at the end of the counter between a sack of potatoes and a barrel of Canadian apples. 'It's a long time since I've seen you. Still at school?'

David admitted the damning fact. The topic embarrassed him. Every other boy of his age in the street was working, and to be still at school implied ambitions beyond his station or an evasive idleness. Carter seemed to understand his feelings, for he changed the subject at once and asked brightly, 'How's Mark doing, have you heard?'

But there too he blundered. David felt that the neighbours looked on Mark's departure as a simple case of running away from home, perhaps to hide some petty theft, and he felt ashamed of Mark.

'Oh, I don't know anything about Mark,' he said rudely. 'I want some vegetables for soup.'

Carter served him swiftly, helpfully, chattering all the time, and David was glad to get out. It was a new Carter, a different person not only in the build and movement of him but in the whole cut, style, and personality. The boy who had bossed a gang without ever uttering a syllable more than was necessary to express the minimum of meaning was now a youth who seemed to find it impossible to stop talking. It bewildered him a little, but he put the discrepancy aside as merely another of the inconsistencies that seemed so common in life, not understanding that in the few years during which he hadn't seen Carter the victor of the battle of the stone had grown up. Obsessed, indeed, with his own identity, self-centred like anyone else of his age, he didn't see that he himself was growing up and changing in his own way, obedient to the inner laws of his nature as Carter was to his.

It was only when he got home and sorted out his shopping in the kitchen that he saw Carter had charged him rather less than he should have done. He faced another problem. He was apt to create more problems than he had the wit to solve. He brooded: if Carter had done it deliberately, he didn't want the money; he resented being patronized. If it were a mistake, he ought to take the extra money back – especially since it was probable Carter would find out the mistake and think him dishonest if he kept it. But if he took it back, and it turned out to be a genuine slip by Carter, he might embarrass him in front of his uncle. If he were deliberate, he might offend him by rejecting an act of friendliness. Everybody knew they were poor. He didn't know what to do, so he did nothing. But the next time he was in the shop he referred to the matter delicately.

'I think you gave too much change, that's what I mean,' he explained when Carter, baffled by the shy allusion, asked him what he meant.

'Did I?' Carter replied without much interest. 'Oh well, it's not lost what a friend gets.'

There came into David's mind then, dimly and inarticulately, what he learnt later more precisely from experience, that in certain circumstances and at certain times in our life, those who were our rivals and even seemed our most bitter enemies, become naturally and inevitably our friends, or at least come to feel sympathetic towards us, hatred being as much a bond as love, and when the hatred is gone the bond itself remains, as it doesn't always do when love goes, for the death of love is accompanied usually by feelings of disappointment, disillusion, and finally disinterest. But our vanity isn't hurt when we find we are no longer hated nor is our ideal shattered when we discover we no longer hate. In the latter situation the heart, instead of feeling empty, feels a mild impulse towards the person it once abhorred and desires to make up for what has come to seem a misjudgement, however excusable the error was, and it wishes not only that the dead should bury the dead but the living should live in amity. We have oftener a common past with those we have long hated than with those we have briefly loved.

Unable to reply to Carter's remark, he smiled it off, but in doing so he accepted it, and he became a regular customer.

'You go to Mrs Ruthven a lot, don't you?' Carter asked him on another occasion.

'Oh, quite often,' David answered defensively, disturbed that his visits to a widow old enough to be his mother should be commented on.

'How's Mary?' Carter asked, weighing potatoes, his eyes on the scale, his tone conversational.

'She keeps well,' he answered primly. Then moved by a malice that was at least half conscious, for he thought he saw through Carter's pretence of asking merely a neighbourly question, he added: 'I don't see much of her. She's usually out with her boy-friend when I go to see her mother. I think she has a new one every week.'

'Yes, she seems to have, doesn't she,' Carter murmured, showing no particular concern, and David wondered if he had erred in thinking he was interested in Mary Ruthven.

He had wilfully lied in saying he seldom saw her. In fact he saw just as much of her as he did of her mother, and he was entranced to be the witness of the mutual trust of the mother and daughter, a complete frankness and peace between them. It made him aware how distrustful his own nature was, how secretive he was with his father, and even with Paul, and how much his own home was disturbed by the intemperate habits of his father, in whom neither he nor Paul would ever have confided.

Half-way through his teens at this time, and three or four years younger than Mary Ruthven, he was delighted to see her relaxed in her own house, to watch the neatness and grace of her as she did little domestic tasks, to see the style and elegance of her when she prepared to go out for the evening. Coming from a womanless house he was more susceptible even than any other adolescent would have been in such privileged observation of a young woman who at times, wearing the great gift of youth, looked bright and beautiful. She would leave the front room where he sat with her mother and go into the kitchen to wash and change; and when she came back to take leave of her mother the boy looked at her in silent pleasure. She seemed to him then the personification of all that was clean, fresh, and radiant, smelling delightfully and to his inexperienced eye dressed in perfect taste. When he thought of what she had been wearing when she left the room and looked at what she had on when she came back it was as if he had seen her undress and dress again. Only the necessities of propriety prevented him from seeing her change her clothes, necessities that indeed a stranger too would have to observe but that he observed entirely for their own sake, not because he was a stranger in the house.

At such times he seemed to himself to belong to her family, and he felt no jealously of her successive escorts, nor did he even wonder if they were her lovers. He was not in competition with them, he was too young and she was too old, and the thought of going out for the evening with any girl was an absurdity to him, so conscious was he of his immaturity and his poverty. In any case he felt himself better off than any of the young men she went out with, none of whom kept her interested for long. He had known her longer than any of them, he was her youthful confidant and heard the long monologues she addressed to her mother every night when she came home from her work. Alone with him, she chattered to him too and spoke to him as if instead of being her junior he were an old man whose judgement was worth listening to. She met him in the street one evening and greeted him warmly.

'Oh, Davie! You must come up and see the new blouse I've bought. I got it at a wonderful sale.'

She had an eye for a bargain, and her wardrobe, though not expensive, had such variety that she seemed always to be wearing something new or at least not quite old. If it wasn't a blouse she wanted him to praise it was a new hat, or a jumper she had knitted, but her greatest self-indulgence was in shoes and he was often called in to admire the smartness of her feet. She taught him by her sisterly manner to notice what she was wearing and to say something complimentary, so that although he remained churlish with others he was always courteous and even gallant with her. But it was done with a smile that made it all a family joke, and she would laugh with pleasure whenever he managed to turn a compliment without floundering into a cliché.

She was playing in the kitchen with a neighbour's child, a little girl four years old with a sticky jam-tart in her hand, when he returned one evening from going an errand for her mother. In the course of their frolicking the child put her arms round Mary Ruthven, but was big enough to embrace her only round the thighs, and the tart slipped from her limp grasp and fell on the carpet.

'What a mess!' said Mary Ruthven, acting horrified. Then without acting she cried: 'My skirt! My good skirt!'

She plucked her skirt round, trying to see the back of it, where the child's hands had been, craning her neck and moving her lips as if she could walk round herself if she tried hard enough.

'Can you see any jam on my skirt?' she appealed to David in alarm.

He looked gravely at her skirt, noticing with a pure, disinterested admiration how she was showing off her legs as she gathered her skirt round them.

'No, no,' he said slowly. 'There's no jam there, but you do look sweet.'

'You're growing up, aren't you!' she answered, laughing, shaking her skirt evenly around her and turning to the child. 'Come on, child! It's time you went back to your mama.'

She put the child out gently and handed her in next door where she belonged.

'Do you like children?' he asked when she came in again.

'That's a silly question,' she said, yawning so that her words were slightly distorted. 'There are children and children. Some of them are horrors. That wee girl is a pretty child, but she would be none the worse for a wash. I don't like sticky children.'

'No, but of your own, I mean,' he said.

She looked at him strangely for a moment before she answered.

'I suppose like any other girl my age I want to get married, one day,' she said. 'And I should hope to have children.'

'Suppose they were little horrors?' he persisted.

'You don't understand,' she said with a smile. 'A woman's own children are never horrors. I suppose there are children born every minute of the day, but a woman's own child is always something that never happened before.'

'And when do you intend to get married?' he asked lightly stoking the kitchen fire for her.

'When I meet the right man,' she said. 'I don't intend to get married for the sake of getting married. Don't worry, you'll have me around for a long time yet.'

Her last words gratified him by implying that she knew he was used to seeing her and listening to her and that he would be sorry when she went away.

'You know that wee one's big sister, the one that's about ten or eleven?' Mary Ruthven asked him as he was putting the shovel back in the coal-bunker. 'The little besom cost me seven bob last week. She's in some junior club and they were giving a concert. She needed sequins for her dress, and the mother gave me five bob to get them in town for her. I was all round the town looking for them, and finally I had to pay eleven and ninepence for them.'

'Why didn't you say so and get your money back?' he retorted, unsympathetically.

'Oh, she hasn't got it to give me. She had trouble enough getting five shillings together, the poor woman. And you know what her man's like. If he knew she had spent even five bob on sequins he'd bawl the roof down.'

She was always helping the neighbours in trivial ways like that. Last winter, he knew, she had bought a hot-water bottle for an elderly widow, living alone on her old-age pension, who happened to say she couldn't sleep for the cold. She liked to be giving.

'Away into the front room and talk to Mother,' she turned on him briskly. 'I'm going to wash and change. Come on, out!'

4

Paul was happy out working and thriving on it. He was as keen as ever Mark was to be smartly dressed and he added to the smartness a touch of style, an air of foppery almost, that Mark had never thought of. He did it by the colour of a tie, by the shade of a shirt, and he was so tall and graceful and carried his clothes so well that he seemed already a tastefully dressed young man. To David, who saw more with his one eye than many people saw with two, Paul's sketchy approximation to the style of a dandy made him look like a younger version of their father. But it would have hurt Paul if he had said so, and he never mentioned the likeness. He didn't want to antagonize Paul and lose him too, as he had lost Mark, for his conscience sometimes whispered he hadn't been guiltless there. He was fond of Paul as he had never been fond of Mark, even though he felt an occasional spasm of irritation at the way he fussed in front of a mirror before he went out for the evening. He was glad when he was left alone in the house, but he was glad too when Paul stayed in and they talked of books and politics, of matters they never heard their father mention and could never have mentioned to him. They shared a belief that in the fullness of time, when they reached man's estate, they would be able to move from the shabby tenements of their childhood and meet more intelligent company, though they had no idea how it would come about.

It was the example of Mary Ruthven's flowing conversation with her mother that made David begin to talk more frankly to Paul of his

66

interests and daydreams and Paul responded with an equal frankness. When they spoke of their ambition to better themselves it was Paul who encouraged David to stay at school and insisted nobody bothered that he brought no money into the house.

'Well, he nags sometimes,' said David wearily, referring to their father.

'I know, I've heard him,' said Paul. 'Little dirty hints. Oh, I know them all! He's got a mean mind. Don't let him worry you.'

'It's easy for you to talk,' David retorted. 'He doesn't nag you. And if he did, you would be more placid than I am.'

'You mean I wouldn't be so bad-tempered,' Paul smiled.

'I suppose you can say it that way,' David admitted.

'You sulk too much,' said Paul. 'And you keep turning over what people say. You should forget it. Folk say more than their prayers, and mean it even less. You'd be silly to leave school now, when you've stuck it so long.'

'Oh, what's the use?' David cried rhetorically.

'Well, I'd like to see one of the family have some kind of education,' Paul answered him.

The answer pleased David. It encouraged him to see that Paul shared his own love of learning for the sake of learning. Even although he knew there were whole realms of study that bored and distressed him because he lacked the ability to conquer them, he was contented and at peace when he was coping with something within his range and interest, without worrying what use he might ever have for the knowledge gained. He was glad Paul hadn't said the whole purpose of his schooling was to help him to pass examinations and then get a good job.

'Anyway,' Paul was saying, 'if he spent less on drink he could have let us all stay on at school. We wouldn't be bringing in anything, but we wouldn't be costing him anything, and he earns enough to keep the house going – not in luxury, but he could keep out of debt. He wouldn't need my few shillings if he didn't waste pounds in that damned club every week. And he's too stupid to see that even from the point of view of his own self-interest he would get a far better return later on if he had let us all get some decent schooling. He would be better off today if he had treated Mark better, instead of nagging him the way he did to get out and earn some money. Mark was clever.'

'Mark wanted to leave,' David said abruptly, disliking the mention of the name. 'All he could think of was getting on and getting money.'

'Oh, he wanted to leave and he didn't want to leave,' said Paul. 'He shouldn't have been asked what he wanted. He should have been made to stay at school. It's a damned shame, a fellow of Mark's intelligence starting life as an office-boy. Do you want to see his last letter?'

'No,' said David, making a show of writing attentively as if taking notes from the textbook in front of him on the kitchen-table.

It grieved Paul that David would never look at the letters Mark sent. He hid them from his father, who was never first up in the morning and never knew what the postman brought, but he persisted in offering them to David, who persisted in refusing to read them.

'He's got another rise,' said Paul. 'But he's still restless. He wants to get on to one of the company's liners as a steward. Wants to see the world before he dies.'

'Is he ill?' David asked.

Paul shrugged, smiled, and gave it up. He was too peace-loving to make an issue of Mark, and David knew he could safely snub him on that topic. It was the only discord in their collaboration as they passed through adolescence together, growing in a mutual affection that was entirely undemonstrative but very deep.

Taking the air late one night after studying hard for his entrance examination to the Inland Revenue David saw Paul and Mary Ruthven chatting in the street. He joined them, glad to speak to two persons who didn't bore him and who wouldn't mind his company, and Paul left them in a few minutes.

'I'll make the supper tonight, Davie,' he said. 'Good night, Mary.'

He moved off with a debonair flourish that might have come from his father in the early stages of inebriety.

'You're a wonderful pair of brothers,' said Mary Ruthven. 'You'll both make good wives to some lucky girl.'

David looked at her impassively, refusing to smile at her pleasantry, and she laughed merrily, as much at his refusal to accept her joke as at the joke itself.

'You'll never guess who asked me to go out with him,' she said.

He glowered at her with his good eye and waited silently. For a moment he thought she was going to say Paul, but Paul – though nearer her age than himself – was not of a courting temperament. He was certainly interested in girls, critical of their dress, speech, and intelligence, but he contented himself with going to a weekly dance run by a local church committee. He wasn't likely to be committing himself to one girl for any evening, and Mary Ruthven was perhaps too well known to him, too much a friend of the family, to have the glamour of novelty.

'Carter,' she said to his silence, and for the first time he saw in her smile the vanity of a woman who knows she attracts men. 'You know, Carter in the fruit-shop down the street.'

He was surprised, for if Paul knew her too well to think of asking her to go out with him he would have thought Carter was in the same position. But so swift is thought that even as he answered her he knew he had in fact no idea how well Carter knew her and he remembered that only a little while ago Carter had seemed on the point of showing a great interest in her as if she were not a person he knew but a person he wanted to know.

'I didn't expect it,' he was saying. 'But why not? What's funny about it?'

'There's nothing funny about it,' she answered, her tone implying that nobody but himself had suggested it was funny.

'I thought you were laughing at the idea,' he said, quickly apologizing for having misunderstood her.

'Oh no, I'd never laugh at any man who asked me to go out with him,' she said. 'Still, it is a bit unexpected. We used to play in the back-court together when we were little.'

'That's a long time ago,' he said, and tried to remember if she had witnessed Carter's order to have his hair cut the night they fought the battle of the stone.

She didn't seem to have been there, for she swept on at once: 'I didn't trust him then. He seemed a bit of a bully. Or maybe I judged him by his friend – who was that fellow was put away for robbing his auntie's shop?'

'Menzies?'

'Yes, Menzies,' she agreed. 'But he seems a very pleasant good-natured boy now. He has certainly made a difference to that shop.'

He went upstairs to the supper Paul had made, and already, disposing of the future with the confidence possible only to a boy of sixteen who knows nothing of the world, he had Carter and Mary Ruthven courting, engaged, and married. The idea pleased him by its conventional sentimentality. He would have a house to visit, he would still be able to see her and listen to her, and Carter too would like to have him visit them. Then there would be children, and he could see them too and help them with their lessons and be a kind of uncle to them. But he soon found he had written out the three acts for a drama that wasn't going to be acted. He kept asking her if she had gone out with Carter and she kept on putting him off as apparently she had put Carter off.

Then he saw them out together and he was pleased. Their association went on for nearly a year, longer than he had known any previous one last. His hopes of seeing his two friends married were high, and he asked her one evening if it were time he started saving for a wedding present.

'And whom am I supposed to be marrying?' she articulated slowly, making a joke of her correct grammar.

He had no answer when she snubbed him like that. He could only look discomfited.

'If you mean Carter,' she said, and shook her head with a smile, 'it's odd you should think I would ever marry him. I had a row with him last week. I'm afraid that's one young man I won't be seeing again.'

'Why?' he asked, disappointed in her for not taking the role he had written for her in his private drama. The thought came to him that perhaps there was something wrong with her, not with the young men she met. She never seemed to keep any of them long. Some she no doubt dismissed. But others, he suspected, hadn't waited to be dismissed. It puzzled him, and he wondered if Carter had tired of her or if she had tired of him. He tried to quiz her.

'Oh, he's dull,' she said. 'He's deadly dull. That kind of dullness that comes from trying to be bright all the time. It gets awfully tiresome. And he talks in clichés. Oh, he's too polite, too polite altogether!'

Her description of Carter amazed him. He gaped at her, and she mimicked his bewildered expression.

'You'll never understand me, will you, Davie?' she laughed. 'Maybe you're too young. And yet you're old-fashioned too. That's why I like talking to you. Of course maybe I don't understand myself. But I just feel he's too – well, too good for me.'

'I don't see how he can be too good for you,' he said impatiently. 'He isn't all that good. What's a small shop in the social scale?'

'Who's talking of the social scale?' She derided the phrase he had used. 'I've never thought about the social scale. I've never thought about marrying money, though I suppose it's a good idea – if you get the chance. I've never thought about marrying, if it comes to that.'

'Yes, you have,' he said quickly. 'You told me.'

'Did I?' she asked, still light and laughing with him. 'I don't remember. I think I tell you too much. Anyway, I'm not thinking of it now.'

'I suppose it will be somebody new next week, then,' he said, throwing away his hoarded dream of seeing her married to Carter. 'And somebody new the week after that.'

'I suppose so,' she conceded readily. 'That's where Carter is too good for me.'

'I wish you wouldn't say that,' he said troubledly as a glimmer of the equivocation in her words came through to him.

She spoke frivolously, but he was nonetheless shaken by her words, and he looked at her distressed and mute. He had not long learnt that the lusts into which he was growing were not peculiar and personal but common to his sex. Now it seemed he was to learn they were not confined to his sex alone, but common to women too. The idea disturbed him.

5

For a few coppers Paul bought some tickets in a raffle run by the church committee whose weekly dances were at that time his only social activity. The draw was held and the prizes awarded during an interval in the dancing and Paul came home beaming, thrilled at his good luck in winning a prize and determined to make the most of it.

'See what I've won!' he cried to David, entering the kitchen like a gust of wind and proudly holding up a cheap box-camera for his brother to see.

David straightened, turning from stoking the fire, a shovel in his hand, and inclined his head so that his good eye could recognize what Paul had in his raised hand.

'What is it?' he asked suspiciously.

'A camera,' said Paul, his face radiant as he gloated over the little cubical object.

David went over, still clutching the shovel, and peered at the camera, and Paul magnanimously took the shovel from him and let him take the camera in his hands.

'How do you work it?' David asked. 'I don't know anything about cameras. Do you?'

'No, but we'll soon find out,' Paul answered breezily. 'First we'll have to buy some films.'

'And how much will that cost?' said David, not for the first time aware of his extensive ignorance of everyday things outside the range of his daily shopping. But he was willing to leave all practical matters to Paul and learn from him. It was Paul who got things done, it was Paul who enjoyed novelties and coped with them.

'I've no idea of the cost,' Paul replied, 'but we'll soon find out.'

His continued use of the plural pronoun flattered David. Paul was always kind to him, and here too, with a new gadget that was entirely his own and would certainly give him great pleasure, he spoke of it as something in which David was to share and whose difficulties they would overcome together. They would find out together how to use the camera and how much it would cost to buy film and how to load the film into the camera. Paul was generous as well as kind, and David warmed in his presence. He had himself no particular interest in the camera. He had never wanted to have one, nor did he feel greatly excited to have one in the house, but he was pleased that his brother was so delighted with an instrument he had acquired by the luck of the draw.

The camera satisfied a want in Paul's life. It gave him a hobby. As a schoolboy he had been addicted to quiet domestic pursuits, little inexpensive interests that kept him quiet at the kitchen-table through the serene stretch of uncounted hours between tea-time and bed-time in a winter evening. He had tried stamp-collecting until he found a good collection was beyond his means. He had made an album of photographs and drawings of the birds of Britain and another of historical costumes. But since he could come by the necessary illustrations only when he could afford certain magazines, he let the albums lapse for lack of material.

Yet he had been very happy with scissors and paste, singing and humming softly to himself as he bent over his messy task. In between times, and particularly after the collapse of his various hobbies, he liked to sit drawing and painting. He copied from books, magazines, newspapers, catalogues, calendars – anything with illustrations. But there too his resources were meagre. For pigment he had only an ancient box of water-colours with inadequate brushes, for pencils he had only cheap things with one kind of lead, and although as he grew older he learnt of the various grades of graphite he was unable to afford a supply of different pencils. Once he bought a bottle of Indian ink and tried to copy line illustrations and cartoons, but he was handicapped by lacking the proper nibs and the right kind of board to draw on. Once he managed to buy a drawing block of cartridge paper instead of drawing on pages torn from one of David's discarded exercise books, and it was then he saw that with one cheap pencil he would never get the shading necessary to achieve anything like a resemblance to the half-tone illustrations he was copying.

A more discouraging handicap finally made him give up drawing altogether: he found he had no talent for it. There was always something stiff, disproportionate, and laboured in his efforts, and even in limiting himself to copying someone else's drawing he never seemed to get the result quite right. To draw anything actually in front of him, a scene, a person, an object, proved beyond his ability. The translation of the solid and spatial into terms of line and colour on a plane surface had always to be done for him.

So it was that his album of drawings consisted solely of copies of illustrations in books and magazines. He thoroughly enjoyed the exercise of restating a translation he was unable to effect for himself, and he would show his drawings to David, holding up the original in one hand and his copy in the other, and solicit his young brother's comments. But David too had no talent for drawing and little visual taste; he could neither correct Paul's work with a pencil nor improve it by advice. All he could see was that the copies suggested rather than imitated the originals.

'Not bad,' he would mutter diffidently, embarrassed at being conscripted as a critic. 'Seems a bit out of proportion somehow.'

'Yes, it's hard to get it just right,' Paul would admit readily, quite unoffended.

Yet the urge to put something together, to make something remained with him. It was his restlessness to be doing something, were it only pasting pictures in a home-made album, that made him sometimes irritate David, who was content to sit and read all evening. He would moon through the house, tired of reading, unoccupied and unable to settle, and sigh, 'Oh, I wish I had something to do!' Then David would mutter crossly, 'I wish you would sit down and be quiet.'

The camera came as a boon and an inspiration to him. Here was an instrument that could copy directly, immediately, and accurately, and give him the satisfaction he longed for, the satisfaction of obtaining on paper through an operation carried out entirely by himself an exact image of what lay before his eyes. At first, buying films only irregularly out of his scanty pocket money, he was content to take occasional snaps of David in the back-court, of the wooden bridge over the canal with the whitewashed house beside it, of Mary Ruthven wearing her best dress at the close-mouth on a Sunday afternoon when the street was quiet, and he put the negatives into the local chemist for development. Then he began to put the purchase of photographic materials first in his list of necessary spending. He had begun to smoke a little, but now he stopped smoking, and he stopped going to the weekly dances he had enjoyed so much. He lived austerely, and all the money he saved went to the furtherance of his hobby. Like Mark before him he trimmed the money he gave to his father and arbitrarily increased his personal allowance. Mr Heylyn, afraid of losing Paul's contribution altogether, made no comment in front of Paul but behind his back he muttered crossly to David.

'Three sons!' he would say to the mirror beside the kitchen sink as he shaved on a Saturday morning when David was in the house alone with him and Paul was at work. 'Three sons, and not one of them worth a damn. The first leaves the house the minute he starts to earn a little money, the next keeps all he earns, and the last doesn't earn anything. Aye, gratitude! You bring them up and deny them nothing, and that's the thanks you get.'

David was indisposed to defend Mark, unwilling to think Paul needed any defence, and too aware of his own dependence to defend himself. And although he raged inwardly at his father's words and phrased a full and bitter rebuttal of them, he said nothing aloud.

In the summer, though he couldn't afford to go anywhere for a holiday, Paul spent a day here and there, visiting for a few hours many of the famous seaside resorts of the Firth of Clyde, and he always took his camera with him, primed for use. Then, without telling David in case it all came to nothing, he had an enlargement made of one of the snaps he took and sent it to the weekly edition of a local paper. The weekly edition was heavily illustrated and intended mainly for export to exiled Scots, whose relatives posted it to them to keep them in touch with their native land, for nobody loves his birthplace so much as a Scotsman or leaves it with such eagerness. In those summer months the paper offered prizes for the best holiday pictures, and Paul came in one Saturday at lunchtime smirking with pride and handed David the newspaper open at the centre pages. There was Paul's snap, three columns broad and four inches deep, and there below it was his name, with the award of the first prize.

'Ten pounds!' cried David. 'Well, glory hallelujah!'

Even his dull dead eye shone for a moment with pleasure, and he shook his brother's hand warmly, sincerely, delighted in the trivial success. To Paul it wasn't trivial, it was important. It marked the beginning of a new stage in his life and opened the door to the fulfilment of ambitions he had been brooding over for a long time. Sensing something of his inspired excitement David smiled in sympathy. He looked at the paper again, amused at the novelty of seeing Paul's name in print, and then suddenly, reading the amount of the cash prize, he cried in dismay: 'You'd better hide it from him! He'll want the money from you if he sees that!'

Like certain African women who avoid mentioning their husband's name, submitting to an immemorial tabu, so were these two youths accustomed from childhood to avoid referring to their father by any word that denoted his relationship to them.

'He won't see it,' said Paul offhandedly. 'He won't look at the paper. He never reads it. He never reads anything.'

'Still, you had better be safe,' David muttered, more easily given to fretting. 'Why not just cut out the picture, and burn the rest of the paper?'

'Oh, don't worry about trifles,' Paul retorted. 'Just study that picture, will you. Do you see how clever it is?'

David stared hard at the page and wished he knew what he was supposed to see that was clever, and hoped he would say the right thing. He came to some degree of appreciation of the skill involved and managed to please Paul by commenting adequately on it, by using some of the jargon he had heard him use about photography and murmuring vaguely about composition, balance, light and shade, and focus of interest.

There were seven or eight swans in the water and a couple more standing on an islet.

'It's on the Kelvin, up past the paper-mill at Dawsholm,' Paul explained. 'I had to do a little trespassing to get there.'

The grouping of the swans made a pleasing pattern, and the mould of their graceful necks and the soft tone of their plumage were delightfully brought out in the picture.

'Only the camera could convey such beauty,' said Paul proudly. 'Try doing it with words – you just couldn't. It's so – so utterly visual. You could never describe that scene, now could you?'

'No, I don't suppose you could,' David answered dubiously.

'It was a sheer stroke of luck I got them grouped like that,' said Paul, eager to live through the moment of his triumph again by talking about it. 'See the lovely effect of recession in it. I hardly dared breathe in case I frightened them away. You should have seen me, on my hands and knees practically, hiding behind the bushes. Then I had to snap them quick before they spread out and spoiled the pattern. Isn't it entrancing?'

'It's a most impressive picture,' David agreed, and to lessen the solemnity of the moment he added, 'but shouldn't you buy some buns out of your prize money and go back and give the swans a real good feed?'

'When you think what a cheap camera I used, it's an amazing picture,' Paul went on, too rapt to bother about his brother's levity. 'It's really a masterpiece. There are few things lovelier than a swan gliding on the water, and I've captured the beauty in that scene better than any artist could do.'

David shifted his weight from one foot to the other uneasily. Paul seemed to imply that a mysterious skill on his part had overcome the deficiencies of the instrument and got a better result from it than anyone else could have done. The implication seemed unwarranted, but he was too fond of Paul to want to argue about it. Paul was staring again at the prize-winning picture, but David saw he wasn't really looking at it. There was a dream in his eyes, a new-born fantasy, a cold hard ambition.

'I must get a better camera,' he said, and with the longing in his voice there was mingled a deep-abiding resolution.

From his inside pocket he took out a photographic wallet and showed David the contact print.

'There, that's what it looked like before I had it enlarged and sent it in,' he said. 'It takes good judgement to see just what it's worth when it's as small as that. I must get a good lens so as I can examine the prints properly before I spend money getting them enlarged.'

Later on David found out Paul had shown their father the picture and told him of the prize money after all. It depressed him a little that Paul could be so quickly disloyal to their common bond of dislike for a man who was excluded from their counsels and ambitions because of his unfatherliness. He began to see that Paul suffered an almost compulsive urge to seek praise, to be taken notice of, even if only by their father who didn't really notice anything or anyone that contributed nothing to his own comfort. With a short struggle he reached a position of tolerance and forgiveness. If that was how Paul was there was nothing he could do but accept it. There was no need to quarrel about it. Yet he couldn't

77

help letting Paul see by a casual word that he knew their father had been told about the picture.

'Oh, you can't hide that kind of thing,' Paul answered lightly. 'Somebody would be bound to mention it to him sooner or later. You'd only look silly or mean if you tried to keep it from him. And I'll be doing more of that, a lot more. And anyway—'

He broke off and took out his wallet. Opening it he let David see two five-pound notes inside.

'I got that out of him,' he said, smiling at his own skill in getting money out of their father.

'How on earth did you manage that?' David asked. 'I didn't think he had that much money.'

'Of course he's got the money,' Paul retorted briskly. 'He isn't as foolish as you think when he gambles. He always salts so much away. I know what he's got hidden in that drawer he keeps locked. You'd be surprised. Of course, you're a simple soul!'

He smiled, and patted his brother affectionately on the shoulder.

'I offered him a share of the prize money,' he explained, 'knowing damn' fine he didn't really need it. Then I gave him a long spiel about how much money I could win in these competitions, and earn too in the summer by freelance photography, if I had a good camera. And how much would that cost, says he. Oh, between twenty and thirty pounds, I told him. I'm trying to save up, says I. I kept at him steadily, and I got that ten pounds out of him.'

'You're a financial genius as well as a great photographer,' said David, laughing it off, yet troubled that Paul should make use of someone he despised.

6

That summer Paul earned more money with his camera. Besides the weekly ten pounds, the paper gave a guinea for every snap used and Paul sent in photographs regularly, glad to pick up a guinea if he didn't win the ten pounds. To conceal the fact that he was sending in so many photographs he asked David for help.

'Your girl-friend could help us,' he said. 'Mary Ruthven.'

'Mary Ruthven isn't my girl-friend,' David said, rejecting the absurd phrase by the tone of his voice and the look on his face. He had just started work in the Inland Revenue offices, and the idea of him having a girl-friend was ridiculous. He was too conscious of his lack of pocket money and of the lopsided look of his face, with one eye dead and the other still alive. 'Why, she's five, well, four – at least three years older than me.'

'But you're friends,' Paul insisted quietly, soothingly. 'You see Mrs Ruthven every day practically. And you see Mary. Do you think she would let me use her name for some of the photographs I send in? The editor won't want the same name appearing every week, even every two weeks. I'm sure I could double what I win if I could use some other names. I could give her commission on it.'

'She wouldn't want commission,' David said, unhappy at the proposal, but willing to accept it since it was Paul's, and after all it did seem unfair if Paul's photographs earned less money than they deserved just because they went in with the same name every time.

'Will you ask her?' Paul persisted.

'Of course I'll ask her,' David answered loyally.

He did it timidly, coming to the point after much circling round it. He feared she would refuse, or be unwilling, or even say it was dishonest, but she was only amused. She laughed, and he liked to see her laugh because her lips were so fresh and her teeth so good.

'I think he's born to get on, your big brother Paul,' she said. 'He can use my name if he wants to. But of course the neighbours will guess the truth.'

'I don't think it worries Paul what the neighbours think,' David commented.

'Well, even at that, they needn't,' Mary Ruthven cried, suddenly remembering something. 'I have an old camera myself, one of those folding models. It never took very good snaps. But it's a camera. I'll fetch it out, and let the neighbours see me with it now and again.'

'Well, thanks very much then,' said David, and turned to go.

'That's a fine thing!' Mary Ruthven exclaimed. 'Am I never going to teach you how to behave?'

He stopped awkwardly at the door, stared at her wonderingly, and only her teasing smile assured him he hadn't made some mysterious social blunder.

'You come here asking me to do you a favour,' she said, 'and the moment I agree you want to be up and away.'

'To do Paul a favour,' he corrected her.

'Oh, but you two are one,' she laughed. 'Brothers in everything. Sit down and talk to me. You've never told me about your job. I'll make a cup of tea. Mother's lying down in the front room. I'll take her one through if she's awake.'

She was always making cups of tea. Neighbours popped in for a chat and she made them a cup of tea. Her mother sat knitting or reading, or lay down for an hour, and she made her a cup of tea. He himself called as a matter of routine, and she wouldn't let him go till she had given him a cup of tea. And over that cup of tea she chattered till he was past taking in what she was saying, but was aware only of the rise and fall of her pleasant fluent voice, of the fascinating way she emphasized certain words, spoke quickly, spoke slowly, pursed her lips, retracted them, showed her teeth occasionally as she spoke, and used her fine hands to add a significance that lay beyond words. Even her throat and bosom, when she wore a low-necked dress, as she often did, held his attention more than her words, because they seemed at some points of her chattering to convey more than she was saying, so alive did they seem as she quivered and panted in her energetic style of expressing herself. At such times she seemed to be an actress, performing because she was born to perform, just as Paul was born to get on, caring no more for an audience than Paul cared for having his name printed so long as his photographs were accepted and paid for. Yet since he happened to be there her entire act was for his benefit.

'Oh, I'm only a clerk,' he said, trying to answer her question about his job but sadly aware he had nothing to say that could come anywhere near the exciting way she could describe the most trivial occurrences of her daily life. 'A very junior clerk. But I should get more to do later on, and of course more money, if I pass my departmental exams. I've one on elementary accountancy and office organization, and then I've one on tax law.'

'More exams!' she cried with horrified emphasis. 'I'm glad I'm only a shorthand typist. I've been promised a move up to private secretary to the area manager, but I've been promised it for so long and nothing has happened that I've given up thinking about it.'

'Aren't you a bit fed up with the job then?' he asked.

'I might be if I were in another office,' she answered, pouring the tea. 'But the company's good, and there's plenty of variety, and then – tell me, do you think a married man can love two women at once?'

The question was beyond his answering. He was too young, too ignorant of the world of men and women, to grasp the implication of her question or even to make a hedging reply. He just sat and looked at her. She rose abruptly and took a cup of tea through to her mother, but came back still carrying it.

'Mother's sleeping. I won't disturb her,' she said, and sat down across from him.

His heart quickened as he looked at her, she seemed at once so young and so old, so wise and so simple, so womanly and so sexless, at least as far as he was concerned, since he felt he was still to her the grubby urchin she had once washed and she was still the big girl who had taken him to her mother when he lost the boxing match. The kitchen was very quiet and they seemed alone in the world.

'What has a married man to do with you?' he asked diffidently.

'Men are lucky,' she said, looking into her cup. 'I can't tell my mother. I can't tell anybody. And yet I've got to speak.'

'All right,' he said, seeing his cue at last. 'Speak to me.'

'There's a married man works beside me,' she said, stirring her tea and looking at it rather than at him. 'Oh, he isn't high up in the firm and he isn't all that well paid, but he's very clever and he can still get on if they play fair with him. Maybe I encouraged him. Maybe it's my own fault. But now he says he loves me. I feel sorry for him. He looks so neglected. Why can't women look after a man when they've got him? One thing leads to another.'

'What on earth's going on?' he asked in dismay.

'Nothing, Davie, nothing,' she answered, looking up at him and smiling again. 'Don't get alarmed. There's nothing wrong, not yet anyway. But I'm in such a muddle I must talk to somebody. It's been like this for months now. He says he loves me, but he loves his wife too. He wouldn't hurt her for the world.'

'Oh, this is silly,' he muttered resentfully. 'What can ever come of it?'

'I know it's silly,' she answered calmly. 'I know nothing can come of it. I laughed it off at first. I laughed at him. But now I can't stop thinking about him. Is that love?'

'How should I know?' he demanded, cross with her. 'Why couldn't you keep going with Carter?'

'Him!' she cried, raising her eyes from her cup to the ceiling. 'He's too good for me. I told you. Much too good. He bores me.'

As abruptly as she had raised the topic she dropped it and he saw he was dismissed. He told Paul Mary Ruthven was willing to let him use her name but told him nothing more, feeling himself a privileged confidant who must keep a discreet silence.

7

In the winter of that year, when the long hours of darkness kept him from using his camera, Paul read extensively in the history, theory, and practice of photography, communicating to David the odd items of information that interested him.

'You know,' he said in a peaceful evening in the front room, 'I hadn't realized photography was so old. Daguerre's first efforts were over a hundred years ago.'

'Well!' said David with emphatically acted surprise. 'I never knew that.'

He was in fact uninterested in the venerability of photography, but if it interested Paul he was at once committed to taking an interest in it too.

'Yes,' said Paul. 'It's in this book. And Delaroche said that after Daguerre painting was dead. The artists of those days called it the invention of the devil.'

'That was a strange thing to say, as if it were evil,' David answered for the sake of saying something and fidgeting to return to his own book.

'Yes, but there's a lot of truth in it,' said Paul sagely. 'It's a deep saying when you think it over.'

He plunged deeper and deeper into reading about photography, coming to the surface only to report his soundings to David, who remained on the shore and watched him lovingly. Whenever he had a couple of shillings to spare he bought a glossy magazine devoted entirely to the subject. Its small ads fascinated him even more than its highly stylized and eccentric photographs. Hypnotized by those advertisements he embarked on a long and arduous course of saving.

'I think I've got ideas that will pay,' he confided to David one evening when their father had gone out to his gambling-club. 'I want to get them worked out before the spring, and then I can get started. I think I can earn good money if I get a good camera. This cheap thing I won, it has a moulded lens.'

'Oh yes,' said David. 'That's not much use?'

'Not really,' said Paul. 'What I want is a good precision camera. A proper lens is made of ground glass, you know.'

'Yes, I know,' said David. 'Spinoza was a lens-grinder.'

'Was he?' Paul answered politely. 'Anyway, the money's there for the taking. I'm sure of it. And I'm sure I could take it with any luck at all.'

'Tell me what you have in mind,' said David encouragingly. He was learning that Paul was under a compulsion to talk about his chaotic plans and reduce them to some kind of order by the very act of talking about them. His own role was to be that of listener, and he was content to play it. His only difficulty was how far to respond without being so critical that he discouraged his brother. The tense application with which Paul studied textbooks, handbooks, yearbooks and catalogues of photography, and photographic apparatus seemed to make his own utilitarian studies an unimportant drudgery, and he yielded gladly to his brother's enthusiasm.

With the money borrowed from his father and the hoarded earnings of the summer Paul bought a precision camera in the spring.

'It cost me a lot of money,' he told David.

'It must have,' David agreed, handling it uncomprehendingly.

'But apart from the money,' said Paul, 'it raises infinite vistas.'

Infinite vistas, thought David silently. That's a good phrase, that could come from a book.

'I mean to say,' Paul rambled on, running his fingers through his hair, eager to express his deepest thought but not sure David had the intelligence to understand him: 'the camera is really an instrument, an instrument for an artist, a new kind of artist. Delaroche said it meant the death of painting, of the old style of artist. I told you that.'

'Yes, so you did,' David said, remembering the reference because he thought the artist mentioned had the same Christian name as his brother.

'You give a pencil to a person who can't draw,' Paul went doggedly on, 'a brush to a person who can't paint. What will you get? You'll get nothing. It's the same with a camera. A camera needs an artist. A camera will give mediocre results in the hands of a mediocrity. But put a camera in the hands of an artist!'

He exclaimed the last sentence, clenching his fist and vibrating it in mid-air.

'You'll get art?' asked David helpfully, supplying an answer as if the exclamation were a question.

'Exactly!' said Paul. 'That's what I mean. It needs the eye, the judgement, the skill, the sense of construction that you find in an artist. It's all a question of style. There's style in the use of a brush or pencil, and there's style in the use of a camera. Every artist has his own instrument, that's all. His own medium.'

'I suppose that's right,' said David.

'You need sensitivity and intuition as well as mere skill to use a pencil like an artist, and it's the same using a camera. You must have a vision, a sense of what makes a picture – composition. You take a still life by Cézanne. What makes it? The composition. Nothing else.'

Paul was far away as he spoke, seeing possibilities beyond the sight of his brother.

'True,' said David, who had read from the library the same illustrated histories of modern art as Paul had read, and envied him the ease with which he assimilated their language.

'All great art,' said Paul, still in a trance, 'is impersonal.'

He said it twice to make it unanswerable. David was too inarticulate to answer. He wanted to mention Shakespeare's sonnets, but he didn't want to argue, so he said nothing.

'And what's more impersonal than a camera?' Paul asked a half-present David. 'All that's personal is the vision involved in the scene to be photographed. And that's all that's personal with a painter. He selects the scene he wants to paint. But it's his vision makes it a picture.'

'But after the selection comes the interpretation,' said David, trying to make a discussion of it, if the effort would help his brother.

'It's the same thing,' Paul flourished. 'The act of selection is the act of interpretation. It's all in the moment of choice. That's where the art lies. You see it, if you're an artist. The ordinary eye doesn't see the possibility. It's like fencing.'

He stopped and posed, then moved in a demonstration of his argument.

'You're on guard, you wait. You keep your distance. Then when you see your chance you attack!'

He attacked, thrusting quickly in the void.

'That's what does it, the attack. Wipe out the personality, don't drag in preconceived ideas. Never look for a sweet picture or a sentimental picture, or even an ironic picture. Leave it to the eye of the moment. The whole secret of the art lies in the moment of choice.'

'The moment, the living actual moment eternalized in a photographic print,' said David, suddenly thrilled by the idea of fixing for ever the transience of the visual. 'The beauty and mystery of the vanishing moment frozen into permanence, like an ancient Greek frieze, like the maidens in Keats's urn.'

'Yes, that's it,' cried Paul. 'That's what I'm trying to say. And what the old-fashioned artist did with his pigments is the same thing as a modern artist does with his camera. The man with a camera is the artist of our time.'

'I suppose so,' said David, losing the point of the discussion and willing to end it in agreement with his beloved brother.

'And I'm going to be a photographic artist,' said Paul. 'Maybe I can't draw very good, but I know how to use a camera. It may take time, it will take time, I'll have to do a lot of pot-boiling stuff first I've no doubt, but I'll manage it, I'll manage it.'

8

From that time Paul was a youth with an obsession. When the return of the sun to their grey dismal city allowed him to resume his hobby he was no longer content to have his negatives developed and printed by the local chemist. He did his own developing, printing, and enlarging. Still learning from books, he made his first enlarger from an old camera and with some difficulty and considerable ingenuity he converted the small bathroom into a dark room.

In the spring and summer he earned a little money by taking wedding-groups. It was left to David, who had more leisure, to study the banns in the local registrar's window and keep Paul informed. Then Paul solicited the commission, and by providing good photographs cheaply and promptly he was soon so well known in the district that he no longer needed to go out and look for commissions.

'It's just as Whowozzit said,' Paul remarked to his brother as he stood glazing some prints. 'Make a better mouse-trap than your neighbour and the world will beat a path to your door. If this doesn't ease up I'll have to teach you the art and employ you as my assistant.'

'It's the spring, that's all,' said David. 'You'll find there are less weddings in the winter.'

'I don't think the human species mates only according to the season,' Paul retorted. 'The making of families is like the making of books, there's no end to it.'

From weddings he went on to births and took photographs of babies a few weeks old, and there too the quality, speed, and cheapness of his work brought him unsolicited custom.

'Well, you see,' he explained apologetically to David, who sighed at the development of yet another infantile face, 'we've got to get some money in the bank first before we can do the kind of thing we want to do. All this commercial stuff, there's nothing to it but the money. But the money's useful, and so is the experience. You've got to be a craftsman before you can be an artist.'

As always, David was impressed by his brother's easy and confident manner, by his charming frankness, by the way he seemed to know precisely where he was going and yet to allow for every obstacle and forestall any criticism.

'It's a pity they don't go in for deaths too,' he remarked, watching Paul rub his hands in pleasure at a particularly successful enlargement of a sleeping infant.

'Oh, they do,' said Paul, 'they do. Pictures of the grave, and the headstone and all the wreaths. But damn it all, we must draw the line somewhere. An infant, yes. There's some human interest. There's catching the right moment, the expression, a pose. But a tombstone! No thank you.'

He stopped and looked up warily as their father came into the room, dressed to go out, well-shaven and jovial. He looked at the prints Paul had spread out on the table and commented on them inanely, wagging his head approvingly over them and humming a music-hall tune. Then he came to the point.

'I wonder could you lend me a couple of quid till the end of the week, Paul?' he said softly and casually.

Paul looked at his father and waited, silently bidding him down.

'Or even one,' Mr Heylyn conceded.

Paul fumbled in the inside pocket of his jacket and came out with a pound note between his long fingers.

'I don't understand it,' David said crossly when they were alone again. 'One month he's lending you money, even giving you money. Then he comes borrowing a miserable pound.'

'Your trouble is you don't understand human nature,' Paul said, smiling. 'And you're all worked up about it too! Keep calm, Davie boy, keep calm! That's just his way of getting something for nothing, or some of his money back. It was supposed to be a gift, what he gave me, but he always likes some return for a gift. He'll use that quid for a hand at cards, and if he loses, well, it's my quid, he's none the worse. If he wins he'll enjoy the win all the more. He hates touching his savings, you know. He's careful enough in his own way. But not for your sake or mine.'

'Human nature!' muttered David. 'Him – he's not human.'

'What I was going to say,' said Paul, 'was that apart from all this routine stuff, I was thinking of joining a camera club. I could learn a lot

87

from people who take photography seriously. I know a club that has a monthly competition. That would be useful experience. If I'm to get on the sooner I meet some stiff competition the better. It's a competitive world. I'd like to see how I get on against some of these supposed experts. Then I could try the newspapers again. Professionally this time. I've got lots of ideas now.'

He discussed them with David, whose job it became to trim them and make them ready for marketing. They met with rebuffs for weeks on end, and Paul bitterly remarked he could paper the front room with the accumulation of rejection slips.

'Take down some headings,' he instructed his brother, 'and let's see what comes out of it. Topographical, architectural, nature study—'

'People and Places?' said David.

'That's it!' Paul cried happily. 'That's a good title. Suppose we start with George Square. I'll take the pictures, and you write the text.'

David read up on the characters whose statues were stuck in the Square and under Paul's guidance he wrote a series of biographies, half flippant, half didactic. They all came back.

'That was a silly idea,' Paul said. 'Too much of the classroom about it. Or guide-book stuff. And who would want to visit Glasgow anyway?'

'It's what geographers call a nodal town,' David said. 'A good place to get out of.'

'I'll try nature study,' said Paul, and became a bird-watcher, wandering at week-ends over the glens and bens just outside the city, tramping from Balloch round the shores of Loch Lomond, ranging from Arrochar to Tarbet and round the loch to Balmaha. Some of his pictures were rejected, some were accepted.

'The unpredictability of editors!' he exclaimed. 'They printed that and returned this, and the one they've sent back is far superior. How are you ever to know what they want?'

'How about a sociological series?' suggested David.

Paul repeated the word blankly.

'What on earth do you mean?'

'I mean beggars, navvies, transport workers, the catering trade,' said David. 'Children in the park, slum-mothers at the close-mouth.'

'Ah, the arithmetical types, put down four and carry one!' Paul cried, laughing boisterously. 'I've got you now! You've got an idea there!'

'The docks, the Forth and Clyde Canal, the subway at tea-time,' said David.

'We can do it, we can do it,' Paul whispered, the faraway look in his eyes again. 'Even a hackneyed subject, if you approach it with honesty, originality, talent, you can create something. Something new. I could make a damn' good series of camera studies out of that idea of yours. A series that would sell, and yet have some artistic merit too.'

Once again David was given the task of writing a brief text to go with the photographs, but he found he had no talent for writing. Just as Paul had found that although he liked to look at drawings and paintings he could neither draw nor paint, so David found that although he liked to read he couldn't write. His sentences were stiff, his vocabulary flat and academic, the sequence of his words tedious to the reader. The series of pictures earned Paul a lot of money, but many of them were used with extensive cuts in the prose David had laboriously put together, and others were published without any text at all. At that point Paul tactfully sacked his brother.

'Of course I'm more than grateful to you, Davie,' he said. 'I'll always remember it was your idea in the first place, and without your help I would never have got it started. But a good photograph, the kind I take, is really self-explanatory. It doesn't need an article to go with it.'

He prepared another series of pictures, a dozen altogether, and all of them well done. They made the most ordinary scenes appear new, so good was Paul's eye for picking a fresh angle on daily incidents, and they were accepted *en bloc*. David's duties became purely secretarial. He had to buy strong envelopes of the right size and see to the delivery of the precious photographs. He had to compose the covering letter and then type it on a second-hand machine Paul had bought. He didn't mind being his brother's office-boy, for he was obliging by nature beneath his defensive surliness, and he had come to believe it was his place in life to further Paul's great talents. All he didn't like was the way Paul was dressing. There was too much style in it, too much of the self-conscious art-student, and he could never understand why Paul fussed so much about the colour of a tie. Going to a tailor now, instead of buying a ready-made suit, Paul had a cut in the lapels of his jacket, a width in the foot of his trousers, that was always just ahead of the fashion. Sometimes David felt slightly embarrassed by his brother's appearance. His hair too became a matter of concern, and when he began to have it waved regularly by a city hairdresser David almost relapsed into juvenile jeering. But he was prepared to put up with anything rather than quarrel with Paul. In self-defence he emphasized his own untidiness, and yet he came to admire the grace and confidence, the sheer style, and even the manicured hands of his successful brother.

For by David's standards Paul was successful. He always had money in his pocket. He was now fairly well established on a local paper which took everything he sent it, so that he had a regular monthly cheque besides the weekly wages from his bread-and-butter job. But Paul himself lamented his lack of money, even although he had a little in the bank, and spoke more and more of how much better he could do if only he could afford to give up his job in the warehouse and have his own studio and become a full-time professional photographer. A prospect that seemed to David to offer only disappointments and insecurity was to Paul the only desirable life. Paul had no doubts at all that if he were his own master he could guarantee his fame and prosperity. David admired his confidence, but he was temperamentally unable to share it. And sometimes Paul's confidence seemed to him sheer nerve, as when he submitted a photograph to a weekly paper and offered the editor a series of six.

'But you haven't got six,' David objected when he was told what to say in the covering letter. 'You're taking an awful risk! Suppose he accepts?'

'Suppose he doesn't?' said Paul. 'What have we lost? And if he does accept, well – we'll damn' soon find another five pictures. Don't you worry! That's your trouble, Davie. You worry too much.'

Yet David remembered that when they were boys together it was he who was rash and Paul who was prudent. Now they seemed to have exchanged natures, and it was Paul who was keen to fight the world while all he himself wanted was peace and quiet. He remembered too that Paul had accepted defeat at once in the battle of the stone, while he had preferred to keep up his own private fight. They were all changed, just as Black Carter had changed from a silent gang-leader into a talkative shopkeeper. But he was surprised when Paul told him he had approached Carter for a loan.

'Carter's got the money,' said Paul. 'That wee shop of his is a gold mine. It's his now – his uncle gave it to him. And did you know he has opened another shop over in Govan? He's got that van his uncle had, and he's got a car of his own now.'

'I didn't know that,' said David. 'I seldom see him in the shop.'

'He's over in Govan most of the time,' Paul said. 'Oh, he must be making plenty of money. I asked him for a loan. But the bastard wouldn't pay.'

'No?' said David, slightly shocked at language he had never heard Paul use before. It reminded him of Mark who had thrown the word at him nearly five years ago, and he didn't like to be reminded of Mark.

'The point is,' Paul complained bitterly, 'I need a studio before I can cash in on what I know I can do. I want to quit my job and do photography all the time. But I must have a studio. I've been looking around. There's a little place in town would suit me fine. Oh, it's not much more than an attic. But it would do me to start with. Only they want six months' rent in advance, because I'm so young and because I've no references. Carter has the money. I haven't.'

'I thought you had,' David was about to say and then decided to say nothing. He disliked discussing money with Paul. To say he thought Paul had enough money in the bank to pay a six months' rent for an attic might seem to be a hint that he thought he should be paid for acting as his secretary.

'I explained it all to him,' Paul went on. 'I offered him it all back at the end of six months, with interest if he wanted it that way. And the bastard hedged. So much for the friends of your boyhood.'

He mooned about the room gloomily, his hands deep in the pockets of his smart flannels, his handsome face scowling.

Their father came in from the kitchen, snooping in a pretence of paternal interest.

'What are you two always plotting in here?' he asked, looking from one to the other with beaming benevolence.

'Nothing, nothing at all, Dad,' said Paul while David moved away. 'It's just a question of how to make more money.'

'Aye, money,' Mr Heylyn smiled. 'We all want to make more money. The odd thing is it takes money to make money.'

'That's just what I was saying, Dad,' Paul smiled back.

'Now if I had a fiver,' said Mr Heylyn, 'I could make it a tenner. At the club. There's to be a good night tonight. How are you off, Paul?'

'Sorry, Dad, I just haven't got it,' answered Paul, mixing a show of regret with the insincere sweetness of his smile. 'The extra money I earn hardly buys my materials these days. Sorry and all that.'

'Oh, it doesn't matter,' said Mr Heylyn. 'I know it's an expensive hobby, photography.'

Brushing off the topic as he might brush cigarette ash off his waistcoat he began to sing an old ballad, and did a little tap-dance as he stood in front of the fireplace. Then he fussed round the room, pointlessly moving a chair and rearranging the ornaments on the mantelpiece.

'I think I'll get away out,' he murmured soon and left them.

'A hobby!' cried Paul, running his long-fingered hands through the waves of his long hair. 'A hobby! I eat, sleep, and dream photography. I want to be a camera artist. And he calls it a hobby! To hell with it all! I think I'll write to Mark. Not that he has any money, bless him.'

Ever since Mark went away Paul had kept up a regular correspondence with him, and he would leave Mark's chatty letters in David's way though he had stopped offering them to him. But David still ignored them, stubbornly nourishing his hatred of Mark. His life was at peace with Mark out of the house. But sometimes he suffered from nightmares wherein he was face to face with Mark again and their enmity had a violent outcome. They fought ruthlessly and it ended with him killing Mark, usually by choking him. So in the hinterlands of his mind he carried the guilt of a fratricide he had failed to commit only because the victim was beyond his reach. He had no idea where Mark was, or what he was doing.

9

'You'll never guess who's back!' Paul called happily through to David, banging the front door as he breezed in.

'No, who?' asked David, busy preparing the evening meal.

'Menzies,' said Paul. 'Remember Menzies? And by God he's well-off too. Dressed to kill and rolling in money.'

'Doing what?' David enquired sceptically. He had little interest in Menzies. All he could remember of the days when Menzies had cheated him in the boxing tournament seemed to concern strangers. But the name itself aroused a spasm of distrust, a lurking hostility.

'He has something to do with a bookie,' Paul explained. 'I've just left him in town. I met him in a little pub I sometimes go to on my way home. He gave me his card. See, here it is. Commission Agent and Turf Accountant.'

It was the first time Paul had ever mentioned he went into a public house, and perhaps David's surprise was clear to him. Anyway, he said no more that evening about meeting Menzies.

But in the weeks that followed David learned that Paul and Menzies had become drinking companions, meeting most nights in the week. Paul came home slightly drunk one evening, looking remarkably like his father, debonair, elegant, well-spoken, confident – and swaying a little.

'I was just telling Menzies,' he said, beaming at David. 'I meant nothing of course. I wasn't hinting. Please God, I don't have to hint. If I want anything I'll ask straight out, and to hell with the bastard that refuses. Make a cup of tea, Davie, just a cup of tea, I don't want anything to eat. There's a good fellow! I was just telling Menzies because he knows Carter. He knows how well-off Carter is. And by God, was he shocked!'

'About what? What are you talking about?' David said patiently, brewing a pot of tea quickly.

'About Carter, about Menzies,' said Paul. 'Menzies knows I'm no small-time amateur photographer taking holiday snaps. All I need is my own place and I could make a good living, aye, and a good name, out of my camera. I was just telling Menzies about Carter refusing to lend me the money for that little studio I told you about.'

'Yes, I remember,' David answered. 'Here, drink this – and sit down before you fall down.'

'Oh, you're a good fellow,' said Paul, lurching to the tea-cup. 'You've a lot to learn, you poor kid. But you're a good fellow.'

'And what did Menzies say?' David asked, sitting facing his brother across the little kitchen table.

'Ah now, there's a pal for you!' Paul cried, beaming again and nodding his head happily at the rim of the cup. 'There's a real pal! We were just having a quiet drink. You must come out with us some night, Davie. You stay indoors too much. You ought to get out more. You're a bit of a puritan, you know. Life is meant to be enjoyed, old boy. Wine, women, song!'

'And what did Menzies say?' David repeated.

'There's something generous about Menzies,' Paul said. 'He's the kind of man who could have been a patron of the arts. But Carter – that bastard is just mean. All he can think of is his wee shop and how much profit it's making. No vision, no imagination.'

'Maybe he's a bit limited,' David agreed unhappily. 'But why do you say Menzies is generous?'

'Well, he offered to set me up in that studio right away,' said Paul. 'We're even thinking about a partnership. Menzies supplies the capital and I supply the talent. You know, he's got a good business head, that fellow. I could do worse than set up with him.'

He left his job in a few weeks and went to his studio as punctually and regularly as if he were still a wage-earner who had to clock in every morning. David wasn't told the precise terms of Paul's arrangement with Menzies, and he didn't like to ask. He wasn't even sure what Paul was doing in the studio all day long, and he felt rather snubbed at losing his job as secretary. Mr Heylyn wasn't told anything about the studio and apparently remained completely ignorant of it. Every week Paul gave him the same amount of money towards the housekeeping as he had always done, not a shilling more or less. David watched his brother anxiously, disliking – though for no good reason – the association with Menzies, and when Paul began to come in later and later every evening, looking pale, drawn, and worried, he was concerned for his brother's health.

'Well, maybe I am working too hard,' Paul said, 'but if I can't work hard when I'm only twenty, when will I ever work hard? It isn't easy, you know. I'm trying to keep the studio open for commissions and I'm trying to steal time off to get out and do some field work. Then I've got to develop, print, and do any touching up in the evenings. I'll take it a bit easier now the autumn is coming on. But I must build up a connection now. Now or never. It's worth it, Davie. Don't you worry about me. How about joining Menzies and me next Friday night? That's the only night off I'm allowing myself now. Once a week, Friday night. You must come out. You'll like Menzies when you get to know him.'

Flattered to have the invitation repeated, David forgot he had taken it as a slightly drunken gesture when it was first made. He accepted shyly and Paul slapped him on the back and said: 'Now mind! You're our guest. Menzies and I are better off than you.'

'Not at all,' David answered hastily. 'I'll pay my share surely.'

In the upshot it was too much for him. Except for a glass of beer on rare occasions he was unacquainted with drink. And now he was expected to drink too much too quickly, whisky and beer together at each round. He sat with Paul and Menzies at a little table across from the bar, and the place was noisy and crowded and the air dim with smoke. He began to feel squeamish, and he lost interest in Paul's witticisms and Menzies' bawdry. The joviality of the conversation de-pressed him and he wanted to be alone, to be sick. He thought that if he could only slip away and be sick in private he could return and perhaps be a match for them. But his companions kept him at it with a merry ruthlessness.

'That dame of yours,' said Menzies, bringing over three whiskies and three beers from the bar. 'I wouldn't mind a night in bed with her. What a figure she has! You know, that was one of the pleasant things about coming back to this bloody city – seeing that wench again. Even as a kid she had something, but now! I could lose a lot of sleep on her.'

David grued as he raised the glass of whisky to his lips and hiccupped uncontrollably. He thought Menzies was talking to Paul and supposed the reference was to some girl Paul knew. Through the confusion of his brain there floated vaguely the question how Paul found time for a girl-friend and why he had never mentioned her. But he was too tired to think of an answer. He wanted to be alone, to close his eyes and sleep. Paul nudged him in the ribs.

'Yes?' he said. 'Yes?'

He looked blearily from one to the other, trying to sound alert.

'I was talking to you,' said Menzies, smiling broadly and fondling his whisky between his large hands. 'That dame of yours.'

'Me? I haven't got a dame,' David answered, disliking the word and Menzies equally.

'You're in Mary Ruthven's house every night in the week, aren't you?' said Menzies, fixing him with an insolent stare.

'In Mrs Ruthven's house,' he answered pedantically. 'It's Mrs Ruthven I go to see. I've known her since—'

He stopped. He suddenly remembered that his first visit to Mrs Ruthven was when she dressed his injured eye after Menzies' boxing tournament. He glowered at Menzies aggressively, ready to quarrel with him. The man looked ugly to him, the eyes small, the nose like a beak, the mouth long and thin under it, the whole face predatory and hard, alien to all human kindness. The hands cradling the whisky-glass looked like claws. Menzies answered the glower with a derisive grin.

'That's a good story,' he said. 'I know who I would be going to see in that house.'

'Oh, I don't doubt Davie has a soft spot for Mary,' Paul said lightly, sensing a touchiness in his brother's mood. He patted David on the shoulder to assure him he was his friend.

'It isn't a soft spot I'd have for her,' said Menzies and leaned back in his chair and cackled.

Withdrawn into himself again after Paul's comforting touch, David missed Menzies' comment. He finished his whisky and looked helplessly at the beer. He had no idea how he was ever going to drink it. But he couldn't let Paul down. He raised it and sipped a little, carefully. The world about him advanced and receded, became remote and unreal. The only reality external to his own blurred consciousness was the leering face of Menzies.

'The trouble with you, Menzies, is,' he said, and stopped. There was a vicious and brilliant attack buzzing in his head, but all the words were darting about in complete disorder and refused to come under his control. He tried again.

'Mary Ruthven isn't my dame. She isn't anybody's dame. She doesn't live at that level of language. She's that much older than me, but I know her – I know her well, I think. And if you're interested I'll tell you what I'll do for you.'

'Yes,' said Menzies, laughing at him. 'What will you do for me? Money's no object.'

'I'll give you a piece of advice,' said David. 'You can save yourself the trouble of thinking any more about her. I know her. I know her tastes. And I can tell you the thought of having anything to do with you would make her ill.'

Menzies laughed loud and long and slammed the table with his palm in sheer enjoyment of David's attempt to be rude.

'Well, it's time we were going,' he said to Paul. 'Are you coming too, Davie? Do you feel fit?'

Menzies rose steadily to his feet, completely master of himself, and broke up the session. It was all David had been waiting for. The movement did what he had wanted to do but lacked the experience: it ended the drinking. At once he felt he would live a little longer, and he wouldn't be sick after all – not at once anyway. But he knew he must take the chance quickly and get away, away to his own corner and recover in solitude.

'No, I won't come with you,' he said hastily, rising and falling back on his chair again. He tried once more and came round the edge of the table, feeling his way slowly.

'I think you need a tug to guide you into harbour,' said Menzies softly, watching him with a little smile.

'I think I'll go home now,' David said. He stumbled against Paul and hung on to him for a moment. 'I'll see you later, Paul. But I really must go home now.'

'We can fix you up too if you like,' Menzies remarked casually. 'Can't we, Paul?'

'No, I think Davie had better go home,' Paul said. 'I think he wants to go home.'

He helped his brother through the crowd three and four deep at the bar and ushered him through the swing-doors to the dark street. David stood for a moment and panted.

'Fresh air!' he said foolishly. 'It's fresh air, that's what it is. It's a wonderful thing.'

'Are you all right?' Paul whispered anxiously, divided between his loyalty to his brother and his eagerness to be gone with Menzies.

'Yes, yes, of course,' said David. 'I'm tightly slight but I can walk straight.'

He showed them, and they laughed. Then they were gone, and he lurched home to the empty house, afraid to take a bus in case he made a public fool of himself. He lay on his bed fully dressed, watching the ceiling come down and the walls change places. It was only as he lay there that Menzies' words came back to him and he understood the meaning of what had been said to him. 'We can fix you up too. We can fix you up too. Can't we, Paul? Can't we, Paul?' He shook his head to shake the words away and fell into a troubled sleep.

He wakened an hour later, sufficiently sobered to undress and get into bed properly before his father came in. He didn't hear Paul come in, but in the morning there he was, huddled in his own bed at the other side of the room, fast asleep.

10

By the time autumn was creeping into winter Paul was no longer regular and punctual in going to his studio. Just as his father started and finished in his own time, satisfied so long as he earned a certain minimum commission, so Paul came to make the most of his freedom from compulsory office-hours. He was his own boss and wallowed in his independence. He flaunted it so much that his father commented on it.

'I don't understand how you're allowed to go in whenever you like in the morning,' he said querulously. 'There's something fishy going on, if you ask me.'

'You take a long time to smell fish, Dad,' Paul replied calmly. 'I'm under nobody's orders. I'm a self-employed person, I am. A ruddy little capitalist.'

'You mean you're living off your photography?' said Mr Heylyn, giving a good imitation of a man who was surprised.

'That's right,' said Paul.

'Oh, I see,' said Mr Heylyn. 'Well, I hope you know what you're doing. I can't say you've treated me any worse than before. You've always been very faithful with the money.'

'And that's the main thing, isn't it?' said Paul.

He didn't see that in breaking away from the discipline of regular office-hours he was following in the steps of a father he despised, for he saw himself in terms of a talent and skill his father lacked. David saw the likeness dimly at times but avoided making anything of it. To follow the erratic working-hours of their father was not in itself wrong, he thought, and he believed Paul had a greater power for self-discipline and hard work than ever their father had. He also believed, just as much as Paul did, in Paul's future as a camera-artist.

The fact that he could go out to work when he pleased made Paul a distinguished character in a street of undistinguished wage-earners, and he enjoyed his role. His manner became a mannerism, airy and slightly patronizing. The local fame he had won by his prize photographs, by his wedding-pictures and baby-pictures, and then by his regular work on a local newspaper, took on a deeper and more respectful note. He was esteemed as a successful young man who by his own efforts had built up a small but flourishing business. David was proud of his brother's fame, entirely free from jealousy. But sometimes it irked him to be known only as Paul's brother. When he was introduced to anyone the mention of his surname usually provoked the friendly question: 'Heylyn? That's an unusual name in these parts. Are you Paul Heylyn's brother?'

'That's fame,' said Paul when David remarked on the frequency of the question. 'When people know you that don't know you. Never mind, Davie! Don't take it to heart. I'll make you proud one day to be known as my brother. I'll be really famous one day, not just known in this city.'

'Oh, I don't complain,' said David, pleased when Paul was happy.

It was just after the turn of the year that Paul told him Menzies had gone to London.

'It's promotion for him he says,' Paul explained. 'The firm he's working for here is really owned by a big firm in London. Different names, you know, but the same people behind them. He's got a first-class business head, Menzies has.'

'You'll miss him?' David asked kindly.

'Oh, I don't know,' Paul said, brooding a little. 'He got in my hair sometimes. Some of his ideas – oh, no doubt good commercial propositions, but he just can't see the art side. I couldn't go all the way with him. Artistic conscience, you know. And then he was taking more money out latterly than was fair.'

David looked at his brother, surprised at the casual way he mentioned Menzies' greed. He waited for details, but Paul said no more.

Then in the spring there was a letter for him from London.

'From Menzies,' he told David.

He walked round and round the room where he had spent so many peaceful evenings with his brother. David watched him all the way with his good eye and felt an excited quivering in his midriff. He knew what was coming before Paul said it.

'I'm going to London, I'm going to join up with Menzies. He has everything organized. It's too good a chance to turn down.'

'I thought you didn't trust him,' David said plaintively. 'I thought you said he took too much money from you when he was here.'

'Oh, there'll be plenty of money for both of us in London,' said Paul. 'This town's finished for me. I'll get no further here, I can see that.'

'It means dropping all your newspaper work here,' David pointed out quickly. 'Oh, I know it's stuff you don't think much of now. But you know it has always been a regular income. You could always be sure of so much.'

'We needn't lose it completely,' Paul answered with a wave of his clean-cuffed hand. 'Not immediately anyway. I'll keep on the present series. I'll post on the proofs to you and you can deliver them as usual. They'll send the cheques here and you can post them on to me.'

'Yes, I suppose we can do it that way,' David answered glumly.

He went through to the kitchen to make a cup of tea, a habit he had picked up from Mary Ruthven, and to which he had recourse whenever he was upset.

He came back with a tray, and Paul smiled.

'No, no, no!' he cried gaily. 'You'll never learn, Davie! This calls for something better than tea.'

He crossed to a shelf where all his books on the history, theory, and practice of photography were ranged, and from behind them he fetched out a half-bottle of whisky.

'Come on now, smartly!' he said, prodding his brother affectionately. 'Glasses!'

David brought glasses and Paul filled them.

'To London,' he said, raising his glass.

'To fame and fortune,' said David.

The brothers clinked glasses and drank together.

'It's as well the old man doesn't know you've got a shebeen behind those books,' said David, trying hard to be flippant.

'There's a hell of a lot the old man doesn't know,' said Paul. 'Just watch his act when I tell him I'm going to London.'

He threw out his arms, the glass of whisky still in his right hand, and hammed a speech.

'So, has it come to this? You too would fly, just like your brother Mark? Oh, sharper than a serpent's tooth it is! God help me, what shall I do? Who shall I do? My sons desert me in my hour of need! Is this the thanks I get for working hard, for slaving day and night to bring you up in the lack of luxury? Left in the winter of my discontent, am I to pay the butcher, pay the rent, all by myself? Begone, ungrateful wretch, and never darken my door again! For never be it said that I required help from a son like you. Begone, get out, and see a father's fond tears fall in floods upon your selfish head.'

He stopped. Then imitating a drunken whisper he added, 'But don't forget to send some money every week, my son.'

David forced a smile and shook his head.

'Oh, be fair!' he protested. 'He isn't as bad as all that.'

'He is as bad as all that,' Paul insisted. 'It's an actor he should have been. A ham actor. It's an odd thing, you know, and it would be worth looking into – I'm sure that somehow the Henry Irving tradition, the old Lyceum style of melodrama, survives in our Dad. How he came by it is a mystery. I wonder what his father did.'

'No, we don't know that, do we?' said David. 'That's the odd thing, I should say. Not knowing a thing about your family past your own father. Not even remembering your mother.'

'The family fame will start with me,' Paul replied, only half joking.

Mr Heylyn was too surprised to put on an act when Paul told him of his decision to go and work in London. He was silent, and looked at his son steadily before he spoke.

'I hope you know what you're doing,' he said slowly, his usual comment when the actions of his sons were beyond his understanding. 'It isn't an easy city to live in, or to work in either. You'll find it a jungle, my boy. I know. I had a year there with the Acme Supplies Company, and damn' glad I was to come back here.'

'Oh, I'll be all right,' Paul answered airily. 'I'm young, and I've got something to sell.'

'So had I,' said Mr Heylyn. 'The trouble is to find somebody to buy it.'

'We're not selling the same thing,' Paul retorted bluntly.

He was gone in a week, travelling light. He gave David instructions about the suits and shirts he wanted sent on when he had a settled address, the few books he would like parcelled. There was nothing more. Clearing out his papers, he left with David an enormous heap of magazines, newspaper cuttings, old drawings, and discarded photographs to be burnt. David went with him to the station on a Saturday morning when Mr Heylyn was still in bed.

'Look after the old man,' Paul said from the carriage window. 'He isn't a bad sort really. Don't take him too seriously.'

David shook hands with his brother as the train began to move, and when he left the station and returned to the traffic and the people in the street outside he felt very lonely.

3

Mary Ruthven

1

'IT ISN'T just pity,' said Mary Ruthven. 'But he looks so neglected I feel I would like to mother him.'

'And what's that but pity?' David asked her, annoyed to hear her talk of the married man after nearly a year in which she had never mentioned him.

Now she was in one of her confessional moods and told him of three men she had met at a staff-dance. She was amused at them, and amused too at David's disapproval when she described their frantic attempts to make love to her.

'If they could only see themselves!' she exclaimed, brewing a pot of tea at the kitchen grate. 'They think they're looking tenderly at a woman, and they only look hungry!'

On the mantelpiece the old marble clock, with its shepherdess at one side and a shepherd at the other, still ticked away contentedly, and the male and female figures seemed contented too, as if they had all the time in the world to get together. The small room was a kernel of peace in a disorderly world. Leaning against the dresser, David watched her move from the fire to the table, from the table to the sink, from the sink to the fireside again. She moved gracefully and always dressed well, and the way she laughed at the sexual excitement of men made him hope he would never give any woman the chance to laugh at him behind his back.

'If it's as funny as all that,' he commented, 'why do you do it at all?'

'I sometimes wonder,' she said, and sighed, filling his cup. 'What does it matter? If they want the body beautiful, they can have it!'

He stared at her, and she laughed in his face.

'Well, up to a point at least,' she said. 'You take everything so literally!

All I mean is, if they want to put their arms round me, it's hardly worth making an issue of it, is it?'

'I don't know,' he said.

'The only man I'm safe with is you,' she murmured casually, and for the first time he saw himself as a man after all – a young man, but still a man. And with his growth to manhood her seniority had come to have little significance. It was no longer absurd, as it would have been once, to think of a love-affair being carried on between them. But the habit of years wasn't to be broken just because the difference in their ages was no longer of much importance, and he knew that whatever temptations he might come to suffer he would suffer none from her. She would neither try to tempt him, nor would he ever feel tempted by her. Perhaps, knowing her so well for so long, he was unable to see her with the romantic illusions, with the novelty and mystery, that made young men run after a strange girl and ignore the much prettier girl who lived next door. Perhaps he was inhibited because he felt sure she saw him as he saw her, as someone too familiar to be a desirable partner in love-making.

At the same time he had no difficulty in understanding why men found her attractive, and he believed without question her stories of all men who wanted to make love to her. The point where she stopped them remained vague to him, and he was bewildered by her mixture of licence and restraint. He believed, in spite of his habit of taking her too literally, that she remained chaste. Her countless love-affairs, if associations as transient as the ones she formed could ever be called love-affairs, were merely a function of her joy in life. She was always in good spirits, always happy, and when she entered a room she brought with her a gust from an outer world of merry-making and sociability.

'I think it's the black tulle does it,' she said. 'It seems to do something to them. You've never seen it, have you? I must put it on and show you it. It's off the shoulder, and I think it's the contrast hits them. The white shoulders and the dark materials.'

She was, he knew, proud of her shoulders and of the whiteness of her skin.

After frivolous boasting and trivial confession about the staff-dance, she had gone on to mention the married man again, and her tone changed and her eyes were looking at her thoughts, and her words came out as if she were no longer chatting for his diversion but arguing with herself. She told him more than she had ever told him before.

'He wants to leave his wife,' she said.

'To do what?' he asked unsympathetically. 'To live with you?'

She shrugged off the question, but he persisted.

'Would you live with him?'

'No, I wouldn't,' she answered sharply, 'I couldn't – not while my mother is alive. I shouldn't like her to know that's how things had turned out. If my mother were dead. I don't know what I'd do.'

'How much does your mother know of this man?'

'His name, and that's about all. How can I tell my mother I'm in love with a married man, fifteen years older than me?'

'So you are in love with him,' he pointed out. 'A moment ago it was only pity.'

'Oh, I don't know what it is!' she retorted, laughing it off. 'If it's pity it can't be love, can it?'

She went through to the front room to have a word with her mother, who liked to sit alone with her book or her knitting at the window overlooking the busy main street, and when she came back she said: 'I don't know if it's because I've put all my worries on to your shoulders, but I feel a lot happier now. I had a dreadful headache before you came in, and now it's gone.'

He hadn't noticed she was unhappy or seen signs of a headache, but before he could argue the point, she asked him abruptly, 'And how's Paul?'

He gave her Paul's last letter and she read it through quickly, smiling at Paul's little jokes.

'I'm glad he's settling down so comfortably,' she remarked, returning the sheets. 'There's no need to worry about Paul. Paul was born for success. I see he mentions Menzies a lot. I'm not awfully keen on Menzies, but I suppose it's wrong to keep things up against him. He may be all right now.'

He heard no more about the married man for a while. She seemed to forget him again, resuming her earlier habit of going through a series of brief associations with handsome young men on the threshold of a career, meeting them as tangents to the various circles in

107

which her numerous girl-friends moved. There was an honours graduate in modern languages who had won a year's scholarship to a German university and hoped to enter the Foreign Office. He went to Germany in a few months, and she seemed not to miss him. Anyway, she never wrote to him. There was final-year medical student who wanted to specialize in skin diseases; there was (rather older) the area manager of a firm of biscuit manufacturers, there was a science graduate doing post-graduate work at the Royal Technical College, and there was a young lawyer, the son of a lawyer. All these came and went in the space of a year, and David scolded her, only half jesting. He would have liked to see her married to any of these men, men of good education and good prospects. It interested him that the men she picked up and then threw overboard were usually men of high intelligence with good academic qualifications. He liked to think it proved that she too was intelligent when she could interest such men. They were either of a higher social standing than she was, or at least equipped to move into a higher class once they began to practise their profession, and he found great comfort in imagining her married to someone who would take her out of the tenements and into a bigger house in the suburbs where the well-to-do lived. And there she would be a hostess to cultured visitors, and he had no doubt she would be a success. Her speech and manners were not inferior to her appearance. But when he lamented she was letting so many opportunities slip she snubbed him.

'I don't know why you're so anxious to see me married,' she said impatiently. 'I'm not all that keen on it myself. And as for any of these fellows – well, they may be clever, but they're so immature!'

Having found the word she seemed pleased with it. She repeated it and repeated it, throwing back her head and throwing out her hands, her lips moving forcefully, so that she was like an actress in a play.

'So immature! So immature!'

'Well then, why bother with them at all?' he asked curiously, really wanting to know. Then in case he seemed too serious, and knowing she disliked solemnity, he added lightly, 'Don't you ever get tired of these sordid amours?'

'They're not amours,' she answered indignantly. 'And they're

108

certainly not sordid. These young men are amusing for a time, but they're too immature, that's all.'

'But surely that's to be expected,' he said warmly, feeling a strong sympathy with these rejected admirers. 'They've been students for so long, they've lived a sheltered life, they're bound to be immature in some respects. But look ahead! They won't always be immature. Think of the future!'

'Would any woman get married if she thought of the future?' she asked lightly and dismissed him.

He felt she thought he too was immature, too immature to understand what she wanted. All he wanted was to see her settled with one man or another. Her unending flirtations distressed him, and he was afraid that the married man would turn up once more. He was the only one she ever spoke of seriously, and when she spoke of him she was careful to insist that she found an older man better company than a young one.

2

Without Paul, he lived a lonely life and visited nobody but the Ruthvens. In his uneventful loneliness he had fallen into the habit of going out for a walk on Friday evenings. He would take a bus into the city centre, stroll along the busy streets and admire the crowds, the courting couples, the cinema queues, the drunk men, and the street-corner revivalists. Then he would go into a public-house for half an hour, sit across from the bar with a glass of beer, and read the evening paper. Occasionally, in an extravagant mood, he would order a whisky-and-soda. He never drank much, and he liked to drink slowly. It gave him the illusion of leisure and well-being, and he liked to linger in a quiet bar and remember with disdain the overcrowded, noisy, and dingy pub where Menzies had made him drink too much too quickly. He was sure his own way was more civilized. In a silent backwater near the city centre he found a place he particularly liked, with a barmaid who was pleasant to look at, a place that was never so empty that he felt conspicuous and never so busy he felt crowded out. He sat there once a week, enjoying the safety of being in a place where no acquaintance would ever come in and bore him with small talk.

It was with mixed feelings, half dismayed at the prospect of having to make conversation, and half glad at seeing a known face after all, that looking up from his paper as the swing-door was pushed open he saw Carter come in. He watched him go to the bar and order his drink there. He didn't want to hide behind his paper and he didn't want to go over and greet him. He compromised, and looked steadily at him until Carter seemed to become aware of it. He turned his head and saw him, and at once the unhappy set of his almost ugly face loosened to a smile and he came over with a flourish. He was quietly dressed, in sedate good taste, and his overcoat was obviously expensive. There was an air of unostentatious prosperity about him. Dressed as he was, and tall and broad in build, he was a smart-looking young man and his unhandsome features merely emphasized his masculine strength.

'So you've found this place too?' he remarked brightly. 'I like it. It's quiet and the beer's good. I haven't been in for a month or two, you know. Two shops to look after keep me busy. But I like a drink once in a while. Just a couple, you know. I never abuse it. You can't drink and run a business. But a little refreshment once in a while is good for you. What do you think?'

Without waiting for an opinion he chatted on, treating David to the talk of a shopkeeper who knows his customers well and keeps their goodwill by his talent for easy conversation, talking a lot without saying much. David remembered Mary Ruthven had said once that he was deadly dull, and he feared she was right. Carter finished his first drink quickly, all too clearly determined to be sociable and stand a round, but when David returned the compliment he became less talkative. He sat and brooded over a glass of whisky and David feared they were a couple of bores who lacked the skill to disentangle themselves. Then Carter moved his glass in a little circle on the board and spoke with obvious impulsiveness.

'Who's this married man Mary Ruthven is going about with?'

'How do you know about a married man?' David asked, hedging to gain time to think how much he should tell. He had thought he was the only one who knew.

110

'I got it from one of her girl-friends who comes into the shop,' Carter explained, waving his hand to dismiss the question. 'Don't try and box clever, Davie. Just tell me. Who is he, what is he?'

'I don't know, I've never seen him,' David answered shortly, disliking the conversation. 'Anyway, as far as I know she isn't seeing him just now.'

'Oh but she is,' Carter retorted. 'She was out with him last week. A man old enough to be her father.'

'He isn't,' David protested. 'He's only about ten years or so older than her.'

'And the rest,' said Carter. 'I was talking to Agnes – Agnes Taylor. You know Agnes Taylor?'

'I've heard of her, I've never met her.'

'It was Agnes who was telling me. She doesn't like it. None of her friends like it. And I don't like it.'

'Is it any of your business?' David asked with a deliberately rude tone.

Carter looked at him long and straight, and sighed.

'I asked her to marry me,' he said. 'She refused. That's three years ago now, and she hasn't changed. But I haven't changed either. I could give her a good home, I could take care of her mother too. I told her that. I've a great respect for Mrs Ruthven. She's a fine woman. When you think what she went through with her husband—'

'What did she go through?' David demanded. He was annoyed to learn so casually that Carter had proposed to Mary Ruthven. He had thought she told him everything, and that was something she ought never to have kept from him. And he was annoyed to learn that he knew less of Mrs Ruthven's life than Carter. He had never thought of asking her about her husband. He had assumed she had lost him as he lost his mother, in a forgotten past.

'Her husband was a rotter,' said Carter, full of the simple virtue of youth and damning by a borrowed word a man he had never known. 'A woman-chaser. He was always in the town with some other woman. He walked out on Mrs Ruthven when Mary was only a baby. Off with one of his lady-friends. Mrs Ruthven went out to work, and she got herself trained as a midwife, and she kept the house going till Mary was old enough to help. But that's not the point. You keep trying to put me off.'

He finished his whisky and David saw he was slightly drunk. He went over to the bar and came back with two large whiskies.

'The point is,' he resumed doggedly, 'can't you stop Mary being so damned foolish as to get involved with a married man?'

'Me? I wouldn't dream of it!' David was indignant, aware that he himself wasn't completely sober. He tried to speak slowly and firmly. 'She's old enough to go her own way. She knows what she's doing – if she's doing it. And it's none of my business in any case.'

'It is your business,' Carter answered, almost angrily. 'She's your friend. She's been your friend for years, and so has Mrs Ruthven. Doesn't that leave you with a duty to perform? How do you think her mother would like it if she knew?'

'You mean I've to tell her to stop seeing this married man and marry you?' David asked with a sarcastic smile, quite forgetting that once he had hoped that was what she would do.

'I wish to God you would,' Carter said vehemently, inflamed by the whisky to complete frankness. He began to speak quickly, his eyes on his glass, rehearsing his sorrows to himself rather than explaining them to his companion.

'Sometimes I think she's just a bitch. Then I don't know. It's a new man every month, and this married man keeps turning up like a bad ha'penny. What does she want from life? I know what I want. I want her. Bitch or not. I would give my right hand to have her.'

'That's a silly thing to say,' David interrupted, shocked at such extravagant language. 'You don't understand what you're saying.'

'I was jogging along,' said Carter. 'I wasn't bothered. I liked the look of her. She amused me. She's good company. Not that she ever gave me much of it. Not after I got serious. That's what frightens her, if you get serious. I was jogging along when I first began to take her out. Maybe I took her for granted. I thought it would go on and on. I never thought about it ending. Then she began to put me off. I got a fright. Maybe I took it the wrong way. She turned on me. She was nasty. She insulted me. I'm deadly dull. That's me. Deadly dull. Tied me up in two words and threw me away.'

He lost count of whose turn it was and went off for another two whiskies, leaving David fretting behind him. It was clear he hadn't come in with the intention of drinking so much, but having found someone he could confide in he had gone on drinking to make his unburdening easier, and he would go on drinking till he talked himself dry. At that moment, when Carter returned from the bar with another two glasses in his hands, the evening seemed ruined to David.

But before the bar closed he was distressed with sympathy for the man. He had heard Menzies talk lustfully of Mary Ruthven, and it always upset him to hear her spoken of as merely a female body. Sometimes he wished the build and make of her were less conspicuously attractive to men, because in their admiration of her body men seemed to ignore what he had seen when he was too young to see anything else: the brightness of her personality, the goodness of her heart, the humour of her conversation. But in Carter the sexual admiration for her had become so much a part of his emotional life that it was no longer possible to dismiss it as only lust and nothing else. He was a man who was suffering on every level.

'It's not just to have her,' said Carter. 'To have her once and forget it. If that's all it was it would be nothing. If it was just a case of getting a woman I can get one any night I want one. But I don't want one. Not since she turned on me. It isn't just her body. It's body, mind, and soul, everything, I want. And I wasn't even allowed to touch her.'

There seemed a discrepancy there to David. From all Mary Ruthven had ever told him she wasn't bothered about the mere touch. It was strange if only in Carter's case the touch was something she couldn't bear. But he was glad later that he restrained himself from saying, 'Well, you must be the only one that wasn't allowed to make love to her.' For as Carter rambled on David saw it was his manhood had been undermined somewhere in his short association, and apparently she who had injured him had alone the power to cure him. She had hurled him down to a pit of despair when she refused him, and as he tried to clamber out of it, with a frantic longing for her, she was above and beyond him as something he had to have. Only when he reached her would he vindicate his manhood. Otherwise his life was an accident with no meaning. Separated from her, he created her anew in the narrow limits of his own skull, and to that private creation he had given infinite importance.

It was some time since he had last seen her, even from a distance, but he still loved her, and he suffered. So much was painfully clear from his whisky-begotten confession, a lifetime told in an evening's surrender.

'Even a shopkeeper can fall in love, you know,' he muttered.

He pressed his lips together and jutted out his chin as if he were proud of his misery. 'I wasn't in love to begin with. It was just a calm feeling of being fond of her. Then when I was taking it for granted she would never refuse to go out with me she began to make excuses and put me off. That's when I knew I had to have her. That's when I asked her to marry me. And that's when she turned on me.'

'I don't think she turned on you,' David said gently. 'You must have misunderstood her. She isn't the kind to turn on a man who has just proposed to her.'

'Well, we won't go into it,' Carter answered, tired after telling so much. 'I know what she said and you don't. We'll leave it at that.'

But he couldn't leave it so abruptly. He delved into his boyhood and seemed inclined to find the root of his obsession with Mary Ruthven in the days when they were children.

'She was always so clean, so pretty. Maybe she thinks I'm just a roughneck because I bossed a gang when I was a boy. Maybe she thinks I'm like Menzies. You know I've always been sorry about that time I stood and watched them tie you to the pole and cut your hair.'

The apology seemed absurdly late to David. He hadn't thought of the barbarous act for years.

'I don't think Mary Ruthven was there at the time,' he said uncertainly.

'Wasn't she?' said Carter. 'I'm not sure. I thought she was. I hope she wasn't.'

He harped on it, as if he could reach Mary Ruthven through David. Because when they were all children she had perhaps witnessed the shearing of a small boy who had dared oppose him he wanted to insist he wasn't cruel, he wanted to prove to her that he was kind, affectionate, and generous and that he was the fit male equivalent of her womanliness. But he had made nothing clear to her. She had only found him dull.

The two young men rose when the barmaid called time, felt their way round the table where they had been sitting, and continued their talk in the street outside. David saw Carter on to a bus and plodded

114

carefully home alone, saddened by what he had listened to. He had no doubt that Carter loved Mary Ruthven at every level where sexual love operated, and he had no doubt Mary Ruthven had wronged him. But he was equally sure that Mary Ruthven could do no wrong and that she knew best who suited her. He could easily believe Carter was a fit and proper mate for her, but he believed also that since she had rejected him he must have failed somewhere to justify his claim. Getting nowhere in the contradictions of what he believed, abandoning equally his faith in Carter's love and Mary Ruthven's discrimination, he undressed in darkness and sidled wearily into bed.

3

He was all alone except for letters from Paul, and he looked forward to them morbidly. Even when he had just had one he would look out for the postman the next day, as if Paul would have bothered to write again so soon. At first he replied to Paul within a week, but Paul took longer and longer between his letters, so that David had to learn not to answer at once. By an effort of will, a deliberate procrastination, he put off writing until a week became a month. Then he had to control his impatience for Paul's reply. When it came he had to exercise his restraint all over again and leave it decently unanswered for a while.

In their correspondence he met once more the trouble he had when he used to write little articles to go with Paul's press-photographs. He lacked the wit of brevity. But Paul, who had been so many years less at school, was the more accomplished writer. He was amusing, chatty, and quite unlaboured. He could write so vividly about his Sunday strolls round the literary landmarks of London that he made David see the places they had read about when they were boys, living on books from the public library.

'You must come down on your next holiday,' Paul wrote. 'I mean must. Stir your lazy bones, you fossil! If not this summer then next. You find your fare and I'll find you a bed.'

He was sharing a place with Menzies, getting it cheap, he said, because Menzies' firm held the lease and charged him only a nominal rent. There was plenty of room. True, he had no extra bed or bedding, but he had the room. If it meant sleeping on the floor, would David mind?

David explained, in two and a half pages, that he wouldn't mind at all, and in another three pages he explained why he would enjoy a holiday in London. To see London is always a thrill to the provincial, especially one as bookish as he was. To see the house where Dr Johnson lived, to walk the streets that Dickens had walked, to see the Adelphi and Albany, and even (though he smiled to remember they had ever read Conan Doyle's stories, so distant those days seemed) to see Baker Street – it meant more to him than seeing Naples could ever do. The prospect of seeing London in the company of a brother so loved and knowledgeable as Paul was an added pleasure, an exquisite refinement that his natural pessimism could not quite believe in. Such things could never be, no matter how eager Paul might be to have him come down. Something, he was sure, would turn up to prevent it.

Paul answered him two months later, scolding him for his doubts and assuring him you had only to believe in a thing hard enough and it would come to pass. He referred to his own success, and David accepted the rebuke.

In his solitary state he looked for company in books. He read indiscriminately and often without profit, for much of what he read was beyond his understanding. For a time he lost his way in the relativity of ethics. He knew that certain things were wrong. But he found he couldn't say why they were wrong. And if circumstances condoned an act that was normally wrong what became of the intrinsic wrongness of the act? He couldn't explain to himself just what happened, and it interested him. Were there actions that were always wrong, wrong in all times and in all places? He believed there were, but he couldn't prove it. His flirtation with ethics didn't seem to lead him anywhere, and he ended where he began, with a firm conviction that certain things were wrong and it was useless to argue about them.

He read many, perhaps too many, books about books, so that he was better acquainted with the conventional opinion of great works than the works themselves. Distrusting his own unaided taste, he had a weakness for literary criticism, so that he read a lot about Milton without ever

116

having read *Paradise Lost*, and he was well up in all the chatter about Harriet without ever having read *Queen Mab*. He was a provincial trying to acquire a shareholder's interest in English literature. At least he thought he was a shareholder, since his teachers had introduced him to the company. But he found it dull work when he could no longer share his discoveries with Paul. His final revulsion came when he spent half a crown on a literary monthly because it had a long article on George Eliot. Ever since he had read that Lord Acton, Gladstone, and John Morley thought *Middlemarch* a masterpiece he had intended to read it. He never had. Perhaps this article would help him. The writer was a lady, herself a novelist and a member of a literary family with generations of good feeding behind it. He waited till his father had gone out for the evening and then settled down to read the article in the peace and quiet of the front room.

He found that to the writer of the article George Eliot wasn't a great English novelist nor *Middlemarch* a great novel. George Eliot was merely Marian Evans, whom the writer's grandmother had known well, and the article was made up of trivial family reminiscences in which George Eliot belonged not to the stream of English literature but to the writer's family. He felt that in thinking of reading George Eliot because she had written a masterpiece he was an uninvited guest, an intruder in a country house whose owner would almost certainly have refused to have him about the place even as an assistant gardener. The whole article was written in a proprietary tone as if the writer were describing a family heirloom. He felt then the full isolation of the provincial whose utilitarian schooling has given him a nodding acquaintance with the great English writers. They remain English writers. They are not, as the lady-novelist made clear, ever to be approached on equal terms by those whose grandmother hadn't moved in literary circles. He had made a mistake in thinking literature was meant for anyone who could read. The lady showed him literature was meant for literary people.

It was only by chance that round about the same time he found he had an ear. Neither he nor Paul had ever bothered about music, and though Paul could date and grade every European painter since the Renaissance and he himself could give the reference-book information on the great European writers, they were both entirely ignorant of the development of music and the order of the great musicians. Their father had a good repertoire of airs from musical plays and the Savoy operas, but that was all.

David would no doubt have continued to live in a soundless world if he hadn't confessed his ignorance to a middle-aged lady with whom he worked a lot in his department at the Inland Revenue offices. She was pleasant-voiced, broad-faced, just going grey and still trimly attractive, a widow with a daughter at the university. She was shocked. She liked 'young Mr Heylyn', as she always called him, because he did his work conscientiously and was always polite and obliging, showing an old-fashioned respect for her sex and seniority. She insisted he go with her to an orchestral concert. Weak-willed where he saw no issue of principle, he agreed to go, although the invitation embarrassed him. He felt rather silly going out for the evening with a woman old enough to be his mother. But Mrs Marchbanks was so natural with him, so easy to talk to, and so manifestly beyond any awkwardness with a young man, that he enjoyed his evening. Mrs Marchbanks had picked a concert when the programme was within the capacity of a novice.

'If you don't like this,' she told him with friendly sternness. 'I'll never speak to you again. There would be no point speaking to you again – because if you don't enjoy this you'll only prove you're stone-deaf!'

He heard a Mozart violin concerto, a Beethoven symphony, and a dance by Ravel. He didn't need to put on an act. Mrs Marchbanks saw by his face that he was excited and she was pleased with him. It was then he found he had an ear and a musical memory. He surprised her by humming odd phrases from the music in the office next day, not to show off but because he couldn't get away from it. She took him out again and gave him little lectures on what he was going to hear and who wrote it. She was never pretentious, and she had no great technical knowledge though she played the piano with considerable skill, as he heard when he was invited round for tea, for their friendship developed quickly when they found a common interest.

She had a record-player and hundreds of good records.

'Mummy would rather have a new record than a new hat,' said her daughter, a chubby brunette, who wore glasses when she was studying.

David feared he might be expected to pay attention to the daughter, but there too he was wrong. The girl was as uninterested in him sexually as her mother. She was fond of her mother, tolerant of her oddities, and if her mother wanted to improve the musical taste of a young man it was something perfectly fit and proper. It involved neither of them in any other relations with him. The only love in question was a love of music, which she shared with her mother.

The little record-player then became such a source of pleasure to him as he sat in Mrs Marchbanks' flat and listened to the concerts she devised for him that he longed to have one of his own.

He began to save, he studied the windows of music-shops, a thing he had never expected he would do, and slowly, like a bather approaching the water for the first dip of the season, he edged his mind towards a model he could afford. He bought it on the instalment system, and for a time he had a record-player and only one record. Mrs Marchbanks laughed and her daughter Muriel laughed when he told them. He meant it to be an amusing confession, and he was pleased when they laughed. But in a moment he was red-faced with confusion and feared they thought he had been cadging, for the mother and daughter insisted he take half a dozen records they knew he liked. They fetched them out excitedly, declaiming the titles on the sleeves for his approval, and brushing away his explanations with their chatter.

'Not at all, no!' Mrs Marchbanks exclaimed, her rather large bosom rising in indignation at the mere suggestion he had been cadging. 'We never thought that for a moment. You must take them. It's so nice to find someone who appreciates music.'

'And it'll give Mummy room for some new records if you take these,' Muriel added slyly, her eyes glinting behind her horn-rimmed glasses, whose legs were oddly fashioned in the form of a snake.

He took the records home, carefully parcelled, and at the first opportunity, when his father was out, he played them through – all of them, in one hungry, greedy session. He was drunk with music when he went to bed.

He didn't have to read about it. No book could pretend to be a substitute for the music, as books about a novelist or a poet might persuade the reader he was now acquainted with the novels or poems.

Whatever he had to learn technically he learnt from Mrs Marchbanks, and he felt no great need for anything more. He was on terms of direct encounter with the works, and the records were his. They weren't the property of a book-producing group whose parents had produced books, and whose grandparents had produced book-producers and entertained writers to afternoon tea.

The strange thing was he couldn't tell Paul much about it. He could say he had bought a record-player and had a few records and was on the way to building up a little library of good music. But to tell Paul of the perfection he heard in the air, of the ordered world of supreme delight and confidence created by the opening bars of Mozart's last violin concertos, of the excitement in his blood every time he heard the beginning of Beethoven's violin concerto, was completely beyond him. It lay outside words, and that was not the least of its mysterious beauty. It was another world, a life that had nothing to do with the space and time wherein he earned his living, though sometimes it seemed to bring him to the verge of recalling something that happened a long, long time ago, when he was very small and his mother was still living.

Mrs Marchbanks had to educate him out of preferring Mozart to Beethoven, and then she made a strong effort to prevent him stopping there. But he learned. His taste widened as his knowledge deepened, and in his solitary unsocial evenings his record-player was his constant companion.

Mary Ruthven called on him and caught him with a record of Schubert's ninth symphony on. She seemed surprised.

'I didn't know you were musical,' she said, looking vaguely about the room as if unable to understand where the music was coming from.

For the first time in his life he felt a spasm of impatience with her. She had interrupted the movement he particularly wanted to listen to closely, and her remark sounded silly to his pedantic ear. It made him think of someone who emitted a musical note if he were prodded in the middle, or played a little tune if he were wound up like a cigarette-box.

She had on a low-necked short-sleeved blouse and a flared skirt, and she obviously had something on her mind too. She looked as elegant as ever, and her bearing and carriage always pleased him. Yet there was an air of confusion about her. He recognized the signs, and waited for her to start talking. As he expected, it was the married man again.

'It can't go on,' she said. 'It's one row after another at home. She does nothing but nag, nag, nag. She has never loved him, not since they were married. She told him straight out. She can't be bothered with him in the house. She has no interest in him. Or in any man. She made it quite clear. She has no use for a man in the house. She can live without a man, says she. And if he can't live without a woman he knows what he can do. She's not bothered.'

He tried to suggest she had only the married man's word for it all, he tried to hint that the evidence was incomplete and to that extent unsatisfactory, and anyway a married man shouldn't tell her such things.

She didn't trouble to answer his comments. Clearly, whatever she was told she believed implicitly was the complete truth.

'You can see she has no interest in him,' she said. 'He isn't even being fed now.'

'What's he going to do?' David asked, trying to hide his want of sympathy for the married man. A man who could complain of not being fed seemed to him either an unmanly grumbler or a handless fool. He himself had made his own meals since he was a boy.

'He told her the best thing he could do would be to get a divorce, and she said go right ahead and get one.'

'But he can't just go and get a divorce as simply as that,' he protested. 'He can divorce her if she'll leave him for long enough, or they can do it the other way round, but he can't—'

'That would take too long,' Mary Ruthven interrupted. 'He wants her to divorce him just as soon as it can be managed.'

'On what grounds?' he asked, looking at her with his head inclined, so that his good eye was on her – his usual habit when he was unhappy in a conversation.

'She knows about me.'

'Knowing about you proves nothing,' he said. 'Unless she knows more than I do.'

'There's nothing more to know, not yet,' she answered. 'But if he could get a divorce I would marry him tomorrow.'

'I didn't know it had got to that stage,' he muttered, surprised. However much she told him there was always more he didn't know. 'The last time you spoke about it you were just sorry for him. I thought you had stopped seeing him, for all I heard.'

'I tried that,' she said. 'He got a shift to another branch, to help us both. But it didn't work out. He phoned me at the office after the most miserable month I've spent in my life. And when I heard his voice my stomach turned over.'

'Is that a sign of true love?' he asked curiously.

She smiled, her full red mouth coming to a pucker of amusement as she shook her head in despair of ever making him understand her feelings.

'Maybe it's one of the symptoms,' she answered. 'But there you are. We started all over again. And now I want to marry him. That's all I want to do. I don't care what else I do or don't do so long as I marry him.'

'And before you can marry him,' he went over it doggedly, 'he'll have to get a divorce. And before he can get a divorce you'll have to provide the evidence.'

Summarizing the situation, he looked longingly at his silenced record-player in the corner.

'That's what it comes to,' she admitted. 'You always like to put things bluntly, don't you? His wife says it's to be me, or there's no divorce. We thought we could fix something to keep me out of it. But she won't have that. She insists it's me and nobody else or she won't do it.'

'A one-night cheap hotel,' he said softly.

'I know it sounds sordid.' She was troubled and kept turning a dress-ring round and round her finger. 'It's something I swore I'd never do. Not with anybody. And now I'll do it with a married man.'

'Women always say they never will and they always do,' he remarked, and immediately wondered if he had read it somewhere.

'I haven't done it yet,' she retorted.

'But aren't you telling me you will?'

'I suppose I am,' she said and gave it up.

4

Later in the year when he was visiting her and her mother in the normal course of his routine, she spoke again of her trouble. The married man had made plans for a divorce. All that remained to settle was the date when they would go away together. From the way she spoke he saw she was obsessed by this man just as much as Carter was obsessed by her. He had never told her of Carter's confession in the pub, and determined he never would. He had never told Paul either, feeling it would be wrong to repeat such confidences on paper. And it struck him as rather sad that she and Carter were suffering from the same incapacity to see things as the world saw them. To most men, he knew, Mary Ruthven was merely a woman of considerable sexual attractiveness, and they let it go at that. There was no world-shortage of attractive women.

They did not become obsessed by her as the only woman in the world they could ever sleep with. To most women, he believed, the married man would be a second-hand male, full of self-pity and guilty of an error in taste by telling tales about his wife. They would never have looked on him as the ideal husband, especially since he had failed so miserably in his first attempt that his wife's idea of domestic bliss was to have him out of the house. But he knew he could no more cure Mary Ruthven than he could cure Carter.

He believed she was wading deeper into a sea of sorrow by determining to marry her married man, but he kept his thoughts to himself. He was afraid to say bluntly to her, 'The whole thing's absurd, and you're being utterly foolish.' He didn't know what she might do then. But if he said nothing she would at least keep on speaking to him.

'There's only one thing he's sorry about,' Mary Ruthven was saying. 'His little girl will take it very badly. He's awfully fond of her.'

It was the first he had heard of a little girl, and he was amazed at the offhand way people came out with the most important facts about a situation. It came out she was a child of twelve who wanted to be an actress.

'But his wife says she won't keep the child from him,' said Mary Ruthven. 'He can see her as often as he likes.'

'And what do you think of the child?' he asked.

'I've never seen her, but I would love to have her live with us. She's the only one gives him any affection.'

'I wish I could meet this man,' he said impulsively, puzzled by the picture of a man approaching middle-age who could complain he was badly fed and not getting enough loving. It seemed to him slightly ridiculous.

'Oh, you wouldn't find anything special in him to look at,' she said hastily, almost defensively. 'Nobody can say it's an infatuation because he's handsome. He isn't. There's nothing particular about him, not to look at. Nobody can say it's just sex. If it were only that there are lots of other men I could get if I wanted to. But I'm in love with him, and that's all that's to it.'

She came back to his remark.

'I wish you could meet him. I'd like you to meet him. But I can't bring him here. Not yet anyway.'

'When do you mean to tell your mother?' he asked gently.

'I've thought about that,' she said. 'I'll tell her when the divorce is definitely on the way. I'll tell her I'm involved. But I won't tell her before I go away for that week-end – whenever it is. There's no point in that. If she cares to work it out afterwards – well, it'll be too late to matter. She knows about him. She knows his marriage isn't a great success. She may have guessed the rest. I don't know. But she'll know when it all comes out that it wasn't a case of me breaking up a happy marriage. Because that marriage isn't happy. Anyone can see that. And surely a man has a right to expect some love from his wife.'

'And if it turned out you were breaking up a happy marriage?' he asked.

'You mean if he were telling me a lot of lies?'

'It's always possible,' he said.

'You have a horrible mind,' she laughed.

'But suppose he were?' he persisted. 'Suppose you found you were breaking up a happy home?'

'I wouldn't go through with it, that's all,' she answered at once, firmly.

He went home and found his father sitting in the kitchen, beside a low fire, staring at the wall, shivering now and again and making at the same time a quavering moan.

'I thought you would be out,' said David crossly, annoyed not to have the house to himself.

'I don't think I'll go out tonight,' Mr Heylyn whispered, and shivered again. 'I don't feel well.'

He didn't feel well three or four times a year, and then his pathetic sighs and wheezing groans, and the way he tottered round the kitchen, ostentatiously groping for support on the table or the back of a chair, made his sons smile behind his back.

'He gives a brilliant performance when he's ill,' Mark used to say. 'But he always recovers when it's time to go out in the evening.'

And indeed his sons could count and remember the evenings he had spent at home, so rare were they.

But ever since he had to cope alone with his father David had found he lacked Mark's critical attitude just as much as he lacked Paul's indifference. He had no more patience than they had with his father's tendency to over-act, but his reaction was more cautious. He was afraid to remain unsympathetic too long in case his father were really ill after all. If that ever happened his want of sympathy would look like mere callousness to outsiders, and it would be small comfort that his absent brothers would easily understand his misjudgement.

'You must be bad if you don't want to go out,' he said, half sarcastic, half solicitous.

Mr Heylyn tried to rise and collapsed in his chair with a cough and a wheeze. David knew Mark would have called it a piece of ham-acting. 'It's not a doctor he wants,' he had said in such a situation. 'It's a drama critic.' But David couldn't be so witty. He was alarmed at his father's behaviour. He put the back of his hand against his father's head, he felt his pulse, and Mr Heylyn moaned gratefully at these gestures of recognition that he was a sick man, as if his son were an audience applauding a good actor.

'What time did you come in last night?' David asked curtly. 'Or this morning rather.'

'Oh, the back of two,' Mr Heylyn croaked with difficulty. 'I was just a wee bit later than usual.'

'And you walked home? In all that rain? Without your hat? At your age?'

'What do you mean, at my age?' Mr Heylyn said with a spasm of spirited indignation. 'You'd think I was an old man the way you talk. And I never wear a hat. You know I never wear a hat.'

He was too proud of his hair to hide it, and he despised bald men, especially bald men who were younger than himself, as if their lack of hair denoted a fundamental weakness of character.

'I think you've got a temperature,' said David. 'You would be better in your bed than sitting there.'

He helped him to bed, built up the fire, gave him a hot drink of whisky and sugar, and went to his own room. He didn't like to put a record on in case it kept his father from sleeping, and he sat staring at the wall, just as he had seen his father do, brooding over Mary Ruthven and her married man.

When he came home from work the next night his father was still in bed, wheezing rather than breathing.

'Have you had nothing to eat all day?' David asked, angry with him for being so helpless.

His father gave a longer and louder wheeze that seemed to end in 'No,' and David bustled round the kitchen preparing a suitably light meal for an invalid. He sent for a doctor and he asked Mrs Ruthven to look in on his father the next day and give him something to eat.

'In the first place it's pneumonia,' the doctor said. 'In the second place there are complications. He has been a heavy drinker, your father, hasn't he?'

'I shouldn't say heavy,' David answered judiciously. 'Regular, but not heavy.'

'I see,' said the doctor, smiling at the ancient wallpaper in the lobby where they stood whispering. 'Well, be that as it may, he's seriously ill, you know. If you're going to be out all day you'd better get a nurse in tomorrow. And if there's no improvement in the next two or three days he'll have to go into hospital.'

There was no time to get anyone in. Mr Heylyn died at one o'clock in the morning. When David looked in before going to bed he moaned: 'Don't go away. Don't leave me. Just sit there a bit. I won't keep you long.'

He dozed, and he muttered in his sleep. He wakened and muttered some more. Then he held out his hand and it was shaking.

'It's getting dark, Davie,' he said, and his open eyes seemed to see nothing. 'Put the light on. I can't see.'

The light was on. David rose, walked across the room, pretended to lower the light switch, and returned to the bedside.

'Hold on to me,' said Mr Heylyn.

David clasped the hand that was held out to him and sat on the edge of the bed. He found it most uncomfortable, and yet he could not keep awake. He came to with a jolt as his head nodded violently, wondered where he was for a moment, and became aware that the hand he was holding was limp and useless. He folded the arm gently across his father's chest, and as did so he heard a deep tired groaning in the throat and he knew his father was dead.

He felt strangely unmoved, and amidst the distractions of having the doctor sign a death certificate, seeing an undertaker, and making arrangements for the funeral, he wondered guiltily if he were incapable of love or affection for anyone. But when he looked at his father lying in the unlidded coffin he knew there had been no communication between them, ever, and he could only suppose that a man who lived so entirely to himself as his father had done, must in the end die only to himself. To others, in whom he had never lived, he could not cause any anguish merely by the banal act of dying.

He sent a telegram to Paul and Paul came home for the funeral.

'You shouldn't have bothered,' said David. 'It's a lot of money to spend, a return fare to London, just to attend a funeral.'

'Oh, there are some things that have got to be done,' Paul answered airily. 'When you took the trouble to send me a wire saying the old boy was dead I couldn't just wire back, O.K. Bury him. Could I?'

'No, I don't suppose you could. But if you had I don't know I would have blamed you.'

Paul stayed overnight with David after the funeral and took the train back to London at ten o'clock in the morning.

'I'll write and tell Mark when I get back to London,' he said. 'I haven't had time to think since I got your wire. Not that it matters. Mark couldn't have come anyway. He's in Adelaide now.'

'Oh!' said David blankly, and only then did he realize he hadn't thought of Mark when his father died.

'I wish I could take you to London with me,' Paul said. 'I think a couple of days in London would do you a world of good. Cheer you up a bit after this dismal business. But it isn't convenient just now. Menzies is putting a friend up this week.'

'Well, it wouldn't suit me just now,' David answered quickly, unwilling to let Menzies have anything to do with it. 'I've got today and tomorrow off, but that's all. If I spend the fare at all I'd rather come down for more than a couple of days. But we can worry about that when the time comes.'

'I like the way you say worry,' Paul commented, smiling. 'And time. I never realized how Glasgow you sound till I came back.'

Afraid to speak after that, David stood at the carriage door thinking that for his part he had been noticing a bogus element in Paul's English accent. His vocabulary too had changed, his style of dress had changed, more loudly artistic than ever. A bastard accent, a bastard vocabulary, and bastard clothes, David thought sadly.

'The trouble with this train is it'll get me in just after five,' Paul was saying, 'and I'll have to get across London at rush-hour.'

Distracted by the imminence of their parting, by his consciousness of having a broad accent, and by his disloyal thoughts, David was baffled at the reference to Russia.

'Oh, I see!' he said, suddenly inspired, and blushing at his stupidity. 'Rush-hour!'

The guard blew his whistle, the brothers shook hands, and the train moved out of the station.

David walked through the town before going back to his empty house. He was distressed at Paul's patronizing comments on his speech. He had believed he loved reading poetry aloud to himself when he was alone. But what value could there be in his love of spoken verse if he were in fact reciting the poet's words in an accent that had no resemblance to the sounds the poet had in mind? He was discouraged, and when he was in such a depressed mood he was troubled by shooting pains in his defective eye.

He waited till the evening, afraid he might seem irreverent to his dead father if he were too hasty, and then unable to resist his longing he put a record on his record-player.

'At least I don't play Mozart with a Glasgow accent,' he murmured to the gracious opening bars, and sat and listened, alone, all alone.

5

He wished Mary Ruthven would go and get it over with. She kept on talking about a divorce, but nothing seemed to be happening.

'It doesn't look as if you'll ever go away with him,' he remarked. 'You talk about it and you brood about it but you don't seem inclined to do anything.'

'I don't brood,' she objected. 'And I'll do it when the time comes. I can't just go away any week-end. I've got to have some pretext. I've my mother to think of.'

There were no young men distracting her now. She was entirely engrossed in her married man and talked of nobody else, so that he missed the old diversity and humour of her gossip.

'We've fixed a date at last,' she told him later in the spring. 'He's got a transfer to the head-office in London, and I'll join him for part of my holiday. His wife can divorce him just as soon after that as she likes.'

'And your mother?' he asked.

'I won't tell her,' she said. 'I can't. Certainly not before I do it, and maybe not at all afterwards. Mother's all right. Up to a point. She's very tolerant.'

The jerky way she said it left him not knowing if her mother was all right up to a point or tolerant up to a point, or both.

'But she has a very old-fashioned attitude to divorce. It just isn't done. I suppose that's why she never divorced my father. I'm sure she thinks only a wicked woman would marry a divorced man. Especially when I've got to go away with him first. She'll have to know sooner or later who I'm marrying, but I'd rather keep the rest of it from her as long as I can. Oh, I wish there were some other way!'

'Suppose his wife won't divorce him?' he asked.

'Suppose night doesn't follow day?' she retorted. 'All she's waiting for is the chance to divorce him. She keeps asking him when we're going away for a week-end so as she can get rid of him.'

'But isn't that collusion, so there couldn't be a divorce?'

'Oh, I suppose it would be collusion if it was on paper,' she admitted. 'If it ever came out. But it's only when they're alone she says things like that.'

'Why can't he just leave her and be done with it?'

'That's what he's going to do, isn't it?' she parried.

'But I mean now, right now,' he insisted. 'She could divorce him for desertion surely, and that would keep you out of it.'

'Oh, it would take years doing it that way,' she protested. 'We can't wait that long. And anyway, she might not bother divorcing him if he just walked out and said nothing. She might just ask for a legal separation, and then we could never get married.'

'But I thought you said she was just waiting for the chance to divorce him?'

He was puzzled at the contradiction, surprised she didn't see the muddle she was in.

'Yes, that's what she says,' Mary Ruthven admitted calmly. 'But if he just left her and said nothing – well, we couldn't be sure what she would do.'

He was still puzzled. He didn't see how they could be sure what she would do even if they went away together. In that case too the wife might refuse to divorce him, either from malice or because she didn't approve of divorce. But he was afraid to nag at the point in case he made her cross or in case he was missing some subtle distinction.

'Well then, I don't see how he can go on living in that house if things are as bad as you say,' he remarked, baffled.

'Oh, they are as bad as I say, there's no question about that,' she answered.

By the time the summer came, making the tenement look dingier than ever in the broad sunshine, he had moved from the house where he had lived since childhood with his brothers and father. He wanted to escape from the rooms that reminded him of all he preferred to forget. He wanted to complete his liberation from the incubus of his father by moving to a house that had never known his father's presence. He didn't move far – only a few hundred yards down the street and round the corner – but far enough to make his routine visits to the Ruthvens less convenient. And besides, he was busy settling himself in his new home, shifting the few pieces of furniture that had been his father's, having the rooms papered and painted, too pleased to have at last a place of his own to call on the Ruthvens – though he planned to have them as his guests for a house-warming.

He was on his knees re-tiling the hearth in his new sitting-room when Mary Ruthven rang the bell. He hurried to make her a cup of tea, but she couldn't wait, she said. She had some packing to finish. She was leaving the next morning, ostensibly for her summer holiday. In fact she was going to join the married man, who was already in London. She was still uncertain whether or not she would spend her whole holiday with him.

'You don't seem to be looking forward to it,' he couldn't help saying, looking at her curiously. He had never seen her look so pale before. She moved her hand in a little waving gesture as if to put the remark aside.

'I don't want to be sentimental,' she said, 'but I'll miss you. Oh, I'll be back again after my holiday – for a while, anyway, until the divorce. But I can't help feeling I'm saying goodbye to you, because when I come back I'll be—'

She stopped and tried again.

'I was just thinking of you last night. Thinking how long I've known you. You were a little grubby boy when I took you upstairs to my mother, and I was in my first job. I had just left school. And look at you now! A handsome young bachelor.'

'A bachelor,' he corrected, disliking the jocular inaccuracy of the other word. But she was being flippant only because she had difficulty in saying what she wanted to say.

'I used to blether to you as if you were my little brother,' she said, smiling at his glowering face. 'You made me wish I had a brother. Then as you got older you became my confidant. I've never understood why I always told you so much. Like telling you now I'm going way with a married man. But I'll miss you. I'll have no one to tell my troubles to.'

'I hope you'll have none to tell,' he said.

He gave her Paul's address and she promised to visit him when she was in London.

She dithered and swithered, unwilling to go and too upset to stay, took a cup of tea with him after all, and he saw her to the door. They parted on the threshold and she gave him a wave and a smile as she went downstairs. He returned to his task, and when he had finished it he washed and changed and sat down to write to Paul:

So here I am installed in my own home, which by definition (though strictly speaking I am not an Englishman) is my castle, even though it is only the first storey flat of a three storey tenement. But the close is clean and tiled and the windows on the stairhead have lozenges of stained glass, so that I feel I have risen in the social scale and can invite my friends here to a humble supper, if I had any friends, without blushing for the dingy entrance to a flight of stairs that were never quite clean, as was the case in our ancestral abode. Which abode, as you know, is scarce one-quarter of a mile from here, and yet I feel I have travelled as long a journey as ever Marco Polo did, for the longest journeys are not always those we make in space.

He scribbled on, enjoying writing his letter, spreading himself over many pages with literary graces and allusions. Paul would bear with his long-windedness if nobody else would. He didn't mention Mary Ruthven because her plans seemed to him still confidential. Later on, when the divorce was through and she was married, he would perhaps mention casually that she had left the city and was married now, but say no more.

Paul replied with unusual promptness and congratulated him on having bought a castle on a junior clerk's salary, poked gentle fun at his 'travels' and told him he had perhaps travelled further than Mark, who had now been practically all round the world but who from his letters sometimes seemed never to have left home, not mentally, for he always spoke a lot of the days when they were boys together and even wrote kindly of their father.

As for your humble servant [he wrote], *I am thriving well and drinking moderately. If you won't come to London I may do a Mahomet on you and take a few days off and come up and see you, and we'll reminisce over a bottle of brandy – which I will supply.*

David was offended at the gratuitous reference to Mark and brooded over the actual words of it, trying to make sure of their tone and intention. He didn't mind Paul making fun of him, but he did mind being mentioned in the same sentence as Mark.

He refused to go to London and stay with Paul for a week on the grounds that the expenses of moving had wiped out his meagre savings. He stayed at home during his fortnight off work, and called on Mrs Ruthven when Mary was still away.

'She's gone to London, you know,' said Mrs Ruthven, and he had never realized before that her hair was so white, her shoulders so bowed, and her wrists so thin. 'I should have thought it a strange place for a holiday. The sea air would do her more good. I wanted her to go down the coast somewhere, but she wanted to see the sights.'

She fetched out a postcard.

'Did you get one?' she asked.

David brought his out, and they exchanged St Paul's for Trafalgar Square. But there was a constraint between them, and he wondered just how much Mrs Ruthven knew. He had a complicated intuition that she knew all he knew but knew he knew she wasn't supposed to know, so that she had to pretend she didn't know he knew while he had to pretend he knew nothing either.

'You've been neglecting me lately,' she complained, smiling to him, and her wise eyes looked at him shrewdly. 'You could at least change my library book for me once a week.'

'I should be glad to,' he answered respectfully.

'I've just been wondering,' Mrs Ruthven went on, 'when that girl of mine is going to get married. If ever. Do you know she's twenty-six this month?'

'Yes, she's four years older than me,' David answered thoughtlessly.

'Oh, that isn't much,' said Mrs Ruthven, polishing her spectacles as she sat with them on her lap, not looking at him, seeming just to think aloud.

He returned to his own room and his record-player, wondering how much he was to admit he had known when Mrs Ruthven found out just where her daughter had been. He put a record on, but for once his attention wasn't absorbed by the music. He sat in a day-dream, thinking of how suddenly Mrs Ruthven had aged, of how pale Mary Ruthven had looked the day before she went away, of Carter doomed to live and die without possessing her, of Paul dragging in Mark and writing of coming to see him with a bottle of brandy. He had a feeling he had lost touch with them all somewhere. Mark was getting on and seeing the world, according to Paul. He knew he would never see the world, and even the noise of children in the street below his window annoyed him. He didn't want to see the world. He wanted to be alone, rooted in one quiet place. But now that he was alone he still wasn't contented.

When the record was played he put it back in its jacket, left the house and went for a stroll through the city in the cool of the summer evening. Just in case Paul kept his promise to come up for a few days and bring a bottle of brandy he thought he had better get acquainted with the liquor. He interrupted his stroll to drink one in the pub where he had met Carter, and the barmaid smiled at his sombre face.

'Cheer up,' she said breezily. 'You'll soon be dead.'

In the morning there was a letter from Mary Ruthven.

It turns out to be goodbye as I thought [she wrote]. *I'm not coming back after all. I don't see any point leaving here just to return here. I'm writing to mother to say I was in at the head-office to see some old friends and I've been offered my promotion here (did I tell you I was due for some promotion?) if I care to take it. I've said I may manage home for a week later on, but privately to you I don't think I'll do that. I would rather not see mother till everything's legal and in order. Meanwhile, I'll carry on working here when my holiday's over, for of course I have got a job in the head-office. I asked for it a long time ago and meant to tell you it was practically settled. Please make sure you go and see mother often and keep her spirits up. Tell her there's no need to worry about me, I'm doing fine. Whatever you do don't tell her anything about the rest of it. I'll tell her myself in good time.*

He knew her swift-flowing handwriting, he knew her notepaper, but the contents seemed to come from a person he had never really known. As a boy he had marvelled at the fullness and frankness of her conversation with her mother. He had admired it so much he was encouraged to imitate her and talk to Paul like that. Now she who had once told her

134

mother everything was telling her nothing. She was even guilty of deceit now, and her letter was a thoughtless assumption that he would help her to deceive her mother.

He knew he would. He couldn't go and tell Mrs Ruthven bluntly that her daughter was living in London with a married man. But he was puzzled at the change in Mary Ruthven's character, and he wondered if the answer was that in fact there was no change: he had merely made a mistake when he thought she was frank and confiding. Perhaps the very quantity of her chatter was itself a technique of deceit. Nobody would ever think that a person who talked so much was hiding anything.

6

A large envelope postmarked London was delivered to David shortly after his holiday was over. He knew at once what it contained. He had often posted one that size when he was Paul's secretary and the sight of it made him smile with happy memories. Paul hadn't sent him many examples of what he was doing since he had gone to London: a few still-lifes, some cloud-studies, a couple of street-scenes, but nothing very exciting.

'Well, let's see what we have,' he murmured, opening the envelope eagerly in his sitting-room, talking aloud to himself in the manner of people accustomed to living alone. 'I hope there's a letter with it. It's time I had a letter.'

There was no letter. There was a bill, charging him for 'six art photographs enclosed as ordered'. He saw the bill before he looked at the photographs, and he stared at the billheading and at the handwriting stating the number and price of the photographs. He didn't understand. Photographs meant Paul, and photographs from London must have come from Paul, but the address on the bill wasn't Paul's, nor was the handwriting, and he disliked the name of the firm on the billheading. Nu-Art as a spelling of New Art seemed silly to him. He had never seen anything clever or amusing in such phonetic trade-names as Kumphy-Kots, Eezy-Kleen, Phit-U-Well, or Brite-Lite. He looked on them as a wanton and unnecessary attack on the conventions of English

135

orthography, and the sight of the Nu-Art Fotografic Agency at the top of the bill put him in an ill-humour at once. He took the tissue wrapping off the photographs, expecting to see something he would recognize as his brother's work, for he assumed they had come, directly or indirectly, from Paul, though the sending of a bill surprised him.

The six photographs were all much the same. They were pictures of nude young women, in various poses, sitting, kneeling, lying down, standing, some full length, some torso only, all marked by an unconvincing coyness. One of them was pensive, with a faraway look in her big dreamy eyes, another smiled roguishly to a corner of the picture as if there were someone just out of the field of the camera. The breasts, belly, and thighs had an unnatural polished look about them, and the bodies of the young women were altogether too perfect to be true. He had seen enough when Paul lived with him to know what was possible in touching up a photograph, and he recognized that these had been improved.

He put them back in the envelope. He felt a flush round his forehead, and he was annoyed to find he was blushing at all at the sight of half a dozen faked nudes. Mark, he remembered suddenly, though it was years since he last had Mark in mind, used to call him a little prig and Paul, more kindly, used to tease him for being too much of a puritan.

'Well, that's how I am,' he remarked defensively, talking aloud to the four walls of his room. 'Why should people criticize me for being a puritan? I don't criticize them for not being one.'

He took the photographs out of their envelope and looked at them again. He was quite sure they were bogus. The girls and women he saw in shops, buses, and offices, the females all around him in the teeming city, were never made like these nudes. No woman ever was. He was still not amused, and his resentment increased when he looked at the bill, with its implication that he had ordered such photographs. He let the matter simmer in his mind for a day or two, then thinking he was in a calmer mood he wrote to Paul. But he wrote more than he intended.

I have received through the post [he wrote], *from an anonymous sender, a set of six photographs of the kind usually, I understand, referred to in the small advertisements of the less intellectual magazines as art studies, though to my untrained eye the art is far to seek and there is nothing studious about them unless it be in the calculated attempt to appeal to the curiosity of adolescents or the jaded appetites of the middle-aged. Can you enlighten me, please, as to the provenance of these photographs? I concede immediately of course that I may be guilty of making unwarranted assumptions when I ask you that question. It may be you are as ignorant as I am of their origin, but by an association of ideas I am sure you will find it easy to understand I thought of you at once when I received an envelope containing photographs, and if the contents are not quite what I should have expected nevertheless it is not to be wondered that I turn to you in my perplexity . . .*

He waddled on, stiff-jointed and verbose. In his innocence he believed his stilted prose was elegant. He believed he was writing with a light tone that couldn't possibly offend anyone. He fussed over clauses and phrases, driving them into the elastic space between two full stops, like a sheep-dog manœuvring sheep into a pen, for he thought that the longer the sentence the more it displayed his urbane control of it. He got himself involved in trying to explain his attitude to nude photographs. But since the nude was an accepted form of Western art he had to explain that he accepted the convention in painting while explaining away the fact that he didn't like it in photographs – especially in ones that came to him through the post without a covering letter.

Unable to stop he hurried on and tripped himself into an essay on the name of the firm, and that led him to dispute the bill. His excitement got worse the longer he wrote. He forgot he was being elegant and urbane, and he failed to see that he was taking two things for granted; that Paul had taken the photographs, and that he knew they had been sent to him. He scolded Paul for wasting his talents on such foolishness and on the third day after he began his letter he posted the twelve pages with a hand that was still shaking a little.

Paul answered his letter within the week, and the speed though not the contents of the reply softened David a little. Paul was brief and light-hearted.

Calm down, me old cock-sparrow [he wrote]. *A tea-cup's not the place for a storm. You lack a sense of proportion, as Cézanne said to Picasso! You're a tiresome moralist at times! I took those art studies as an exercise. It's a common exercise in professional photography. The agency belongs to Menzies. How its name riled you! Or rather to Menzies and some of his friends. It gives me a useful income, and it gives me plenty of scope. I told you I was going to work for Menzies. He has the business side well organized. I suppose Menzies sent you the prints. Next time I see him I'll ask him. I remember I was telling him you had moved, and he was interested because he remembers the district well of course. He asked me just where you had gone. So I gave him the address. Forget the bill,* fratellino mio. *That would be Menzies' little joke.*

David was content to take it as a gratuitous act of malice on the part of Menzies. But when he sat down to reply to Paul's explanation he found his pen take charge of him again. He became discursive and aggressive, ridiculed the agency again, and criticized the photographs in the technical jargon he had learnt from Paul himself. He had a long wait for Paul's next letter, and when it came it didn't please him. Paul was angry with him, and wrote with hurt pride:

I don't know why you take so much pains to criticize my work if it's all that bad. The trouble is you don't know the ABC of what you think you're talking about. I take good photographs and I take bad. I turn out some of high artistic value and others of less. And I know when I do either. You don't understand art, not really. You never have, though I did my best to educate you. But you suffer from illusions of infallibility in matters of taste, matters that in fact are beyond your appreciation altogether. You seem to be suffering from delusions of grandeur too, judging from some of your other remarks. You think fit to run down an agency that operates a large mail-order business Menzies created from scratch by brains and sheer hard work. I am not aware that a person in your sheltered position has the slightest right to criticize a man of Menzies' business ability. Frankly, I think you would have starved before you could have done a quarter of what he has done in building up a business.

The injustice of the reply kept him awake at night and he lay composing replies he never wrote. He had never said he knew the ABC of photography, but that didn't mean he couldn't see when Paul was wasting his time. He had never claimed to be a business man, but that didn't mean he had no right to comment on the taste and value of

Menzies' Nu-Art Agency. The answers went round and round in his head and he went on composing them in his sleep.

Visiting Mrs Ruthven and accompanying Mrs Marchbanks to concerts gave him some distraction, but the topic was always with him, oppressing him to silence. He couldn't tell Mrs Ruthven about his quarrel with Paul because she knew how close they had been. It would only distress her. He couldn't tell Mrs Marchbanks because she had never known Paul, never known how close they had been. She would see nothing to be sorry about. In neither case did he feel he could explain trouble had started over half a dozen photographs of nude women.

Every time he saw Mrs Ruthven there was in any case the shadow of her daughter between them. She had written only one letter home since the summer, three pages of trivial chattering. Mrs Ruthven seldom mentioned her daughter. She seemed preoccupied with something else, something she was unwilling or unable to discuss. He noticed her eyes were often fixed on some point behind him, over his shoulder, as he sat talking with her, so that she hardly seemed to be listening to him. Her lips were tight when she was silent, and a spasm would cross her face as if she were in pain. But since she looked in normal health otherwise, he supposed he was imagining things when he thought he saw an expression of dumb suffering on her ageing face.

He brought a packet of cigarettes every time he called and left them unobtrusively behind him before he went away. He never referred to them nor did she, but it pleased him when she fetched out her cigarette-holder, stuck a cigarette in it, and smoked as she chatted. She seemed to be smoking more and to be more silent every time he visited her. Sometimes he wished Mary Ruthven would write to him, if she didn't want to write to her mother, and then he might have some news to pass on to Mrs Ruthven. But he saw that wouldn't do either. To write to him while she had still to write to her mother would only make things worse. He couldn't, with any tact, say he had heard from Mary when Mrs Ruthven herself hadn't heard. It was as well he knew nothing. It left him with nothing to hide. So he sat with Mrs Ruthven, tried to divert her, played a hand at cards with her, brought her magazines and weekly papers, went to the public library for her, did some shopping for her at week-ends if she was too tired to go out on a Saturday morning.

And both kept on thinking of an absent woman that neither cared to mention.

All that time he put off writing to Paul in case he made bad worse, and while he procrastinated he kept on hoping Paul would write again. Even if he didn't apologize for the harshness of his last letter he might explain it away by using gentler arguments, or he might ignore it altogether and resume their correspondence as if nothing had happened to cause bad feeling between them.

He watched for the postman every morning, and if he left the house before the postman passed he would go home in the evening hoping for a letter and look behind the door, trying to deceive himself by the casual way he did it. But nothing came.

The autumn sidled up against winter. The rain came. It was cold. The clock was put back. He went to work wearing a heavy coat and a scarf Mrs Ruthven knitted for him. It was dark when he rose in the morning and dark again when he went home in the evening. It was at that dead time of the year, when the sun seemed gone for good, that the postman brought him another large envelope. It came on a Saturday morning, when he was off work, and he had just begun to prepare his breakfast when the postman knocked. He knew before he opened the envelope that there would be no letter inside from Paul. He could see it contained photographs and he knew before he removed the tissue-paper that they would be worse than before. He knew it by a painful twilight of intuition, seeming in one moment of time to be living in another before he actually got there. His hand was not quite steady and his heart was beating faster than it should. He put the photographs on his breakfast table and frowned down at them. There were six of them again, but none had the coy poses of the first set. The pretence of art studies was dropped. These were not the pleasant nudes that could offend nobody but a prig. He was faced with six obscene photographs, male nudes and female nudes together, coupled in twisted poses, absurd and ugly.

As he looked at them he remembered Paul's remark about Menzies' little joke. He lifted the envelope and shook it, and a bill fluttered out. It had the same heading and the same handwriting as before. He put the bill and the photographs, one by one, in the kitchen fire and watched them burn slowly, shaking his head over them as the flames leaped eagerly at bare breasts and naked loins.

He went without his breakfast. An elderly widow came to his house every Saturday morning to give the rooms a thorough cleaning, and when she arrived he had a cup of tea with her and that was all. Then he wrote out his shopping list and went round to Mrs Ruthven to see if she wanted anything. The weather seemed to be depressing her and she was coughing a lot. But as he was going out with a note of her requirements she remarked with something like her old smile, 'I wish you'd stop scowling, Davie!' Her smile moved into a little laugh to show she was only teasing him: 'You're supposed to come and cheer me up. And you've a face would turn milk.'

'I'm sorry,' he said, startled that he was showing on his face the unhappiness he felt in his heart.

'Have you heard from Mary?' she asked, and he was sure that the casual way her question came out was an affectation.

'No, not since the summer,' he answered. Mary Ruthven was the least of his worries. He hadn't been thinking of her at all that morning.

'I had a letter this morning,' Mrs Ruthven said slowly, as if she were still trying to make up her mind whether to tell him or not. 'Oh, a very short one. I don't quite understand it, to tell you the truth.'

'Can I see it?' he asked. He trembled a little when she went to the kitchen dresser to fetch the letter, but he supposed he was still shocked by the photographs.

Mrs Ruthven gave him a small sheet of notepaper. In his haste, trying to take in the whole letter in one eager glance, he skipped the address, date, and greeting.

I may be home before Christmas for good. Things haven't worked out as I expected. It's very hard to explain. Tell Davie Heylyn I'll write to him in a day or two. Then maybe he can tell you for me.

'What on earth can she mean?' Mrs Ruthven said, busying herself at the fireside and not looking at him.

'I've no idea,' he answered impulsively, deciding in a fraction of a second that he were better to say nothing till Mary Ruthven wrote to him. 'I don't know what can have gone wrong. Maybe she just doesn't like living in London, even though she has got promotion.'

There was no letter from her in the week that followed, nor in the week after that. His only mail was another large envelope, with four instead of six photographs. The decrease in number was made up for by an increase in the fantastic coarseness of the pictures. He had led so sheltered a life, as Paul had reminded him, that at first they puzzled him, and it was only after a few moments that he understood they were pictures of sexual perverts. Homosexuals and lesbians accounted for two of the pictures. The other two, though heterosexual, remained beyond his comprehension for many years.

He had kept himself from writing to Paul after the last lot of photographs because he was afraid if he wrote in haste he would say all the wrong things. But now he was too angry to care about discretion. He wrote to Paul that evening, forgetting all he had ever learnt about tact and moderation, about the superiority of soft words to harsh ones. He was a pugnacious schoolboy again. He scribbled on so bitterly that before bed-time he was dismayed at the number of pages he had covered. He revised and excised and made a fair copy. It was after midnight, but he worked on. Then he found that for every bitter phrase he had cut out he had written in two elsewhere, and he tried again.

He ended with a long rhetorical passage, imploring Paul to leave Menzies before it was too late.

If you have any respect for yourself or for me or for your dead mother [he wrote] (and even as he wrote he wondered why he dragged in a mother he couldn't remember at all and Paul could remember only dimly, yet he wanted some standard of female dignity to refer to, some sexual symbol that belonged to the normal world and not the world of Menzies' exhibitionists and perverts), *if you have any respect for the talent you once had, if you have any intelligence or integrity left, get out of this ugly business now, at once, without delay. You are co-operating in an agency for the distribution of obscenities.*

He was so taken with the last words that he worked them again.

How can you know the harm you may do, taking, printing and publishing such lies? For they are lies. They are lies about human nature, about the human body, and about human instincts. Sex, yes. Your photographs, no. If you persist in your present course you make yourself nothing but an agent in the circulation of obscenities.

He was exhausted when he finished, trembling with indignation and excitement. Then although it was the small hours of the morning he went to his record-player and put on Mozart's fifth violin concerto. The supreme music, confident in its own beauty, vibrated comfortingly in his ears, and as it went on its happy way it scattered largesse round his room till his impoverished spirit was enriched and he forgot his anger at Paul. In the presence of Mozart Paul hardly seemed to matter. A world with Mozart could put up with several Pauls, even if every one of them had a Menzies for his patron.

He had a long, long wait for his brother's reply, and he went about his daily routine with a dogged, sullen air, convinced he had lost Paul for good. Mrs Marchbanks quizzed him gently about his health and hinted that worries were never so bad once they were confided to somebody else. But he knew that however much he might tell her he could never tell her what Paul had done. It brought a new distress to him: he saw he was ashamed of his brother.

'You're looking awfully tired these days,' Mrs Marchbanks said. 'And you're getting pale. You didn't used to be so pale.'

She began to have him round for tea oftener, with a gramophone recital to follow. Sometimes Muriel entertained them at the piano, though she didn't play as well as her mother, and she would divert them at the table with a university student's innocent gossip about professors and lecturers and the Pelion upon Ossa of term exams and degree exams. She had a turn for mimicry and she travestied the lecturer in metaphysics, complete with an apple in her hand, proving she didn't have an apple at all. She did it amusingly, and her mother and David laughed. In such company Paul's photographs seemed very far away, very unreal.

A reply came when he was no longer expecting one. He opened it still hoping there was some explanation he hadn't thought of, still hoping Paul would say he had left Menzies and had been foolish ever to have got

143

mixed up with him. The first lines showed him it wasn't going to be like that at all. There was no fraternal salutation, but in the top left-hand corner was his full name with his address under it. The letter was typed, and badly typed, and in the occasional solecism and misspelling he recognized Paul's unaided composition.

Your grotesque epistle surpasses all your previous efforts. A lengthy essay in your own peculiar theory of aesthetics (if that's what it was meant to be) apalled me by its humourless pedantry the last time you wrote. The present effusion goes even further in stupidity. When I look over the bombastic passages in it I can only sit back and wonder at your astounding offensiveness. Amid your faraggo of insulting (and from you unexpected) stupidities you should have remembered all the time you are writing to me on questions you want answered. You want to hear my answer. You even demand an answer. Demand, forsooth! You hardly go the right way about getting an answer at all. Your impertinence brings out all too clearly the delusions of infallibility and grandeur I remarked on before. You don't like my work therefore my work must be poor. I am only a hard-working photographer, but you are a gentleman of leisure, fully qualified to teach me how to do my own job. If you had ever to earn your living from scratch the way I have overcame all my handicaps I might consider you worth listening to. But you have always had life easy and you have no knowledge of the world outside the little world in which you have grown up, if you have grown up. Your egotistical tirade proves as much. The sad fact is you are a provincial puritan labouring under the delusion that nudes are improper.

David found he wasn't reading. He was skipping to the end.

I have answered to the best of my ability. What you will think I do not know. My own feeling is you have made a fool of yourself. I am content as to my own reliance on my intelligence and as to my personal integrity. I am an artist and will continue to be an artist. After the manner in which you have conducted this correspondence, the terms you have slung about, the sneers and personal abuse, further correspondence with you is distasteful.

Paul's signature in full followed immediately, abruptly.

7

Mrs Ruthven liked to read long novels that dealt with the rise and fall of a family, with scores of characters over the years, and she was especially pleased if there was a genealogical table inset before the text. David didn't share her tastes, but he tried to be tolerant of them. When he went to the library for her he was careful to pick a book she might like, not one he thought she ought to read. Faced with the need to keep her going in books when she had gone through the local library's stock of suitable fiction he began to bring her popular biographies, and she enjoyed them if they had any scandal. She became quite expert in the ladies of the Regency and in George IV's troubles with Queen Caroline. So he brought her a book about Caroline's daughter, the Princess Charlotte, hardly looking past the title-page before handing it over.

He found out later it had an appendix giving the details of Charlotte's death in childbirth. Mrs Ruthven, with a professional interest in the topic, though she had done no nursing for a long time, seemed fascinated by the fact that even royalty were subject to pain and mortality and at the mercy of their physician. She lamented the lack of medical knowledge in those days, and while David politely agreed it was a pity they knew nothing about hygiene he would gladly have been spared a reading of the more bloody details in the appendix. But Mrs Ruthven enjoyed reading them to him.

'Sheer ignorance killed that poor girl,' she said. 'Listen—'

She read him some more. There was something flushed and strained in her enthusiasm about the book and David was uncomfortable. But if it gave her something to talk about he felt he had to show an interest.

He brought her next a popular account of the courtship and marriage of Victoria and Albert. She found it dull. There was no scandal in it. Yet she was sufficiently interested to ask him how Victoria came to be Queen at all and what would have happened if Charlotte's baby had lived. Not without difficulty, falling back on guesswork where his memory of classroom history failed him, he drew a table for her showing all the relationships she asked about. Once she had a pedigree she was satisfied. But that seemed enough for her on the royal family of England.

By good fortune at that time he saw on a book-barrow a gaudy volume entitled *Moths Round the Flame* and he bought it for a couple of shillings. He would never have bought for himself a book with such a title, but if it pleased Mrs Ruthven it was worth the momentary embarrassment of picking it up. It dealt with the ladies of the court of Louis XIV, and he hoped there would be enough scandal in it to keep her talking for some time. It turned out to be a more substantial book than the title would have suggested. It had plates, appendices, source-references, and genealogical tables. Mrs Ruthven was delighted with it. It was something new for her to have a book to keep, a book of her own, instead of a book on loan from the library.

'This is better than the Sunday papers,' she told him gaily the next time he called on her. He loved her face when she smiled. There seemed to come through her smile all the wisdom and tolerance of the years she had spent watching and nursing people. 'Such goings on! And when they've had their pleasures they all turn to religion. They made the best of both worlds, those women. From the royal bed to the nun's cell!'

But there was always that strained, excited manner in her speaking when she recounted to him some incident in the book, and he wondered how far her interest in the biographies of courtesans was an attempt to distract herself from thinking about her daughter. It was coming near Christmas and she had heard no more from Mary, nor had he ever received the letter promised him. But the matter was never mentioned by either of them.

He himself was less concerned about Mary Ruthven than about Paul. The letter in which Paul had broken off relations with him had become the recurrent substance of disturbed dreams. He slept badly, and as he tossed and turned and heard three and four chime in the dark stillness of the winter night he went over and over the words of it. If further correspondence was distasteful to his brother then certainly he wouldn't write again. But the injustice of leaving him without the right of a reply when he had still so much to say remained as a torment to him. Even if he had nothing to add to what he had said already, Paul's final letter raised a regiment of new questions, and he was baffled by the attitude Paul had taken, by his bland assumption of being in the right when he was so clearly in the wrong.

More than once, unable to sleep, he rose and put the light on, fetched out Paul's last letter and conned the words of it again, although he had them all off by heart.

'Does he really not see what the issue is?' he muttered in his empty room, talking to the sheets of paper spread out on the table before him. 'If he knows the kind of photographs I was getting how can he talk about being an artist and about his integrity and all the rest of it? The thing's absurd. And if he doesn't know, if it was just Menzies and nobody else, why didn't he pick on my complaints about obscene pictures and disown any part of them? He doesn't know what I'll think of his answer, he says. But he hasn't answered anything.'

Every time he looked at the letter he saw a new weakness in it.

'Grotesque,' he said, putting his finger on the word. 'Your grotesque epistle. But if anything is to be called grotesque surely it's those damned photographs! He's using the very word that's fit for them and applying it to my letter. It's as if he saw the truth and deliberately twisted it.'

On another occasion he stopped at the phrase, 'your egotistical tirade', and frowned at it suspiciously.

'That's silly,' he said. 'I hadn't noticed that before. A tirade can't be egotistical. This thing's full of silly phrases. He wants to call my letter a tirade. Maybe it was. But then he wants to call me egotistical, the very word that applies to himself. So he calls my letter an egotistical tirade. He's using words without bothering what they mean. It's the same with that remark about delusions of grandeur. I've got delusions of grandeur. But he's the one that says he's an artist. Now there's a delusion!'

His obsession with Paul's obtuseness was ended for a time when he visited Mrs Ruthven in the week before Christmas. She opened the door promptly enough to his familiar ring but he saw she was in pain the way she tottered at once to her armchair and sat down, panting a little. He was alarmed, and questioned her.

'I had such a night last night,' she said slowly, and as if the admission of an illness she had long concealed was some relief to her she relaxed in her chair. 'I hope I never pass another night like it! The pain – I've never known such pain!'

147

She put a hand across her breast.

He glowered at her, his head half turned to fix her with his good eye. 'Shall I get the doctor?' he asked timidly.

'A doctor?' she said, and smiled. 'What good would a doctor do?'

'That's no way for you to talk,' he said, gathering boldness at the weakness of her smile and the weariness in her voice. 'A trained nurse should have some faith in doctors. I'm going to get Dr Tennant right now.'

He called in the doctor who had attended his father.

'I hope you're not calling me in at the last minute again,' Dr Tennant remarked affably. 'When I saw your father nobody could have helped him.'

He visited Mrs Ruthven early the next morning and when David came home from work and went round to see her after tea she greeted him with mock complaints.

'You're a fine help, I must say!' she scolded him. 'Sending a doctor to see me! I'm all right here in my own corner. But no! That won't do. I'm not to stay here, thanks to you!'

For a moment he thought she had been advised to take an ocean cruise or move to some country place where the air was better, or do something equally impracticable, and he stared at her without speaking.

'I've got to go into hospital the day after tomorrow. Dr Tennant arranged for a bed today. He came back in the afternoon after he had seen me in the morning and told me it was all fixed. I'd better give you my keys, and you can look in here once a week and keep the rooms aired for me. He's a very pleasant young man, your Dr Tennant. I haven't met him before. But he's clever. He knows. Oh yes, he knows all right!'

'He knows what's wrong?' he asked.

'Oh, he knows, and I know too. I've known for a long time,' she answered carelessly. 'Here, have a cigarette.'

It wasn't often he smoked in her company, it was seldom he smoked at all, and he took a cigarette from her feeling she was letting him know the subject was dropped.

But although he was afraid to press Mrs Ruthven with questions he wasn't afraid of Dr Tennant. He went to the doctor's consulting-rooms the evening Mrs Ruthven was removed and sat at the end of a queue of ailing people, poor unhappy bits of humanity, sad-faced men and women who if they didn't seem to have much wrong with them didn't seem to have much right either. There were obviously many regulars amongst them, and he knew he struck them as an odd intruder by not maintaining his place in the queue. Every time a new patient came into the waiting-room he surrendered his seat to him and went to the end of the queue. He believed he would be less of a nuisance to Dr Tennant if he went in last, when the evening's consultations were over, and made it clear he would not detain him long.

His strategy was successful. Glad to have seen the last of his lugubrious patients and written out the last prescription for the evening, Dr Tennant was in no hurry. He saved David the need of any apology by giving him a friendly greeting at once. Perhaps he knew he would save himself from having to listen to some stiff courtesies and punctilious explanations from the young man if he forestalled him.

'Mrs Ruthven?' he said breezily. 'You want to know the verdict, is that it?'

'Yes,' said David. 'If I may, if it's etiquette. I should have asked Mrs Ruthven herself after you had seen her, but she put me off, and I didn't like to persist.'

'Oh, she would put you off,' Dr Tennant said, and laughed. 'She would have put me off too if she could. She's a wily old bitch.'

David was going to resent the word but the doctor chatted on. Obviously he was accustomed to use the word as a pleasantry.

'You'd think some of these women don't want to live. Oh, she hasn't much of a life, I know, shut up there all day alone, a husband that walked out on her and a daughter that just up and went on the pretext of taking a holiday, and nothing left her but her memories. But still . . .'

Just how much had Mrs Ruthven told this free and easy young man David wondered jealously. Mrs Ruthven had never mentioned her husband to him.

'But she isn't all that old,' Dr Tennant was saying. 'Not so old that she should have given up all interest. Not that that's the point.'

'What is the point?' David asked.

'Well, I think she has cancer of the breast,' said Dr Tennant blithely. 'I'm not sure. I'll have to get the specialist to confirm my diagnosis. And her heart's done. I don't know why it should be done in a woman her age, but it is. I suppose there's years of hard work and worry and strain behind her, but she would be a better patient if she wanted to get well. Which she don't.'

Just as he had called Mrs Ruthven a bitch out of sheer good feeling for her, so he ended his remarks with a jocular solecism to take away any appearance of being annoyed with her for not wanting to get well.

'How bad is she?' David asked, none the wiser for the doctor's remarks.

'Bad?' said Dr Tennant. 'She might die tomorrow or she might die next week. I don't know. She might live six months. You can't tell. She hasn't a great future I shouldn't say.'

And while David was trying to sort out the meaning of the double negative, Dr Tennant went fluently on: 'But if I can get her to stay inside for a month it'll be as good as a holiday for her. And it will give them a chance to find out if it's cancer or not. The way she's living just now is silly. Nobody to do a damn' thing for her, and climbing up and down three storeys every day. These tenements were never meant for elderly people. What is she to you anyway? Your aunt?'

'No, she's – she's an old friend of mine,' he answered.

'Well, I've known men pick a worse girl-friend,' Dr Tennant said flippantly. 'She's a great philosopher when she starts talking. You know, Providence, foreknowledge, will, and fate, and all that kind of thing. She was a midwife for years she was telling me. Of course I regard the old generation of tenement midwives as a bloody menace, but I wouldn't hold that against Mrs Ruthven. She's got some good stories. She's seen them come and she's seen them go and she's not bothered. There's a kind of divine detachment about her. She'll watch herself go as if it were somebody else. But if you know where that hard-boiled daughter of hers has got to it might be a good idea to tell her it's time she saw her mama again quick if she wants to see her again alive.'

David went away puzzled almost as much by the doctor as he was by Paul. He had no anger against the doctor, who seemed an amiable young man, doing the best he could and full of good will. But just as with Paul, he had difficulty in understanding what he meant by what he said, if he meant anything at all. He brooded over the doctor's words as he had brooded over Paul's, and regretted his own lack of intelligence that kept him from grasping what was said to him. Mrs Ruthven might die tomorrow, she might die next week, and she might live six months. And in saying so, Dr Tennant appeared to think there was no difference in the three comments. To make it all quite simple, he added he didn't know how long she would live. Then in case that seemed to remove any cause for worry he had suggested Mrs Ruthven's daughter should be told of her mother's illness.

Disturbed as he was by that advice, David put off writing to Mary Ruthven until he saw Mrs Ruthven again. He didn't want to be an alarmist. But when he visited the hospital on Christmas Eve Mrs Ruthven looked so old and tired, so frail a fragment of mortality as she sat up in her nightgown, that he was embarrassed to look at her. It was as if he had intruded on a decent privacy. He was tempera-mentally anxious to do his duty, if only he could be sure what his duty was. In this case it seemed to be to write to Mary Ruthven. Any doubts he had were scattered when as he stood to take his leave and hovered over her Mrs Ruthven said to him softly: 'I feel tired. I've never been so tired. I can't do a thing for myself. Would you write to Mary for me?'

From under her pillow she took the last letter she received, the one she had shown him, and he copied the address. It wasn't the same as the address on the only letter he had from her when she first went to London.

8

He passed Christmas and New Year alone. Mrs Marchbanks had gone out of town over their short office-holiday, taking Muriel with her, to a moneyed relative in North Berwick. He had always been proud of his ability to be alone, but that week was a great strain on him. He wrote to Mary Ruthven on Boxing Day, briefly and calmly, reporting only that her mother was in hospital and that the doctor thought she might get worse. Perhaps she could manage home for a few days soon. There was no reply. Yet once, he remembered, she had never failed to send her friends a card at Christmas, even people next door and people she saw every day.

She was always sending cards – birthday cards, get-well cards, anniversary cards, Christmas cards, New Year cards. It was all part of her sociable, well-wishing nature. But now there was nothing.

Nothing until half-way through the dark days between Christmas and New Year. Then he received a large envelope. His heart dropped when he saw the postman with it and he almost slammed the door in his face. For a moment or two, alone in the kitchen where he had a good fire going, he was tempted to burn the envelope unopened. Then he thought it would be cowardly to shirk seeing just what was in it.

There was only one photograph, not obscene like the second and third sets he had received. It was more like the first lot, only it was not the figure of a young girl hardly out of her teens, with a slim and impossibly perfect body. It was the figure of a mature woman in her late twenties, broad in the hips, rather flabby, and with very large breasts. The very age of the subject seemed to remove the picture from the class of what Paul called art-studies and put it into the class of the indecent. The photograph was obviously retouched to heighten the contrast of the lights and shadows, but no retouching had altered the face. It was unmistakably Mary Ruthven's.

He stood over the photograph as it lay on the kitchen table and looked and looked. A cold implacable hatred of Paul rose in him and he knew it would last the rest of his life, even though the silence that would remain between them would mean he would never find out how Mary Ruthven had ever allowed such a photograph to be taken.

In the evening, although he knew that never again could any spoken words pass between them, he sat down and wrote to Paul.

'Even if it is bombastic,' he said as he addressed the envelope, 'even if it is an egotistical tirade, it's going.'

As always, he wrote more than he intended, but he didn't trouble to cut and re-write.

Just because you tell me you find further correspondence distasteful [he wrote], *doesn't mean I must keep silent about the latest photograph I've received from your agency. If you're still satisfied with your personal integrity, as you*

152

quaintly boasted, then you're easily satisfied. If you think you're being an artist it's high time you were told you're only a conceited ass. I don't know how Mary Ruthven comes to be mixed up in this sordid business and I don't want to know.

He stopped there for a moment, aware he had written a magnificent lie: he was in a torment to think he would never have Mary Ruthven's part explained. But he let it stand. It was the expression of an attitude. He wanted nothing more from Paul.

I think you could have kept her out of it [he went on]. *All I should like to know is that you had no hand in it or that at least you didn't know I had been sent this particular photograph, and I should appreciate a straight answer for once. If it was only due to Menzies that it came to me I think you should say so – though that doesn't absolve you, because it would mean you have no control over him and yet go on working with him.*

So long as you work for Menzies further correspondence is not only distasteful (do you think I find these photographs tasteful?), it is impossible. But before I dismiss you as a hack who fabricates dirty photographs for a living I should like to have your apology for this photograph of Mary Ruthven. I think you are in duty bound to answer this letter, however distasteful you may find it, even if it is only to say you have nothing to say.

He knew as he wrote that for all his anger he still wanted Paul to answer him and explain Mary Ruthven's photograph, or to say he didn't know anything about it. But his abiding fear was that Paul would never answer, and he would be left wondering all his life what the explanation was.

He began to have nightmares again, in which he held Paul a prisoner in the room where they had worked together as boys and tried to compel him by brute force to admit he wasn't an artist. But he always wakened with a jolt before Paul admitted anything. In his waking hours he was left with a futile obsession and he brooded on the matter. How could Paul really believe he was an artist? Was his judgement completely ruined by his vanity? Or was he really innocent? Had he taken only the first half-dozen photographs and was somebody else responsible for the others? But even then Paul was being dishonest about it, for he went on working for Menzies. He had even defended Menzies. And although he had lightheartedly excused the first set of photographs and admitted taking them, he had never replied about the others, not even to disown them. When he reached that point he went back to the beginning and went through it all again, unable to rest in certainty anywhere in the circle.

He visited Mrs Ruthven the day after he received her daughter's photograph, and looking at her old grey face, with the eyes two empty mirrors in it, he remembered the casual way the doctor had said 'cancer of the breast'. He remembered at the same time how the photograph had been posed to emphasize the fullness of the daughter's breasts, and the discrepancy between the two cases seemed to him the discrepancy between truth and falsehood. What Mrs Ruthven was suffering was real and inescapable, part of the pain women were born to. What the photograph stressed was something false and unnecessary, a sham so-phistication meant only for the gloating of mental adolescents. It was the contrast between the real world of human bodies that were fatally flawed and mortal, and an artificial world of bodies faked to appear perfect and please an idiot's lust.

'You're looking grim again,' said Mrs Ruthven, and the shape of a smile was briefly sketched on her patient-eyed face. 'Did you write to Mary?'

'Yes, but it's a bit too soon for an answer,' he said soothingly.

She made a little weak note of disbelief.

'Do you ever see that fellow Harry Carter?' she asked suddenly.

'I see him in the shop occasionally,' he answered, 'and we pass a few words, but nothing much.'

'What happened between him and Mary?' she asked.

She had one arm out on top of the sheet and plucked at the bedclothes nervously. He stared at the movement and noticed how poor her flesh was as he wondered what to say.

'I don't really know – he says one thing and Mary says another.'

Or had they said the same thing, he asked himself. She said he was too good for her and he said she was a bitch. Or had he only said she might be? He couldn't be sure. But it came to him that perhaps Carter had his own kind of shrewdness. Perhaps that was the explanation of the photograph.

'Such as?' Mrs Ruthven prompted him.

'I don't know,' he said, distressed at her persistence. 'It's hard to remember, it's so long ago. Mary thought he was too dull, and he thought Mary was a bit of a gadabout.'

'Oh, she was never a gadabout,' Mrs Ruthven said with a low, tired enunciation that rejected the charge more firmly than a shout would have done. 'She liked people, she liked to meet people, new people. But she was never a gadabout. She was always considerate. I don't know what I would have done without her. She was always a very sensible girl, a good-hearted generous girl.'

'Oh, I'm sure,' David murmured, and wondered fantastically what she would say if he showed her the photograph and said: 'Do you know who that is? That's your daughter.'

'Well, you knew her,' said Mrs Ruthven. 'You knew her better than Carter – or anybody else for that matter.'

'Yes, I suppose that's true,' he said as if he had never thought of it before. 'I did know her well, didn't I?'

'Well, come in on Saturday,' said Mrs Ruthven.

Then to his surprise, for she had never been a demonstrative woman, she held out her hand. He took it, not quite sure what to do. He could hardly shake it vigorously, and to press it would be ridiculous. He held it limply, and it was she who gave his hand a little squeeze, looked up at him, and sighed.

'Goodbye,' she said.

He went back to the hospital on Saturday, and as he came to the threshold of the ward he saw at once that her bed wasn't in its usual place. There was a gap there, but further along the wall, down at the corner, there were screens round a bed.

'Mrs Ruthven?' he said, intoning a question to a nurse who saw him hover and came helpfully forward. He had seen her before and she knew him too.

She looked over her shoulder at the screened bed and said brightly: 'Oh yes! Mrs Ruthven. We were wondering who to get in touch with. Mrs Ruthven died at three o'clock this morning. Are you her son?'

He nodded dumbly, too shocked to speak. He had seen his father die and marvelled he had felt nothing, but the nurse's statement that Mrs

Ruthven was dead hit him in the throat and brought such sorrow to him that he saw the nurse and the ward through unshed tears.

'Do you want to see her?' the nurse asked, and he followed her to the screened bed. For a moment he could have believed it was a tasteless practical joke. There was a waxen face on the figure in the bed when the nurse raised the sheet, and it wasn't a very good likeness of Mrs Ruthven at all.

'She looks so lovely,' said the nurse kindly. 'She has such a sweet face. She was an old dear. She must have suffered something terrible and she never said a word of complaint. You'll want her things, won't you?'

'Yes,' he said. He could just as easily have said no, but her question seemed to expect a yes, and even in uttering the one syllable he found his voice was not his own, but a reedy instrument with a flaw in it.

The nurse had the clothes already parcelled, and she brought out also some miscellaneous articles – a handbag, a wristlet watch, a couple of rings, her spectacles, and a book.

'Mrs Ruthven was letting me read this book,' she said. 'It's quite interesting.'

She handed him *Moths Round the Flame* and he said, 'Oh yes!'

He left the hospital after seeing the matron and getting a death certificate from the doctor in residence, and as he went about the routine of arranging for the funeral he felt absurdly comforted that his father's death had at least taught him what to do to get Mrs Ruthven decently buried. But even as he was doing all that had to be done he kept on saying to himself, 'What am I to do?' It wasn't the funeral that was in his mind. He was thinking only of the loneliness that surrounded him in the crowded tenemented city, and wondering how he would face Mary Ruthven if she came home for her mother's funeral. He wasn't sure she would come, and that misgiving increased his unhappiness.

He stopped at a post-office and sent her a telegram, telling her of the death and the date of the funeral in half a dozen words.

He was coming back from seeing the undertaker and just passing Dr Tennant's consulting-rooms on the main street when a small car drew up at the kerb and the doctor got out. David stopped and the doctor stopped and they spoke for a few minutes.

'I think you should come along on Monday night and join the queue,'

Dr Tennant remarked pleasantly. He knew Mrs Ruthven was dead and seemed to hope to comfort David by being cheerful and friendly. He was so far successful that David found he could speak in a normal voice.

'Join the queue?' he queried. 'Why, what do you mean?'

'Oh, I wouldn't give you a bottle,' Dr Tennant answered. 'But I'm sure I could find something wrong with you, and you'd be none the worse for a few days off work. You look as if you had a bit of a shock, and I think your nerves are in a bad way.'

'Me?' said David, and smiled it off. 'I'm perfectly all right.'

He had never had any dealings with a doctor, and he didn't want any. But he wondered if Dr Tennant would give him anything to stop him having nightmares. He wondered whether there was any use telling him about Paul. He put the idea away as absurd. Nobody could help him about Paul any more than about Mrs Ruthven now.

'I tell you what I'll do,' he said impulsively. 'I'll come and see you the day before I die.'

He said it for the sake of saying something, trying to imitate Dr Tennant's levity, and then he was sorry he had spoken. It sounded as if he were implying a doctor was only a last and useless resort. But Dr Tennant laughed, slapped him on the shoulder, and crossed to his consulting-rooms with a flourish and the parting remark: 'Oh, I hope I'll see you before then! Look in some night when I'm not busy. I'd like a chat with you.'

He phoned his office on Monday morning and got a day off for the funeral and a day before and after it on the plea of being a relative of Mrs Ruthven. The office made no question and he was past caring that he was guilty of deceit in claiming relationship. He had still a lot to do, and he needed the time. For decency's sake the husbands of two of Mrs Ruthven's neighbours took the day off and went to the funeral with him, but there were no other mourners. Mrs Marchbanks sent a wreath, although she had never met Mrs Ruthven, and wrote him a note of sympathy.

On the way back into town from the cemetery the two men quizzed him about Mrs Ruthven's house.

'You have the keys, I believe,' said one of them blandly, passing round cigarettes. 'You'll have to let the factor have them.'

He saw they were already planning to get somebody into the empty house and he resented it.

'Oh no,' he said quickly. 'I can't do that. Mary's coming back to live there.'

He was thinking of the letter she had written saying she might be home for good before Christmas. He no longer believed in that letter, but he was determined to keep the keys of the house until he knew what Mary Ruthven meant to do. He had a wavering hope that something had kept her from the funeral and that she might turn up yet. Her mother's house would be somewhere for her to live till she went back to London or made up her mind what she was going to do. He looked boldly at the two men, silently defying them to contradict him. They looked at each other and then looked at him as they sat facing him in the undertaker's car.

'We were just wondering, the wife and me, why she wasn't up for the funeral,' said the man who had raised the question of the keys, and his tone seemed to demand an explanation rather than simply make a statement.

'You see,' said the other man, 'Willie here has a daughter that was married last week, just at the New Year there, and she's going to live with her man's folks. That house would suit her fine, just one stair up from her mother.'

'Aye, it's hard for a couple to get a house these days,' said Willie with elephantine pathos. 'You know, you were lucky to get a good house the way you did when you moved from our street. It's a nice place you went to. How did you manage it at all? A single young man, and there's couples can't get a house!'

He was going to be rude to them and tell them to mind their own business, but his impulsive lie about Mary Ruthven's return made him feel he had gone far enough. It would be better to avoid antagonizing them in case Mary Ruthven never came home and he had to surrender the keys in the end, and even ask the neighbours for help in disposing of Mrs Ruthven's furniture.

'Ah well, you see,' he explained amiably, 'it was a straightforward exchange. A young couple with a family wanted the extra rooms and I didn't need them.'

'Well, how about the daughter?' Willie insisted. 'Why wasn't she at the funeral? Surely to God she could have got away for her mother's funeral.'

'Oh, she could, of course she could,' David said, and added glibly, startled at the facility of his own invention, 'but as it happens she's ill in London with pneumonia. She just wasn't allowed to travel.'

'Funny we never heard about it,' said Willie.

David was glad when the car stopped at Mrs Ruthven's old close and he got rid of the two neighbours. He too left the car there and walked to his own house with a heart comparatively light after the horror of the interment and the anti-climax of the niggling conversation in the car. But when he closed the door and was again alone he felt the futility of his grief depress him as much as the grief itself. He knelt at the hearth and prepared to light a fire and the tears came into his eyes and he wasn't sure if he were weeping for the death of Mrs Ruthven, for the absence of Mary Ruthven at the funeral, or for Paul's desertion of him. They were all mixed up in his head, three strands of sorrow that twined to a rope constricting him. He saw again the steep sides of the grave, he heard the sound of the spades against the clay and the first scattering of soil on the coffin lid.

He was just sitting down to a frugal tea, with no appetite for a meal, when his bell rang. It was a telegram boy. He read the telegram on the threshold, said, 'No answer, thank you,' and closed the door slowly.

He stood at the fireplace with the slip of paper in his hand, reading and reading it as if it were a long letter. Mary Ruthven was coming home.

9

The morning was cold and squally, and the cheerless sky had never seemed lower. He felt the substantiality of the city, of the world, of all material existence, press in upon him, painfully reminding him that he was still a prisoner in the flesh and that Mrs Ruthven was gone. He went in the late afternoon to her empty house and prepared a fire there against the arrival of Mary Ruthven, tidied the rooms a little, and in good time he went to the station to meet her. It all seemed part of a nightmare, and when he tried to struggle out of it and assert some rational control over his feeling of unreality, all he knew was he didn't want to meet her. But he had to, because there was nobody else.

When she arrived he was struck at once by the fact that she looked bulkier, but smaller in height, and that her features seemed coarser and heavier. He believed he was seeing her for the first time as she really was, and her almost-dowdy appearance gratified his resentment against her. Their greeting was nervous and clumsy. He had the double grudge against her that she allowed the photograph to be taken and that she had missed her mother's funeral. He was in no mood to say much to her, and although she couldn't know of his first grudge he expected she would have some answer to the second. But she had as little to say as he had. He took her for a meal in town, and his lack of experience in city restaurants increased his awkwardness. The meal was badly served and dragged tediously. Once or twice Mary Ruthven tried to make conversation, but since she spoke only of the weather and of her journey he stubbornly refused to encourage her. He thought she should ask him about her mother's illness, tell him why she hadn't come to the funeral, and say what she meant to do and what had become of her intention to marry a married man.

They returned to the station to collect her luggage, and partly to lessen the time he would have to spend with her, partly to show that he wasn't a parsimonious yokel and knew how to treat a visitor from London, he took her home in a taxi – silently. He saw her across the threshold of her mother's house, put a match to the fire he had set, and when it was burning healthily he prepared to leave her.

'Aren't you going to stay a while?' she asked, plainly surprised and even hurt.

He invented an appointment, but since he hadn't mentioned it before and since the evening was now well advanced she didn't believe him. He saw it in her eyes, but she let him go without saying anything more.

He slouched back to his own corner, sullen and lonely, and exasperated to find that leaving her had made him even more unhappy than he had been already. He almost wished he had agreed to stay a little longer with her. But his resentment was still too sharp to let him regret his departure. He fetched out his record-player and played a couple of records. When they were played through he felt in a more forgiving mood, and if he could have seen her then he was sure he could have spoken to her frankly – not concealing his disappointment at her behaviour, but not sulking about it, and she would no doubt have explained everything.

'But no, not that photograph,' he said aloud, brooding in his chair. 'Nothing will ever explain that photograph.'

Three evenings later an urchin came to his door with a scribbled note from her. She wanted to know couldn't he come along and see her. 'I feel desperately alone,' she wrote, and signed it with her regal initials.

'It'll do you good to be alone,' he muttered, but he went. And as he walked the short distance between the tall sombre tenements, he shivered a little in the chill of the winter night. He had a sudden misgiving about his reaction to her photograph. It seemed to imply a lot more than he had ever admitted. He had loved her unwittingly over the years, and his unexamined desire was derided by what she had done. What to him would have been something sacramental she had sold to the anonymous mob. If he hadn't felt that way about her, the photograph wouldn't have bothered him half so much.

'No, that's not true,' he argued with himself. So disputatious was his nature that he spent much of his waking time arguing with himself, and even his dreams were often a quarrel in his own skull. 'I liked her, I admired her. I was very fond of her. But I never wanted her. They're two entirely different things. I was fond of her mother too.'

Mary Ruthven smiled when she opened the door, and he wondered what had happened to her taste in clothes. He didn't think much of the sacklike dress she was wearing. She greeted him brightly, affectionately, and in a moment he was inside and seated on his old chair, where he had so often sat facing Mrs Ruthven. Mary Ruthven's first brightness soon faded, and they were constrained again.

'Why did you send for me?' he asked distrustfully, glowering at her. His bad eye, which had so improved over the years that he was hardly conscious of its defective vision, seemed to return to its old inadequacy and he had to incline his head and squint at her.

'I wanted to see you, I wanted to talk to you,' she answered, surprised at the question. 'You always want the simplest actions to have a precise

161

explanation. The most natural things in the world – and you'll want to know how, why, and wherefore. It isn't necessary, you know. People are human, even if you aren't.'

'Why do you want to see me, to talk to me?' he persisted woodenly.

'You're my friend, Davie, you're my friend,' she murmured, retracting her lips as she finished the words so that she sat smiling at him, showing her strong, perfect teeth. The words were spoken sincerely, but in case they sounded too solemn or sentimental she sent them from her mouth with a smile intended to keep them lighthearted.

'I'm everybody's friend,' he retorted with a dash of bitterness that went ill with what should have been a boast.

'And nobody's sweetheart?' she said slowly, derisively, mocking him with one of her special smiles that she made by puckering her lips, bringing her mouth forward, and laughing without showing her teeth. 'Is that what ails you?'

He resented the question, aware at last that if ever he had a sweetheart, it was herself – and she had ignored and betrayed him. So he said nothing.

'Why were you so strange with me when you met me at the station?' she demanded abruptly through his silence. 'You would hardly speak to me. What have you got against me?'

He felt she had asked for it and he let her have it. The words poured out of him like water from a canted jug. She gaped at him bewildered, overwhelmed, and hurt.

'And you couldn't even come to your mother's funeral,' he ended. 'What were you doing? Having more pictures taken?'

She saw he knew, though how he knew she didn't trouble to ask.

'Go away, go away!' she cried, near sobs. 'Leave me in peace. I thought you would understand if anybody would understand. I've told you everything since you were a boy at school. I don't know why I told you so much. I thought you understood me.'

'I understand you now,' he answered sullenly. 'You said it once, and I was too stupid, or too young, to know what you meant.'

He stopped and then quoted her.

'If they want the body beautiful they can have it.'

She walked to the window and looked down on the main road

between the high tenements. With an irrelevant surprise she noticed how much busier the road seemed than in the dead days when she was a little girl who had played with safety across the tramlines in pursuit of a ball or running away from the boys in games of chase. She turned back to him and spoke in spite of herself, against her preference for silence.

'Now you *are* being stupid. I said that when I was young. I said it when I had more men than I cared for. And what I meant was that if men think a woman is just a body they're welcome to the idea. I said I was a bitch too.'

He scowled at her. He hadn't dared remind her of that.

'I said that because it amused me when they tried to make love,' she went on, her voice tired. 'I suppose it pleased me or flattered me or amused me. I don't know. Most of them had no idea. There was only Alan, and he overdid it. He seemed to think he had to prove how clever he was, how experienced he was. As if I could ever forget he was married! There was no peace from him. A lot of sorrow and little pleasure was all he brought me. What pleasure do you think there was for me in having those pictures taken?'

He noted she said pictures although he had seen only one. He faced the word with self-conscious bravery, learning again that the reality was always worse than he allowed for. In his glowering silence she repeated her question hysterically.

'Do you think I enjoyed it?'

'How should I know?' he retorted. 'You tell me. It was you that did it. Nobody forced you.'

'Oh, Davie, Davie!' she sobbed in anger. 'Nobody forced me? I hadn't a penny in the world. I hadn't a friend. I knew Alan was going to leave me. All that about a divorce, it was all talk. He never really meant it. I needed money. I hadn't even my fare home. I went to see Paul. You gave me his address. I couldn't find him. The people there gave me another address. Some agency. I met Menzies. I tried to borrow money from him. My fare home. And I wanted money for another purpose. But that doesn't matter now. I wanted to come home and see my mother.'

She stopped at the mention of her mother and wept.

'He wouldn't lend me it,' she went on, snivelling into a small handkerchief as she dried her eyes and wiped her nose. 'He said I could earn it. I thought he meant the usual way. The idea made me laugh. Then he said, it isn't what you think, it's quite easy, all you have to do is have your photograph taken.'

She stopped again and looked at him beseechingly.

'Have I got to say any more? How much explanation do you need? I never thought you needed things explained to you in detail. I thought you were intelligent.'

'No, I'm stupid,' he said perversely. 'You've just said I was stupid. All the explanations in the world won't explain what you did.'

'I had something else to tell you,' she said slowly. 'But it's no use now. You would only damn me twice over, you're so straitlaced. You always were.'

She turned away from him and wept without restraint, without trying to hide it, and he heard her wail through her sobs: 'Why did God have to make it men and women? Was there no other way?'

He was baffled, and too disturbed by the agony in her voice to cope with what she meant or what she was trying to tell him.

'I don't understand,' he muttered. 'I don't follow you. It's all too much for me.'

'It's too much for all of us,' she replied, suddenly calm again. 'Sit down and I'll make a cup of tea. Don't stand there brooding over me like Nelson's Column.'

And it was only when he watched her move about the room that he saw she was with child. A piercing sense of his own irrelevance to life, and to the continuation of life, went through him. He felt dumb, sterile, and useless. It was her health and liveliness had made him admire her, and now she was more alive than ever although she had appeared defeated and exhausted. Out of her abundance of life new life was to come, and he would have no more part in it than he had in hers. For what part had he ever had in her life but the part of a convenient friend, receiving the small change of her conversation and nothing more? For the first time it came home to him that he had never even touched her, and now the time for it was past beyond recovery. His chaste imagination turned in distaste from the thought of what she had done. Now that he knew he wanted her he knew also it was too late, far too late. The idea was ridiculous. Their long friendship had never taken that turn. It had grown in such a way that it prevented the aberration into love. He could not unmake the past to allow for a desire he felt too late, and in her present condition his desire could only be an absurdity.

She was in complete control of herself when they sat drinking tea and talking together, and he could hardly believe she had been so hysterical a little while ago. The embarrassing scene had already moved into the limbo of things past and done with. He didn't want to start questioning her again, in case he distressed her, but he was driven by a restless curiosity and spoke without thinking: 'Tell me. What did happen exactly? I thought you were going to get married.'

She answered him calmly, as if she were talking of somebody else. There was no divorce, so there was no marriage. The first differences arose over money. The married man began to see all the difficulties in their way, the cost of the divorce itself, and the expense of keeping two homes. He didn't see how he could manage it. He said it so often she turned on him and told him to go back to his wife.

'But no,' she said. 'He didn't want to do that either. He didn't want to do anything. I had been living with him for three months when it dawned on me he was quite content with things as they were. I was still working, I was keeping myself. But there was nothing being done about a divorce. His wife knew we were living together, but she didn't do anything. I said one night I would have to stop working sooner or later. It was only then I found out she didn't intend to do anything. I don't know if she was trying to punish me, or him, or herself. But she had written to him and said there would be no divorce – ever. She had connived at the situation, she had told him to live with me if he wanted to, she had known all that time we were living together and she had done nothing about it. If she asked for a divorce, all that would come out and they wouldn't get one. So she said. I don't know. Anyway, it all fell apart. I felt I was the innocent abroad. I left him. There was something else we differed about.'

But she said no more at that time, and he gave her the little parcel he had brought with him, containing her mother's handbag, watch, and rings.

'Your mother's wedding-ring is there,' he said.

She shook her head.

'Oh no,' she said.

'I didn't mean you should wear it,' he added hastily, confused at the calm way she snubbed him. In fact, he had meant nothing else.

'You're a very moral man, aren't you?' she said. 'But I'm past caring what the neighbours think. All they can say is a woman of my age should have had more sense – and they would be right.'

And so without either of them mentioning it the fact that she was pregnant was accepted between them.

He went back to her a week later, full of questions, and she welcomed him.

'How are you going to live?' he asked before he was right in the room.

'Mother had a little money saved,' she answered. 'Not much, but enough for me. Even at that, I don't know how she managed it. And there's the insurance. I've ample to see me through till I can go back to work.'

'But the expenses?' he asked. 'When you go in.'

'I have enough,' she said calmly and quietly. 'Why should you start worrying? I'm not worrying.'

'Why didn't you write to me for your fare home? Or to your mother?' he asked, knowing he would get no peace of mind till she had explained everything.

'I didn't want to,' she answered. 'Why should I ask you? It was my business, not yours. And I certainly wasn't going to worry my mother.'

'For your fare from London, a few pounds?' he queried. 'How would that have worried your mother? She would have been only too glad. And why shouldn't you have asked me. I couldn't manage much, but I could have managed that much.'

'It wasn't just my fare,' she said. 'There was more to it than that. I know it sounds silly, but the first two I should have asked, you and my mother, were the last I could have asked.'

He waited, afraid he would put her off if he said anything. If he kept silent she might go on talking. She had the house all cleaned and polished, new curtains on the windows, a shining hearth, and a bright fire. The house looked lived in once again, the old hospitable house he had known.

'You like to probe,' she said and sighed. 'Well, I told you everything before I went away and I might as well tell you everything now I'm back. There was the question of the baby. That's when I said I would have to stop working sooner or later. And that's when it all fell apart in my hands. True love has a queer ending. He said the only thing was not to have it. He seemed to think it was all my fault having it at all. I don't know what possessed me, but when I felt he didn't want the child neither did I. I suppose I was out of my mind. He took me to some doctor. He wanted so much. I hadn't got it, and Alan hadn't got it. So it was left to me to find it. Everything was left to me. I went to see Paul. I thought if he was doing as well as you told me he could maybe lend me so much or give me a chance to earn something. Some photographs – I was supposed to have a face and a figure. I thought Paul might put a few crumbs my way. But it was Menzies I saw. We've gone into all that. I didn't know Paul's business was just that kind of business. You never know how dirty the world is till you mix in it a little. Well, I got the money. I got what that horrible doctor wanted. If he was a doctor. And I no sooner had the money than I came back to my senses. What I had done wasn't wrong. Living with Alan, I mean. But to do what he wanted me to do, not to have the child – that would have been wrong. I was ashamed of myself for even thinking of it. I had thought if he didn't want it neither did I. Then I saw it was as much mine as his, and nobody was going to stop me having it. That's when I left him. As far as I know his wife has gone to London and they're living together again.'

She had spoken without haste, quite self-possessed. She sat at the fire patiently knitting something in white wool, and added: 'I loved him, and I don't love him now. It's as simple as that.'

'I don't know what that means,' he said bleakly. 'People use these everyday phrases and I've never understood them. They say, "Oh, it's just one of those things." What things? They never say. Or they say, "Well, you know how it is." But I don't know how it is – not till they tell me. And they never do. Or they say, "I love him." I don't know. It conveys nothing to me.'

'The desire of the moth for the flame,' she said, and laughed at the phrase.

'For the star,' he said, never able to resist the temptation to be pedantic.

'Whatever it is. I still think flame is better. A moth couldn't reach a star. A flame is nearer. You can't see it attracted by a star, but you can see it wanting to go into the flame. I saw a moth round a candle flame when I was a little girl. It must be something like that. You just can't help it. Some men have it and some haven't. I've had plenty of men want me, but I never wanted anybody till I met Alan. But it's not just the want. Because if it was, anybody would do. There's nothing to it by itself. It isn't just sex. Sex is there. But it isn't enough. I wanted to live with Alan, to look after him, to be with him all the time. Every time we tried to break it off I suffered agonies till I saw him again. Nobody ever knew. I could hide it. But it was as real a pain as toothache. I just felt he was all I wanted out of this world. And then the horrible way it ended. Or the ridiculous way. I suppose with him it was never anything else but sex. I don't know. I give it up. It doesn't matter now.'

'Isn't it all rather like a confidence trick?' he asked with an unreasonable desire to hurt her.

She eased her heel out of the slipper she was wearing and curled her toes till the slipper fell off. She recovered it with her foot and thrust her toes deep into it again, stretching out her leg.

'I suppose it depends on confidence,' she answered. 'Confidence in God and man. Sometimes you find the confidence was misplaced. But it needn't be. And it's still something to have had the confidence.'

'You talk a lot of nonsense sometimes,' he said rudely. He had never been rude to her before, and he was angry with himself for being rude now, but he couldn't stop. He looked coldly at her heavy graceless body and remembered that once she had been vain about it and that Menzies and Carter and others had lusted after her. 'First it's only the heliotropic instinct of a moth, then it's a divine confidence.'

'I don't know what heliotropic means,' she said, and he felt very small and silly. He wasn't sure he had used the right word anyway.

She sent him away, saying it was late and she was tired. He went to a dictionary when he got home and tried to find out what heliotropic meant. It seemed to apply to plants only, and he was sorry he had used it. He looked up 'moth' to see if there were anything there that might justify the word, but what he found was, 'a fragile and frivolous creature, easily dazzled into destruction'.

'But where was the dazzle from a married man fifteen years older than her?' he asked the open dictionary in vain.

Going to bed, he suddenly saw she hadn't yet explained why she had missed her mother's funeral nor had she told him who it was had taken her photograph. The unanswered questions kept him awake for some time and when he fell asleep he dreamed he was in Mrs Ruthven's kitchen and Mrs Ruthven was bathing his eye and he was only a boy at school again, and Mary Ruthven came in in her underwear and started quarrelling with her mother. He had never seen them quarrel before and he was unspeakably miserable to see it then. As they shouted at each other Paul sauntered in, dressed in an expensive-looking light-grey suit, and he had a bowtie and his hair was long. He laughed at them and said: 'Moths round the flame. Silly bitches. But I'm clever. I've got the camera eye. I don't quarrel with anybody. Quarrelling is distasteful. I take pictures, artistic pictures.' He took a flashlight picture of the mother and daughter, and they posed for him, holding the very gestures of their quarrel and then curtseying to him when it was over. He began to cry when he saw Paul smirk at the two women and in a surge of insane violence he rushed at him, threw him to the floor, and began throttling him. Paul's face was getting red and the tongue was lolling out. Another moment and he would have had him choked to death. But he wakened himself with his hate-filled screaming at his brother and lay afraid of the dark and afraid to go to sleep again.

10

The winter passed away and the March winds came, hauling down the chimney-pots and sweeping down a slate here and there, and the gales at night disturbed his sleep. He hadn't the boldness or bluntness to ask her who had taken the photograph, Menzies or Paul. He didn't know if Menzies did any photography, and for all his morbid curiosity he could see it hardly mattered to her who had taken it. The subject was closed, she would much rather never mention it again. Slowly he came to see it the way he supposed she did; it didn't matter whether Paul or somebody else had taken it. Paul had done enough. One offence more or less was negligible in the account.

Then, when he no longer expected it, she spoke of her mother again. April had come, and even in the valley of the tenements there was an elusive feeling of freshness and well-being, and sometimes the sky above the dingy roofs was blue. She asked him to take her to the cemetery and show her where her mother was buried. He couldn't refuse, but he dreaded the outing. He had seen enough when he saw the clay of the open grave in January, and saw Mrs Ruthven's coffin lowered down in the rain by two huge grave-diggers handling the ropes. Wherever Mrs Ruthven was, she wasn't there. He felt no sentiment for the spot where she was buried, and he was surprised Mary Ruthven should suddenly wish to see it.

She stood at the margin of the untidy plot and all she said was: 'I must get a headstone. Even a small one. This is awful.'

He too was depressed at the neglected appearance of the grave, but it meant nothing more to him than another uncouth spot in an uncouth world, and he was impatient with her conventional desire for a headstone.

'Don't be silly,' he said. 'A headstone costs money. Even a small one costs a lot of money. Where would you get the money to waste on a headstone?'

'How would it be wasting money?' she answered his question with another. 'Any money I've got now is what my mother saved. Apart from what I've got for when I've got to go in. And why shouldn't my mother's savings go on a headstone for my mother's grave, tell me?'

He said nothing, and she turned abruptly, and left the grave. As they walked back to the main gate, alone in the deserted paths between the countless graves in the cemetery, humble graves with nothing on them, showy ones with enormous marble slabs, unkempt plots, and trim areas, she began to speak to him as if confessing under hypnosis.

'It was a kind of paralysis. I couldn't move. I couldn't think. I couldn't do anything. I just wanted to die. Or go away and hide somewhere. If

170

there is a hell it must be a place like London, where you've got to be alone, utterly alone. Alone in London is hell on earth. Everything happened at once. Alan sent me to that doctor. I saw Menzies. And when that was over I was just beginning to see daylight for myself. Once I had the money for an operation I knew I could never do such a thing. I left Alan the week before Christmas but it had been coming for a month before that. He stayed on at the address you wrote to, and I don't know whether he did it deliberately or not, but he took his time sending on your letter and the telegram. I got them together and I read the telegram first. My mother died on the Saturday and I got them on the Monday. I suppose I could have got on the night train and been here on Tuesday morning. But I couldn't think. And it didn't seem to matter if I wasn't at the funeral. I don't think my mother would hold that against me, whatever else she might.'

It was a Sunday, and she insisted he spend the evening with her.

'I've nobody else to talk to, you know,' she added lightly. 'The neighbours say good morning if they see me, and that's about all. They don't know what else to say. They look so embarrassed – but they'll get over it.'

There was no mistaking her condition now. Her pregnancy was far advanced, and as she moved heavily about the kitchen and prepared a meal for them both he thought of the photograph, and only then did he understand that the exaggerations he had thought to be a vulgar retouching of the negative were in fact due to her condition at that time. That may have been why Menzies wanted her photograph. Perhaps the nude picture of a pregnant woman had a particular interest to some people, the world was such a strange place.

'Isn't it time you were going to see a doctor?' he said timidly. 'There are all these ante-natal clinics now, and you've never been near one.'

'I'll be all right,' she said. 'There's plenty of time yet.'

Their meal was over and they sat talking dully, a weariness between them as if they had said all there was to say. Her face was puffed up, her eyes looked odd, red-rimmed and heavy, and when she was on her feet the way she stood with her feet apart and splayed out and her front stuck forward seemed ludicrous. Yet, although for the time being she wasn't

171

the smart, lively, light-moving woman he had known, although even her face had lost its attractiveness, he knew he was as much committed to her as ever. The person, the personality, remained the same behind the physical changes, and that was where his loyalty lay. He could never forget she had rescued him when he was the victim of Menzies' boxing tournament.

'Tell me,' she said, and as she stretched her fine legs to the fire he noticed even her ankles looked thicker, 'if anything happens to me will you look after the child?'

Was it the last insult or the last compliment, he wondered.

'You're just after saying you'll be all right,' he answered edgily. 'There's nothing going to happen to you.'

'Maybe not,' she said. 'But if?'

'What could I do?' he asked, appalled at the idea of looking after a baby.

'No, I suppose there's nothing you could do,' she said. 'It was a silly question. It's a pity you aren't married.'

It was only when he had left her he thought he might have said, 'Well, I can marry you if you like.' But that wouldn't have lessened the absurdity of supposing he could bring up a child alone if anything happened to her. And he was inclined to think she would take the offer as an insult. But he brooded over it. He tried to sort out what he was really thinking. People said he was a prig, or a moralist, or a puritan. But he didn't think she had done wrong. All he thought was she had committed a blunder. The affair with a married man was foolish from the start, and he would never understand how a woman of her intelligence failed to see it. Of course her defence was the old one: she was in love. But that was only a phrase. It vaguely described the state of being in error, but it didn't explain why or how the error was made, nor why it took so long to correct. As for the idea of marrying her, he put it away as impossible. He was too used to being alone to put up with someone always with him.

Further meditation over a day or two convinced him he would be glad to marry her. He knew her so well, she would be easy to live with. But he knew she would take a proposal of marriage as a clumsy attempt to protect her. She would reject the patronage. And perhaps she would be right. Perhaps he was only seeing himself acting the part of the upright, loyal, and forgiving man raising a fallen woman to a respectable position in society. A bogus act of loyalty, a piece of ham-acting. With behind it, perhaps, the mean idea that thereafter she could be kept dependent and servile, always liable to be reminded of what she owed to the high-minded man who had made an honest woman of her.

'It's so difficult to make out just what one's real emotions are,' he complained to the mirror, looking at his puzzled face as he was shaving.

He was more concerned than she was about her position, more worried about what the neighbours would say, and he sometimes wished she had worn her mother's ring when he suggested it. But she seemed past caring about anything or anybody, living alone in patience, waiting. She was neither happy nor unhappy. She often smiled and made little jokes with him, but all the time without bothering much about it. Once he stumbled on a confused expression of his fear that the neighbours must be talking about her and would talk more when the child was born. He came near suggesting once more that she should wear her mother's wedding-ring.

'More fool you if you worry what people say,' she answered calmly, knitting. 'Do you think the unmarried mother is something new in the tenements?'

'No, but . . .' he said unhappily, wishing she wouldn't refer to herself so callously.

'But I should have been past it, that's all,' she commented, looking up tranquilly from her knitting. 'At my age. I'm not an ignorant girl in my teens. Even so, it'll be a week's wonder, and then they'll all be in to see the baby. You can't keep women away from a new baby. Stop fretting about me.'

He went round one evening determined to ask her again to visit a doctor. He had never dared ask her straight out when she expected the child, and in his anxiety over her indifference to herself he feared she would make no arrangements and then cause alarm at the last minute. He opened his mouth, the words all prepared, and she spoke first.

'I saw Dr Tennant yesterday, and I was at the clinic in the afternoon. The upshot is I've to go into the maternity hospital at the week-end. Dr

Tennant's idea. I thought I had a bit to go yet, but maybe I'm not good at arithmetic.'

He looked in on Dr Tennant the next night and asked him if she was all right.

'Perfectly all right,' said Dr Tennant. 'A fine strong healthy woman. Why shouldn't she be all right? What did you think would be wrong?'

He had nothing to say to that, but he felt a strange urge to talk, to explain Mary Ruthven's position and defend her.

'She's been let down rather badly,' he said, 'and I was worried about her, that's all.'

He rambled on, sitting alone with the doctor in the shabby consulting-room. He had a guilty feeling that he was being disloyal to her in telling a stranger all about her. But he had to insist she wasn't a stupid woman who hadn't enough sense to keep herself out of trouble, nor was she a woman of immoral habits. He tried to make out it was a case of true love, persuading himself as he spoke that after all the words meant something.

'It wouldn't have happened if she hadn't fully expected to marry the man,' he wound up.

'No doubt,' said Dr Tennant. 'That's what they all say. Which doesn't mean it isn't the truth. But that's none of my business. Her morals aren't my province.'

'But she isn't immoral,' he insisted.

'I never said she was,' Dr Tennant laughed at him in a friendly way. 'It's you that's upset, not me. Look, I haven't the car tonight. I tell you what we'll do. We'll take a bus into town and have a quiet drink.'

They went to a hotel lounge, a place he would never have dared enter alone, so hushed and withdrawn it was, so expensive and well furnished. He had a pleasant hour of conversation with the young doctor, partly literary and partly tenement gossip, and he almost forgot about Paul and Mary Ruthven, too.

He was embarrassed to find that she expected he would accompany her to the maternity hospital. He had no armour against her attack of taking him for granted, and he went without a word of protest. When they left the taxi a fine spring rain was falling and there was the smell of damp gravel and damp laurels on the carriage-way up to the entrance.

'Well, it won't be long now,' she said as they went up the steps to the reception hall. And when at last she was admitted and he had given her the small suitcase he was carrying for her, she turned back from the nurse waiting to escort her and said in a voice so low he couldn't be sure he heard her right, 'You've been too kind to me.' She held out her hand and they shook hands very briefly. It was the first time he had touched her hand. He was aware of that, but it was a purely mental awareness. He felt nothing particular in the touch.

On Monday about noon he was engrossed checking an allowance claim with Mrs Marchbanks when he was called to the phone.

'Oh bother!' she cried. 'I did so want to finish this before lunch. Don't be long!'

He had never before had a phone call at work. Other clerks occasionally had one, and their supervisor made no complaint, although periodically he circulated a memorandum saying in many polysyllables that incoming calls on private business were discouraged and outgoing ones forbidden.

'Your girl-friend's had her baby,' Dr Tennant's voice came over loud and clear, full of breezy good-humour. 'A daughter, seven pounds plus. I've just seen her. I asked them to phone me. The baby's fine. But the mother isn't. I don't understand it. She was a healthy-enough girl. She had everything. The birth wasn't all that difficult. But she's very weak. I think you should go and see her tonight.'

He went, and Mary Ruthven looked at him as if she were in one world and he in another. Her eyes were dull and the hands she had once used for lively gestures were limp on the bedclothes. He didn't know what to talk about. She was always the one that kept a conversation going, and without her help he was ill at ease. He couldn't even praise the baby: he didn't see it.

'You will tomorrow,' she promised him. 'They're so damned careful nowadays – they even ration me with her. But you'll see her tomorrow. You'll come in tomorrow, won't you? And remember you promised to look after her.'

He remembered the point was raised, and he remembered he had dismissed it as absurd. There was no question of a promise. But he didn't like to tell her that.

When he left her he hurried to Dr Tennant's consulting-rooms.

'How is she?' he asked at once.

'Damn it, it's you that has just seen her, not me,' said Dr Tennant defensively.

'Yes, but I'm not a doctor,' he persisted. 'You didn't sound very happy about her when you phoned this morning.'

'I'm not,' said Dr Tennant. 'More important, Dr Graham over there isn't happy either. She saw the baby and gave it a sort of hail-and-farewell look. She didn't seem really bothered about it. And she's been sinking fast ever since. I don't understand it. Like her mother, only worse. Her mother's life was over anyway. Hers shouldn't be. But I think it is. It's just ebbing away.'

He knew then he was losing her as he had lost Paul. But there was nothing wilful in her leaving him, no betrayal of a common past, only a great weariness of the world, the same defeated fatigue as her mother had known. And perhaps for the same reason: that someone loved and trusted had been found wanting.

Prepared by Dr Tennant's words and fortified by a natural pessimism he was neither shocked nor overwhelmed when she died. It was only something more to be endured. He saw her lying dead, and he was allowed to see the baby. He had never seen a baby two days old, and to him it was remarkably ugly sight. But since that was how God had decided things should be there was no point in complaining. He looked at the infant with only a slight feeling of revulsion, persuaded to patience by the death of the mother.

He walked through the park on his way home from the hospital, and it struck him as odd that she had died in the spring when the world was coming to life again. The air in the park was mild, the grass fresh after a late shower the night before, and the clouds in the blue sky were small and harmless. The River Kelvin looked almost clean, and in the Botanic Gardens there were countless prams parked, with well-dressed prattling infants, and young mothers gossiping. As a boy he had played just across the river, in the days when Mark was his boss, but that seemed to belong to a different order of space and time, as if it had happened on a planet that no longer existed.

Driven by the promise he was supposed to have made he went to the local registrar's office and registered the birth of Mary Ruthven's child. Where he had to put the name of the father he wrote his own name, firmly and without hesitation.

His next move was to have the child taken care of till she was out of her infancy. He took counsel from nobody and went his way doggedly and unthinkingly. It was something that had to be done, and there was no one else to do it. He knew there were Corporation homes for infants and orphans and he asked the matron in the hospital which one he should apply to. He had clerks to see and forms to fill in, and the fact that he was in his own small way a practising bureaucrat helped him to deal with the people and papers concerned. Once it had distressed him that Mary Ruthven wasn't married, but now he named himself on paper as the father of the child, though not the husband of the mother, and he wasn't at all embarrassed. He went through it as if he were dreaming it. Within a week he had a child out of the hospital and placed in a Corporation home for three years to begin with. If he hadn't done it the people in the maternity hospital would have done it. But he hadn't let her go there as an orphan, he had claimed her as his own, and he would have her out in due time. So he believed, speaking to himself, explaining it all and justifying his action, and suffering an irregular illusion that he was telling Mary Ruthven.

Dr Tennant stopped him on the street.

'You know it's an offence to make a false declaration when you register a birth,' he said, and the smile on his face showed he was more amused than shocked.

'Yes, I know,' he answered, and added frankly, 'but who's going to say I made a false declaration? And who can prove it?'

'Anybody could prove it that cared to check on the dates,' Dr Tennant said. 'She was in London at the time and you were here. That's all.'

'There's a margin surely,' he said brazenly. 'I was in Mary Ruthven's house regularly and Mary Ruthven was in my house the night before she went to London. You can't pin things down to the very day and hour.'

Dr Tennant laughed.

'You're mad,' he said admiringly. 'Why did you do it?'

'I was reading up the Illegitimate Children Scotland Act,' he said. 'It

177

allows specifically for the putative father to be granted custody and access.'

'Well, I won't challenge you,' the doctor replied. 'And I don't suppose anybody else will. But I don't like it. I don't like false declarations.'

'Neither do I,' he agreed readily. 'But you're begging the question. Who says it's a false declaration?'

He could easily have convinced himself he was telling the truth in claiming paternity, so unreal did he feel the world around at that time, a world so impoverished that it had neither Mary Ruthven nor her mother, but Dr Tennant waved further discussion away with a flourish of his hand in mid-air, and they parted amicably.

He had to tell Mrs Marchbanks the truth. He didn't mind telling the bureaucrats what it suited him to tell them. He knew that all they wanted was a document properly completed and ready for filing. But he couldn't deceive Mrs Marchbanks. It may have been because he was unwilling to have her believe he was the father of an illegitimate child, it may have been because he wanted her sympathy, even her praise. He didn't know. He knew he would have to tell her one day, and the longer he took the harder it would be. He told her everything as soon as he had no more papers to sign. She was shocked.

'But why on earth did you do it?' she demanded. 'You can never bring that child up, so why did you claim her? And suppose you do take her home when she's older, suppose you want to get married one day, how will you explain it? Do you think any girl will believe you?'

He was taken by the paradox that although he could put a lie on paper and have it accepted without any questions, Mrs Marchbanks wouldn't believe the truth when he told her it. Perhaps that was where Paul was better adapted to the world: he had seen that a lie is always marketable, even the lie of pretending that obscene pictures were art-pictures.

'You're not listening to me,' Mrs Marchbanks cried. She was vexed with him.

He tried to explain how he saw it.

'I had no option,' he said. 'It seemed to be my duty. Of course I know it will be difficult for me to bring up the child. It will be difficult, but it won't be impossible. Why shouldn't I manage it when she's older? I'll be seeing her every week from now on. She'll grow up knowing me. She'll accept me. A child takes the world as it finds it. Maybe I'll need a woman in to help. I don't know. It's all very difficult. But I couldn't leave the child to be brought up as an orphan, could I? I couldn't just discard her.'

'She could be adopted,' said Mrs Marchbanks.

'Well, isn't that what I've done?' he asked.

'No, it isn't what you've done,' she retorted. 'There's a world of difference.'

'I don't see it,' he muttered, giving up the argument. So much for the sympathy he had expected, so much for the praise he had hoped for.

'Oh, you're a foolish young man!' Mrs Marchbanks exclaimed impatiently. He saw she was nearly crying, and he turned away in bewilderment.

Yet she insisted on going with him to see the infant, and Muriel went too. They went with him every week.

4

Prologue

1

HE LIVED afraid of a knock at the door. The lie he had written on the child's birth-certificate was always in the hinterland of his mind. He trusted Dr Tennant and he trusted Mrs Marchbanks. But he remained afraid that somehow, sometime, the truth would come out. After all, he thought, there was one man who must know the truth: the child's father. He knew the past could never be buried so deep that its grave was beyond discovery, and he waited over the years for the resurrection he feared was bound to come.

He had just newly managed, after much persistence and overcoming many difficulties, to be allowed to take the child into his house. It meant an official was liable to call on him unannounced to make sure he was providing a satisfactory home. And although he had been used to looking after himself since he was a boy he knew he couldn't look after a girl-child unaided. He went to a friendly garrulous neighbour, a middle-aged widow who lived with her only son, a long-distance lorry-driver who was drunk every time he was home for a few days, and she gladly agreed to help him. She practically lived in his house, arriving first thing in the morning to wash and dress the child, and going away last thing at night after putting her to bed. He was grateful to her and paid her well, apart from whatever she took privately on commission when she bought the child clothes with the money he gave her for that purpose. They were an odd but not unhappy trio, and he let the widow think he was a widower, though he suspected she knew the truth. There are no secrets in the tenements. And knowing that, he was always expecting someone to appear and challenge his right to the child.

So it was with a heart alarmed that he heard a gentle knocking at his door one winter evening and heard the sound of a man clearing his throat. The child, three years old, was asleep in the next room. He had just looked in on her, just returned to his chair at the fireside, and his first fear was that the knocking might waken her. That fear awakened a deeper one, the fear that was always with him. He wasn't expecting any visitor, he had no friend likely to call on him uninvited, no neighbour would presume to come to his door for an idle chat. The knocking was ominous to him.

When he opened the door he saw a tall broad-shouldered man on the stairhead, a man with a smiling mouth, good features, and happy confident eyes. The kind of man who would no doubt be attractive to women, he thought with an immediate hostility. He resented the stranger's good looks, he disliked his expensive-looking clothes, and he prepared himself to deal with Mary Ruthven's married man.

The stranger offered his hand and a disarming smile. David for a moment rejected both, governed by the joint rule of pride and prejudice. But he couldn't stand there like a boor, defying a social convention without any acknowledged reason, and there was a mild hypnotic force in the stranger's benevolent eyes. His hand went up and out to the stranger's hand in a mindless movement, and there was a perfunctory handshake. The stranger shook his head in calm amusement, laughed briefly, and said, 'You can't stand there and pretend you don't know me.'

Only as the words were being spoken did David see it couldn't be Mary Ruthven's married man because it was Mark. Embarrassed at his failure to recognize his brother, he muttered, 'It's the dim light on the stairhead here.'

'The light's fine,' said Mark, and stepping past him into the lobby he waited there to be shown in.

David closed the front door and turned forlornly. He didn't know what to do. But the long years of his dislike of Mark could be brought to life only by an effort of memory, and even then it was with a thin, bloodless, inane existence. As he stood there he felt no hostility at all. Fire drives out fire, love drives out love, and no doubt his hatred of Paul had driven out his earlier hatred of Mark. Or maybe he had just grown out of it. He didn't know. His only feeling was a slight fear that he might prove a dull host to a visitor who appeared to be a man of the world.

'Well, do I just stand here, or are you going to show me in?' Mark asked gently, with a smile that seemed to brighten the twilight of the small lobby, and David noticed at once the smooth, low tone, the pronunciation free from any oddities of dialect. It had nothing of Paul's bogus accent. It had no discernible accent at all.

'Through to the left,' said David, rather abashed, and moved to open the door for him.

'Take my coat first,' said Mark, and David found himself humbly valeting his brisk, masterful brother.

'I didn't expect to see you again,' he remarked grudgingly when they were seated facing each other. 'Ever,' he added after a short pause, and managed in spite of himself to load the word with ungraciousness.

Mark, well dressed and debonair, smiled.

'Go on,' he said encouragingly.

'I'm not sure I've anything more to say,' David replied, and after another short pause he added a couple of sour words. 'To you.'

Mark laughed.

'You do like to keep things up, don't you?' he said. 'You always did. And you haven't grown out of it, I see. Of course, living alone in a backward city – you've had no chance.'

'And you have?' David enquired coldly.

'I think so, I hope so.'

Mark brought out a packet of foreign cigarettes and offered one, but David shook his head.

'I've been in every big port in the world, I should think,' said Mark, leaning well back in his chair, his legs stretched out, utterly relaxed.

'And what are you doing here, in a backward city?'

'I'm on holiday,' said Mark and laughed at his brother's dour face. 'I haven't had a holiday for three years, and now I have six months to myself. Six months to do nothing but spend my money.'

'You're lucky,' said David, and looked distractedly round the room as if he were looking for a way out.

'I suppose I am, but I've worked hard too.'

'Doing what?' Again the question was put ungraciously.

'You don't know? You wouldn't read my letters, would you? Paul told me. You didn't have to, but I thought a spark of brotherly interest might still be struck from your heart of flint.' Mark smiled broadly at his own extravagant metaphor and David looked at him stolidly.

'I worked in that shipping office in Liverpool,' said Mark, 'and I went to sea when I was nineteen. I was cabin-boy, drudge, skivvy, everything. And now I'm a steward on what's probably their best ship, and in a year if all goes well I've a damned good chance of becoming chief steward. It's a good Line and they keep their promises. I'm happy. Why shouldn't I be? I've seen a lot of life and I'll see a lot more. I've friends in Melbourne and I've friends in Singapore. I've friends in Hamburg and I've friends in New York. A bloody cosmopolouse, that's me. And you get the world in a microcosmos in a ship anyway.'

'Microcosmos?' David repeated, startled. 'Microcosm, you mean.'

'Microcosm,' Mark said accepting the correction graciously. 'You know my favourite bedside book is a good dictionary. I like looking into words, finding their roots, if you know what I mean. I may get them wrong now and then, but I left school at fourteen, remember. I didn't have your education. But then if I had, maybe I wouldn't have the good life I have. The best thing ever I did was leave this city.'

'And why did you come back? I asked that already.'

'Nostalgia,' said Mark. 'To see the scenes of my boyhood. And to see you.'

David looked at him again, straight and stolid, trying to understand, and afraid Mark was laughing at him.

'You see,' said Mark, 'when you go all round the world you learn a lot – though actually the most striking thing about a foreign port is the smell and the pimps. But sometimes at night, when you have the sea all round you and the stars so far away, you get overwhelmed with the idea of infinity. Who was it said the silence of the starry heavens terrified him? I've stood often on deck at night and looked at Orion, and looked beyond him for Castor and Pollux. Two brothers, one of them immortal. And Pollux loved Castor so much he was willing to go to Hades to be with him. I used to stand there and look at Castor and Pollux and think of you and Paul.'

David glowered at him, waiting.

'Being at sea like that makes a man want to see his own city again, his own kith and kin. All a man has in the end is his own family. Friends are only a substitute. And the only family I've got is you and Paul. I just longed to see you both.'

'And you've seen Paul?' As he asked the question David felt a quivering in his stomach.

'Yes, I've seen Paul,' Mark answered, 'and that made me the more anxious to come up and see you.'

He seemed to be having trouble with his hip pocket, and after some grimacing and tugging he fetched out a bottle of whisky.

'Have you a couple of glasses?' he asked. 'And will you have a drink with me?'

For a moment that seemed long enough to witness the day of judgement David said nothing. He had never bothered about Mark, never wondered what good or ill fortune had befallen him, never cared. He had lived on the capital of his hatred, and now when he went to draw on it again he found it was all spent, and it had never earned any interest either. He was afraid of making an irrevocable mistake, and although he was by nature unsociable he knew enough of the conventions of society to understand that if he refused to drink with his brother he would be guilty of the extreme insult, and he felt he would put himself beyond the forgiveness of God and man.

'I should be glad to,' he said, defeated.

At one o'clock in the morning they had finished Mark's bottle. David stumbled to his sideboard and brought out a bottle he kept there against an emergency that had never arisen. And now he was glad of it, pleased to think Mark would consider him a civilized being who had always a drink available for a guest.

'It's time I went back to my hotel,' Mark said as David opened the second bottle. But he made no move to go.

They sat up all night. David drew the curtains at seven o'clock in the morning, and the light of a winter dawn looked coldly in on their smoke-laden room.

'It's been an education,' Mark said. 'I've enjoyed talking about the old days at home. Even about our father. He was only a cipher in our life, and yet he was our father. It seems another life altogether now, when you and I looked after him.'

'You remember things I've forgotten,' David said.

'And forget things you remember,' Mark commented. 'I think that's the trouble.'

'Was the trouble,' David answered. 'What I should forget.' He reached for the bottle.

He was thinking that the battle of the stone, which had meant so much to him at the time, had been a comedy, a farce even, to Mark. The way Mark had seen it, his honour was not involved, and his flight from Carter was a laugh of mockery, not a whimper of fear. He had forgotten the sequel, forgotten his brother was tied to a pole and cropped, just as he had forgotten he had destroyed the library book. But he remembered better things, more rewarding things. He remembered their brotherhood and he remembered their father. And at that point David understood how thwarted and bitter Mark must have been, how brave too, when he ran away from home. He deserved sympathy, not hostility. He was to be admired for growing up so sane and affectionate, for taking the trouble to come back and see an unwelcoming brother. There was a grace and generosity in him, a humanity and intelligence. He regretted the years of his absurd hatred, when he had presumed to judge a man by the recollected prejudices of a boy.

'I wronged you,' he said. 'And now I've so much to expiate.'

'Don't talk silly,' said Mark, holding out his glass. 'It's fine to recall the days when we were brothers.'

He broke off and declaimed:

> 'Two lads that thought there was no more behind,
> But such a day tomorrow as today,
> And to be boy eternal.'

'How do you come to be able to say that off by heart?' David asked, puzzled.

Mark shrugged the question away.

'I've a good memory,' he said, 'and I always liked learning lines that took my fancy. When you're off duty on a ship, what can you do but look at the stars or read? Read and think.'

'It's all so different, you're so different, from what I thought,' David muttered. 'But that's not true either. The truth is I never thought.'

'How far back can you remember?' Mark asked him. 'I like to think back and back and try to pin down the very earliest moment I can recall. Just to prove—'

He couldn't complete what he wanted to say, and there was something foreign in the way he used his hands to fill out the thought.

'To prove what?'

'Oh, I don't know. You know—'

With his glass raised he declaimed again.

> 'Not in entire forgetfulness,
> And not in utter nakedness,
> But trailing clouds of glory do we come –
> Heaven lies about us in our infancy.'

'There wasn't much heaven in our house when we were young,' David commented.

'Ah, that's because you can't go back far enough,' Mark replied.

He went away just after seven in the morning, and left alone David splashed cold water on his forehead, behind his ears, and on his wrists. But although his eyes smarted and his head ached he was happier than he had been for many years. He walked round the house, drawing the curtains, stumbling a little now and then, but full of good will, patting forgivingly the chair that tripped him or the door that got in his way. He looked in cautiously on the sleeping child and stood brooding over her for ten minutes. Then he went to his own room and thought of Mark again.

'What manner of man is this,' he asked aloud, 'that comes and quotes Shakespeare at me, alludes to Pascal, lifts a word from Kipling just in passing, hauls in a classical myth, and leaves me with some rhetoric from Wordsworth? An amateur in astronomy too. Castor and Pollux be damned. I wouldn't know where to look for them. I wouldn't know them if I saw them. How much of the sky have I ever seen? How much of the sky can you see between the tops of the tenements?'

He was fascinated by his brother, won over by the vitality and charm of the man, by his easy air of knowledge of the world, and by his slapdash use of literary allusions. It was only when he went in to work and tried to tell Mrs Marchbanks all about Mark that he remembered they hadn't discussed Paul. Mark had referred to him several times in the course of his recollections, but though he hadn't praised him neither had he said a word against him.

2

Mark visited him again, though he had made no promise to come back. He saw the child and David tried to tell him about Mary Ruthven but felt quite sure he had failed to make him understand. He avoided mentioning Paul's photograph of her, thinking that to tell anyone else about it would be like taking her photograph a second time.

'Extraordinary,' said Mark. 'You mean this child was sleeping in the next room the night I called? Extraordinary. You are a secretive fellow, really you are. Of course I remember Mary Ruthven. I can remember her at school. She was supposed to be very clever. I remember her as a striking girl with a graceful way of walking.'

He tried to talk to the child, to play with her, but his attempts were strained, and his admiration seemed wholly conventional.

'It's a pity,' he said, giving up trying to talk to the silent little girl, who simply looked at him with large critical eyes that seemed to be wondering why he was using baby-talk at his age. 'I had hoped to take you out to dinner one night before I go away. I didn't know you were tied down with this—'

He stopped, confused. 'Like this,' he corrected himself.

'I can always manage a night free,' David said stiffly.

Mark was so anxious to take him out that he agreed to a time and place and asked Mrs Marchbanks to sit with the child for an evening. He put on his best suit and went nervously to the rendezvous Mark had named. A traffic jam as he approached the centre of the city made him late, and he almost ran the few yards from the bus stop to the expensive licensed restaurant where he was to meet his brother. He hurried through the public-bar, ran upstairs to the lounge-bar, and went in rather out of breath and looking as if he expected to be challenged and denied service. Mark's loud greeting, his hearty shout of sheer delight at seeing him come in, only increased his confusion. He felt out of place when he saw so many well-dressed women and prosperous-looking men sitting there drinking unknown drinks.

'I've been sitting here telling myself you wouldn't turn up,' Mark said boisterously. 'I was beginning to convince myself you were just being polite to a bloody intruder when you said you'd have dinner with me. I'm so glad you're here! What'll you have?'

He clearly enjoyed playing the host, and after a drink at the bar he led David through to the dining-room with a lordly air and took the welcoming waiter in his stride while David shuffled uneasily behind him. He had never been in such a place before, where the waiters wore long-tailed coats, and although he was slightly uneasy when he was offered a cigar over the coffee he silently admired the suave confidence of his brother. He admired the way he looked at the menu as if he understood what was on it, the way he ordered the wine as if he knew one from another, and the way he spoke to the waiter as if he were used to dining out regularly in the best places in town. When he saw the bill and saw the size of Mark's tip on the salver he was appalled. But Mark's manner remained casual, and David bleakly wondered at the wide experience of people and places his brother must have gained, while he himself remained all his life within a few yards of the house where he was born, drudging along within a narrow groove.

'It's odd,' he remarked. 'You've been out of the city all these years and yet you know where to dine out. I've never been out of the city, and this is the first time I've been in this place.'

'Nothing odd about it,' Mark replied kindly. 'Why should you ever dine in a place like this on your salary? I knew of it when I was a boy. Old Arbuthnot, the lawyer I worked for when I left school, used to come here. I determined to have a meal here myself if ever I came back with some money in my pocket. It's a fine place, and it's worth the money. But I wouldn't make a habit of it. I'm on holiday, remember. And I didn't come all this distance to see you and then talk to you over a cup of tea and a bun. The occasion called for a bit of style.'

He was fond of style, David could see that. The outward show of things appealed to him, he valued the fine things money could buy, and he preferred the tact and diplomacy, the gentle speech and quiet manners of men of the world, to the uncouth ways of his native city. So David was surprised, even shocked a little, when he said abruptly over the brandy, 'Now, about Paul.'

'I saw Paul in London,' he went on unhurriedly. 'I was upset to learn there was some difference between you. I don't quite know what it's all about, and I don't particularly want to know. All I want is to act as peacemaker. It's a great pity there should be bad feeling between you, because a man's own family, his own blood, are all he can depend on in this world. We hadn't much of a family as boys, and none of us have any family of his own yet. All the more reason why we should keep together. Or at least have our differences in a civilized manner. This business of not being on speaking terms – it's barbaric.'

'Very true,' said David. 'You make a good after-dinner speech.'

'Now don't be cynical, David, and don't be rude,' Mark said firmly. 'That's the trouble, so far as I can make out. You were shockingly rude to Paul. Paul didn't tell me much in the way of details, but he was quite objective about the whole business, quite level-headed and normal, quite urbane.'

His hands moved again in the foreign gesture as he tried to find the word to describe the complete propriety of Paul's tone.

'But you,' he went on, 'you, I gather, were simply rude, outrageously rude.'

'Being rude I can't be right,' David commented, half making a statement, half asking a question.

'In so far as you were rude you weren't right,' Mark replied judiciously. 'Look, tell me what your grievance is and let me see if I can help. Paul said you tried to patronize him in your letters, to teach him his job, and ended up by being unpardonably rude. But I'd like to hear your side of it. What were you rude about, what made you so rude? Paul was rather vague there. But I'm not all that dumb. There must be your side to it too. I suppose you must have had some provocation. Though I can't imagine how anyone as easy-going as Paul could ever provoke anybody.'

'Let's go home and talk about it, if we must,' David answered, rising to postpone the distasteful topic.

They went to his flat and he was proud to introduce his handsome brother to Mrs Marchbanks. But when she left, Mark said once more, 'Now, about Paul.'

They sat face to face again, a bottle of whisky between them, and David went back to the day when Paul won a camera in a raffle and described the years of his collaboration with Paul, the aims and ideals

Paul expressed, his theories about the man with a camera being the true artist of the modern world. He told of Paul's early successes, of how hard he had worked to extend his market and increase his earnings, of his move to London to join Menzies, and then the arrival of the photographs. But he still wouldn't mention the picture of Mary Ruthven.

'It's a pity you burnt all those photos,' Mark sighed. 'Of course, if they're as bad as you say I suppose you thought it was the only thing to do. But still, I should like to have seen them, just to make sure you're not exaggerating. I don't mean a wilful or malicious exaggeration, but after all you are a bit parochial. It's a common enough trade – artistic nudes, erotic photographs, what have you. The naked truth, you know. Don't you like the naked truth?'

He laughed at his own flippancy, but the laughter was kindly meant and David could take no offence.

'The truth isn't like that,' said David. 'And they weren't artistic. Paul kept on insisting he was an artist. But that's nonsense. That's just his vanity. I told him he wasn't an artist, he was only a damn' fool. I suppose that's where I was rude. Paul seems to think that because nudes are a commonplace in painting every nude in a photograph is also a work of art.'

He poured more whisky into both glasses as he did so he muttered: 'Some nudes are works of art, Paul's photographs are nudes, therefore Paul's photographs are works of art. Bloody rubbish.'

'That's worse than being rude,' Mark said severely. 'That's being smart and harsh and pedantic and stuck-up and everything that's wrong. You can't apply logic to a fellow like Paul. There's an uncivilized bitterness in you, a prim hatred of your brother. After all, he is your brother. Let brotherly love continue. Saint Paul.'

'Even for a brother with as much vanity as Paul?' David asked.

'I don't see what vanity has to do with it,' Mark retorted. 'There's none of us short of vanity.'

'Few of us have his excess of it,' said David. 'It was his vanity made him say he was an artist, and it was the idea that he was an artist made a fool of him, made him do what was wrong. I suppose most of the wrong things done in this world are done through vanity. But if I was rude to him I'm sorry. Rudeness seems a totally inadequate answer to a man who has done what he has done.'

He brooded over his glass and over the memory of Mary Ruthven. She was as much a part of Paul's boyhood and adolescence as of his. She was the truth and beauty that Paul had distorted when he made her the subject of one of his photographs. That was the supreme disloyalty.

'Well, at least I can tell Paul you're sorry you were rude to him,' Mark was saying with a smile.

David looked up at him and shook his head. He saw no communication was possible. The hackneyed quotation about the bell tolling for yourself when the man next door died was quite wrong. Each man was in fact an island, an island where no ship ever called. He could never make Mark understand just what Paul had done unless he could recover from the ashes the photographs he had burned, or unless he told him of the perversions Paul had photographed. The one was as impossible for him as the other.

'You mentioned Menzies,' Mark said through the heavy silence. 'I didn't see him when I saw Paul. But I remember one strange thing Paul said. He was telling me he had a share in a photographic business, and then he said, "But that bastard Menzies spoiled it." It was the only time he showed a spark of temper when he was talking to me. That's why the word has stuck. That bastard Menzies, he said. As far as I can understand Paul simply turned out harmless pictures for mail-orders that Menzies had organized through the usual small ads. And then it seems to have got out of hand, out of Paul's hands anyway. I don't know just how far Paul was involved in the worst of the pictures. He can be as secretive as you when he likes. And of course Paul wasn't the only one taking photographs. You know Menzies was arrested?'

'No, I didn't,' said David in alarm. 'And Paul?'

'Paul left just in time. It was the usual charge against Menzies. Sending obscene pictures through the mail. I've no doubt Menzies went further than Paul ever intended.'

'How far is too far?' David asked. 'And how far did Paul go? Didn't he know what Menzies was doing? Wasn't he doing as much himself? He seems to have left Menzies only when he saw the business was getting dangerous.'

'Could be,' said Mark. 'But after all – feelthy postcards! I've met them in every port. The world is full of these things. Why worry about it, Davie?'

'Because it's wrong,' David said stubbornly.

'I wish I could be as sure as you are what's right and what's wrong,' Mark replied, smiling at his brother's dourness.

'I'm not sure,' David said, and he was confused. 'I'm very far from sure. When Paul first went to London and I was left alone I tried to read books on ethics. I don't know why. I think I wanted to know how you can distinguish right from wrong apart from feeling right and wrong. It didn't get me anywhere. I only tied myself in knots. Is a thing wrong because the laws of God and man forbid it, or do the laws of God and man forbid it because it's wrong? Are some things wrong even though there is no legal or religious prohibition? Are the things that are wrong always wrong? Is killing always murder? If a foreign army occupies a country and a civilian patriot shoots one of the soldiers in the back down a dark street one night, is that murder? The patriot might say he was only doing his duty. It's all very difficult. I know it's difficult. But we still know murder is wrong. I'm sure of it. And I'm just as sure that what Paul was doing is wrong, even though I can't put a name to it and can't prove it.'

'You were a prig as a boy, and I'm afraid you're still one,' Mark murmured, and filled his glass again. David pushed his glass forward and Mark filled it amicably.

'One would think you took Paul's career as a tragedy,' he complained.

'Hardly,' said David. 'Tragedy is supposed to require some nobility of character in the tragic hero. I don't think Paul has any character.'

'It's slowly penetrating,' said Mark, 'that I'm not going to make much of my attempt at reconciling you two. You're almost persuading me you don't like Paul.'

'I despise him,' David said.

'All right, you despise him. And where does that take you? Say he's silly, say he's conceited. He's like his father then, that's all. I suppose we're all like our father in one way or another. Why despise him for that? None of us can escape it. You're young yet to set up for despising people. But I suppose it's because you're young you talk like that. Forget it. It's

195

the way of the world for lads with fine ideals to grow up into practical men, turning a penny where they can. There's no point despising a man for exemplifying a platitude.'

'I wouldn't despise him if he were sorry for what he has done,' said David. 'I wouldn't despise him if he found that was the only way he could earn his living. I despise him for trying to defend himself. I despise him for admitting nothing. He has the lie in the soul. I wouldn't despise him if he didn't believe he was a fine fellow.'

'We're all fine fellows in our own eyes,' Mark replied. 'Paul worked for a mail-order business in art-nudes. All right! Is it worth all this fuss? I wonder you can be so innocent, so naïve in some things, and so intelligent in others. I don't blame you, of course. It isn't your fault. You were at school till you were seventeen or eighteen, and then you went straight into a nice, safe job. And you've been there ever since. You've led a sheltered life, a bookish life, not even a love-affair to broaden your mind! Anyway, Paul's doing well now, and I still think it's a pity you two can't get together. He's getting big money in an advertising agency. High-class photographs.'

He reached for an illustrated paper that lay on the floor beside his chair, a woman's magazine that Mrs Marchbanks had inadvertently left behind her, and turned over the pages quickly.

'Yes, I knew I'd find something,' he cried, smiling. 'There, look at that! That's Paul.'

He pointed to an advertisement for a new kind of girdle. David turned his bad eye from the glossy page and squinted at the photograph of a faceless woman's hips and part of her thighs.

'Has he changed his sex too?' he asked.

'It's a picture by Paul, not a picture of Paul,' Mark explained patiently, refusing to acknowledge the sarcasm.

'I see,' said David. 'It's very interesting.'

'It's very well paid,' said Mark.

'I don't doubt it,' David replied. 'The odd thing is, he wanted to be famous – and yet all that kind of work is anonymous. I remember when he earned his first fee for a photograph he had to tell everybody. Even his father. We were going to keep it from him in case he tried to borrow some of the money. You know what he was like about money. But in the end Paul had to tell him. He had to have people admire him. He liked to be told how clever he was. But if his name were known it wouldn't make him famous. It would only make him notorious.'

Mark sighed and stubbed his cigarette in the overflowing ashtray with unhappy vigour.

'Paul wanted to get on,' he said. 'He had ambition. Is that a fault?'

'Ambition isn't a duty,' David answered. 'Not even for a man who has talent. And I doubt Paul's.'

'There seems no use talking any more about it,' Mark said.

David, who had said so much, felt he had said nothing, but he was afraid of boring his brother if he said any more.

3

Mark went off to London but returned in time to attend the wedding of Mrs Marchbanks' daughter. It was Muriel who insisted David should bring his brother, and at the reception it was Mark who seemed the old friend of the family and David the stranger. He was sociable with everyone, thoroughly enjoying the company and the drink, and though David feared he was perhaps a bit loud now and again, even a bit off key, Mark himself was quite sure he was hitting the right note every time.

'Now don't stand in a corner blushing for me,' he whispered, as he passed David stuck alone in a corner with a glass in his hand wishing he was home again. 'Everybody thinks I'm just wonderful. I know what I'm doing, Davie. It's all a matter of being in character. I'm supposed to be the breezy man-of-the-world type, and the way I carry on helps you to keep in character as the lonely thoughtful type. And yet, God knows, I've been alone often enough, and maybe I've been thoughtful too sometimes.'

He squeezed his brother's arm and moved on to banter the bridesmaids again. He hadn't said if he had visited Paul in London and David didn't like to ask him.

Mrs Marchbanks came to his side, her eyes bright with uncertain tears and unaccustomed liquor, and murmured vaguely to him.

'Well, if she's going to marry at all she's better marrying now than when she's older. She's old enough, goodness knows. Some folk are saying it's a fine return to her mother, only a year or two since she took her degree and then she goes off and gets married. Oh, I know what they're thinking, though they don't dare come and say it to me. Silly people! I don't mind Muriel marrying. I wouldn't have minded even if she had married before she took her degree, though I'm glad she didn't.'

'A good education is never wasted,' said David, and then felt very conscious he was standing awkwardly in a corner offering platitudes while Mark moved around full of merry remarks and friendly witticisms. Mark was at ease among a crowd of strangers, while he himself was still stiff with an old friend.

'I'll miss her,' said Mrs Marchbanks. 'But for her company, not for her salary. I can keep myself, and Ian can keep Muriel. And if anything ever happens to him Muriel will always be able to earn her living. I don't mind at all. I only wish her father were still here to see her this day.'

It was the first time she had ever mentioned her husband to him, and he glanced sideways at her curiously. She wiped the corner of her eyes neatly with one finger and went off to have her glass refilled.

Muriel came along with her husband, a tall rugby-playing type and a civil engineer whose father was on the board of directors of an engineering firm. She was anxious for David to be quite sure he must be one of the first to visit them in their new house when they returned from their honeymoon, and the young engineer smiled benignly, showing a mouthful of good teeth, and nodded his head vigorously to italicize his wife's invitation.

It was a year later, after Mark was gone, that on one of his rare visits to Muriel he found Mrs Marchbanks there too. He had come in obedience to a special invitation, and he was aware of a tension in the room that warned him he was walking into something awkward. He became more ill at ease after an almost silent meal when the husband excused himself as they lingered at table over coffee and went to another room on the pretext that he had some drawings to finish.

'We didn't want to bring Ian into this just yet,' said Muriel, innocently admitting her husband had left them alone by previous arrangement.

'We want to talk to you first as old friends,' said Mrs Marchbanks. 'Ian agrees with every word we're going to say, but we thought you would take it better if it came from us alone.'

'If what came?' he asked, looking from one to the other suspiciously. He had a feeling that once again it was time to distrust everybody.

'First of all,' said Muriel, 'I should tell you something I don't enjoy telling you. But it may make you take the rest of it better. It may help you to understand.'

He waited. She was plainly embarrassed, and he believed the only way to treat embarrassed people was to leave them to find their own way out of their difficulty. So he waited, deliberately unhelpful.

'I've been told,' said Muriel, and moved a salt-cellar pointlessly, 'that I can't have any children. I've seen my doctor. I've seen a specialist. They tried to be nice about it. They wrapped it up well. But that's how it is, I'm afraid.'

He saw it coming before she went on. His nerves stiffened and his stomach turned over, his throat closed up.

'Let me adopt your child,' she said abruptly. 'Please.'

'She isn't my child,' he said, solely to divert her plea.

'We know all about that,' she said, almost impatiently. 'You registered her as your child when she was born. Don't quibble about it now.'

'I'm not quibbling,' he objected. 'If she were my child you would be paying me a compliment in wanting to adopt her. It would mean you thought a child of mine was good enough to take into your own house. The mother was all right. But what do you know of the father? What do any of us know? How can you be sure she won't turn out a liar, a thief, a bitch—'

He stopped. He remembered some people had thought her mother was just that, and he shuddered in a passing agony.

'How do you know what any child will turn out to be?' Mrs Marchbanks intervened. 'Don't talk silly, David. The best of parents might have a pretty worthless son. You drag in heredity as if it were all quite simple when you know perfectly well it isn't. A criminal grandparent might reappear in the child of a respectable, law-abiding couple.'

'If we went out to adopt a strange child we would have no idea of its heredity,' said Muriel. 'We could only go by what we could see. What do any couple know of the heredity of a child they adopt? And yet there are people adopting children every day of the week.'

He saw his stopgap argument thrust aside by their feminine directness, and muttered stubbornly: 'You don't know anything about the child's father. Nor do I. You couldn't be sure what bad streak is in her.'

'We know all we need to know about the father,' Muriel cried impulsively.

'We've always agreed to call her your child,' Mrs Marchbanks said gently. 'That's how you wanted it from the day she was born. Let's keep it that way.'

He looked from the daughter to the mother in dismay. They didn't believe him. They never had believed him. All they knew of Mary Ruthven was what he had told them. They didn't know when she went to London, nor when she came back. They knew he had been close to her for years and was often alone with her. They had only his word that a married man was responsible. To them, it was not only possible but certain that he was the child's father. Why else should he have done what he did? They had never cared to dispute his story, never held the truth against him, but at this moment of stress Muriel revealed their long-concealed belief just as clearly as if she had written it down for him.

'Apart altogether from the question of a bad streak in the father,' Muriel hurried on before he could argue the point, 'the fact remains the child is much more likely to turn out wrong if she stays with you than if she's brought up in a home where she can have a mother's care and affection – even a stepmother's.'

He glowered at her and she swept on boldly.

'We know the child. Mother and I know her well. We've seen her since she was a baby. We love her. Can't you understand what I feel? I'm going to adopt a child sooner or later if I can't have a child of my own. And it's your little girl I want. I can bring her up properly. You can't. Look at the trouble you give yourself. A woman never off your doorstep to help you to look after her. A good-enough woman, no doubt. But she's only doing a job. She's too old to care very much. And it will get worse as the child gets older. It's wrong. It's all wrong. A man in your position bringing up a little girl. And it will get more wrong the older she gets. The child needs a mother. And it isn't as if you'll ever marry.'

Her last words hurt him and he looked at her reproachfully.

'I don't mean no woman would have you,' she added so hastily that he was sure she had meant nothing else. 'I just mean you're not the marrying kind. If you had married before now that would have been the best answer. But you won't marry, you know that. And the child will never have a proper home if you don't give her up. What you're trying to do is wrong, and you know it's wrong.'

'I don't know it's wrong at all,' he protested. 'I made a promise—'

He stopped in confusion, remembering he had never made any promise. One had been ascribed to him, and he had accepted it, that was all.

'Whatever promise you made to Mary Ruthven,' said Mrs Marchbanks softly, 'will be fully kept, better kept than you're keeping it now, if you let Muriel adopt her child. What did you promise? What do you mean by promised? Surely all you could have meant was you would see the child was taken care of, given a good home, and some love and affection. What can you give her that will make up for a mother? Muriel is giving you the best chance you ever had of keeping whatever promise you made.'

He knew he had no answer. They were saying no more than he had often lain awake at night thinking. The girl needed a mother. He felt she was being neglected, looked neglected, and he was grateful to Muriel and her mother for not saying as much straight out.

'Give me time to think about it,' he said, and rose from the table.

Muriel rose too, and her mother, and they stood on either side of him and put their hands on him.

'Whatever you do, don't sulk on us,' said Mrs Marchbanks. 'Don't go away and not come back. We can still be friends.'

'You must agree,' said Muriel, nearly crying. 'You must. But even if you don't it won't make any difference. I'll still want to see you – and the child. But I'll think you're wrong, horribly wrong. Unfair to me and cruel to the child.'

'I think a little music might help us all,' said Mrs Marchbanks, and as always when he visited her or her daughter they dropped all conversation for an hour of music. It thawed him and sobered him. He seemed to see further and see clearer, and to understand the perspective of what he saw. He knew they were right. He agreed, but heavily, unwillingly, wondering if he had failed in his duty.

4

He found it was a relief to have the child off his hands. He saved money on it, and when he was ashamed of his meanness in even thinking of money he defended himself with the argument that he was earning about half of what Muriel's husband earned. It was a pleasure to them to have her. It had been a worry to him.

They told him he could see the child as often as he liked. He acknowledged the invitation, but he felt no great desire to accept it. He was back in his lonely rut, and everything seemed a dead end. Then a bright letter, postmarked Valparaiso, came from Mark. The six pages of elegant penmanship, full of interesting gossip, put some life into him. The very name of the place thrilled him, recalling an elusive odour of happiness.

Do you remember [Mark asked him] *a picture in our school reading book, I think it was facing a poem about a wet sheet and a flowing sea, called 'Off Valparaiso'? I don't know who the artist was. Well, here we are in Valparaiso after all these years! I'll be here for a week at least. Suits me if it's longer. I saw Paul again before my leave was up but when I said I had been drinking with you (cue for song, 'All through the night') he got very chilly. Maybe he was afraid of the old tag about* in vino veritas, omnia veritas. *I had a certain peculiar feeling he wouldn't mind if I didn't bother seeing him again.*

He didn't want to hear about Paul, but he wished Mark had told him more about Valparaiso. Repeating the oddly familiar name to himself he became restless to see someone, to go somewhere. He phoned Muriel and asked her could he come and see the child.

'I was expecting you long ago,' she said, and scolded him. 'Come round here just as soon as you can.'

He went over when he had a day off owing to him for working on a public holiday. The moment he crossed the threshold the child ran to

202

him, but Muriel wasn't jealous. She was wearing her spectacles all the time now, but not the ones with the legs in the form of a snake. He spoke to the child, he played with her, he took her walking round the back garden of the house, and they were soon on the same terms as they had been before he lost her. Slowly and rather timidly he formed the idea of taking her out for a longer walk, for a trip on the bus, for some kind of outing.

'I don't mind, but don't go too far,' said Muriel, and added, half joking and half warning, 'and bring her back!'

She put a hat and coat on the little girl, and looking at her he had to recognize she was better dressed, trimmer, smarter, and cleaner looking, than when she was with him.

'She looks quite pretty,' he said in surprise.

'She always looked pretty,' said Muriel. 'I suppose she takes after her mother.'

She had never seen Mary Ruthven, and she made the remark with the lilt of a question and yet seemed to keep it as a statement too. But the child's face was still too young, too soft, unformed, and baby-like for him to see in it the womanly face of Mary Ruthven.

'Where are we going?' the child asked. She seemed for a moment to be as much nervous as curious, and he patted her shoulder in a clumsy effort to reassure her.

'I don't know,' he said. 'I'll tell you when we get there. But you'll be back here for your tea.'

Once she understood she wasn't leaving her new mother for good the girl was eager to go, and he saw then the full force of the arguments Muriel and her mother had used. They were right. The child was happier in the care of a woman than ever she had been with him. She seemed less bewildered, she was livelier, more talkative and friendly. She chattered to him all the way on the bus till he almost wished she would shut up for a bit, or at least not ask her questions so loudly, especially when he wasn't sure of the answer to most of them.

He had intended only a short trip on the bus, a little walk, and then the bus straight back. But on the journey he remembered the bus would pass near the Botanic Gardens, and he thought it would be a pleasant outing for the child if they went through the park. She would see the strange plants in the hothouses and the goldfish in the ponds. Surely that would interest her.

As it turned out it interested him more. He had wandered forgetfully into the playground of his boyhood, and he found it all changed. The water he had once waded across to warn his brothers that avenging raiders were on the way was now fenced along the stretch of banking where it was most accessible. No other boy would ever do what he had done. The old cast-iron fountain and the metal drinking-cup, an offence to a more hygienic age, were gone. Even the grass was different, less green and less lush. And the handsome houses that had once overlooked the river were shabby and senile, clinging to a fallacious duration like a widowed and deserted old man who still clings to a world that finds him tedious.

Walking slowly in the afternoon sun to keep pace with the child, waiting patiently for her when she wandered away a little to pat a dog or to speak amicably to a stranger of her own age, he brooded over his maimed nature. He had a talent for hating. He had wasted years hating Paul, as once he had wasted years hating Mark. But he had no talent for loving people. Yet why had he hated Paul so much if not for what he had done or caused to be done to Mary Ruthven in that tawdry humiliation of the beauty of her body? And if he hated Paul for degrading Mary Ruthven it was only because he too, as much as Carter, loved and always had loved her. He put aside for ever the gigantic fraud of sex and rested on that other love, which expected nothing and gained nothing, but which served.

The child came running to him, hiding behind his legs from a dog that had come snuffling at her, a dog that was bigger and more frightening than any she had ever seen before. But it was held on a leash by a tall hard-faced woman who spoke to it crossly, yet managed to make it clear she thought the child was to blame for being in the park at all and for being alarmed at a superior form of life.

He sat down on a park bench, calming the awed girl till the woman and her dog were gone, and as he sat there a young mother came along the path, pushing a pram with a sleeping infant in it. Beside her walked a broad-shouldered, well-dressed man with a rather ugly face. He recognized Carter at once, though he hadn't seen him since Mary

Ruthven came back from London. Carter stopped and loomed over him with a smile and a hand held out. David stood up, shook hands, and was introduced. The young mother with the pram, a fresh-faced well-rounded woman with smart shoes, was Carter's wife and the sleeping infant was his second child.

'A boy to carry on the family name,' he said smiling, and his face looked quite different when he smiled. 'The first was a girl, so we had to try again, hadn't we, Margaret?'

He put his arm round her shoulder and pressed it affectionately, and Margaret pushed the pram forward and brought it back and pushed it forward and looked at him with eyes that were laughing while her tongue made reproachful sounds. She spoke with womanly ease and interest to the child, but asked no questions about her. Perhaps, he thought, they had seen him before he saw them and Carter had quickly warned her.

'We're living near the University now,' Carter said. 'I always wanted a house near the University. A good substantial house with plenty of space for a family. I never liked the new scheme houses. And we're handy for the park now. It's good for the children.'

'It's time I turned and got back home,' Margaret said. Her voice, like her face, was fresh and clear, neither pretentious nor common.

'I'm going on through the park,' Carter explained. 'Margaret just came out to keep me company part of the way. I want to cut over and visit the old shop. You know, the one you used to come to.'

'You must come and see us,' Margaret interrupted with such suddenness and emphasis that he almost believed she meant it. 'Harry often speaks of the Heylyn family, especially of you. You must come.'

'I wish he would, Margaret,' Carter said. 'I'd love to have him see our home, and the children. But I think he's a kind of hard person to get to come anywhere.'

'Have you ever asked him?' Margaret asked with a smile. 'Ask him now. You know the nights that suit us. Make it definite. Don't just say sometime. I always think a sometime invitation is a never-never invitation.'

She wheeled the pram round, smiled to the child on the bench, waved to them all, and went away. The sun went behind a cloud.

'She's going to be the image of her mother,' Carter said abruptly and sat down.

David looked from him to the child who had got tired of sitting on the bench and gone for a voyage of exploration round behind it. He wasn't sure how much Carter knew. He was never sure how much anyone knew – about anything.

'You remember the night I met you in the Chatton Bar?' Carter said very softly. 'All that was true. True at the time. But I got over it. Just as you said I would. I suppose the only person that couldn't see that was me. What cured me was that business with the married man. I couldn't understand how any woman could be so stupid. It was her stupidity cured me. I was cured even before I met Margaret.'

'Maybe she felt about him the way you once felt about her,' he suggested coldly, unwilling to leave her undefended.

'I suppose it was something like that,' Carter admitted readily. 'But there was a big difference. She could never have any future with him. I heard about him from Agnes Taylor. He had never had any intention of getting divorced. He had used that patter before, about his wife doesn't love him. A middle-aged sympathy-scrounger. There's plenty could have told her. I've often wondered why you didn't make her see sense.'

He dropped the topic as abruptly as he had lifted it, and when he had obeyed his wife's instruction and pinned David down to a precise evening to visit them, he went away.

It was time for him to go too. He took the child's hand, and as they walked along the bank of the river his mind was occupied with Carter's invitation. The more he thought of it, and remembered Carter's wife had been behind it, the more flattered he felt. He was prepared to believe he wasn't so maimed in solitude after all. He didn't live entirely in a world of shadows, vainly recalling Mary Ruthven and her mother – who had meant more to him in the end than his father had ever meant. He had Mrs Marchbanks and Muriel. Dr Tennant, who had told him that letting Muriel adopt the child was the wisest thing he had ever done, was still his friend. And now he had Carter and his wife. He had gained Mark, who more than made up for the loss of Paul. Mark's letters were not frequent, but they came often enough to make him feel he had a sincere correspondent. He could be worse off. He seldom thought of Paul, of the vanity of ambition without talent, and when he did he rejected Paul's talk of the man with a camera being the artist of the modern world, and all his theories about art, as bogus and question-begging. He believed he was silly ever to have listened to them respectfully. But he was too young then to know any better.

He was so busy with his own rambling thoughts that it was only slowly he became conscious of the child tugging at his hand and trying to tell him something. His mind had jumped from Paul to Menzies, and he was thinking of the rise of Menzies after the battle of the stone and his rude assault on Queenie Crawfurth, when the child's insistent voice and the pull of her hand reached him at last.

'Look! Look!'

She pointed with her free hand and said something in so excited a voice that he couldn't make it out. Instead of looking where she was pointing he bent and looked into her face. He was fascinated by the pitch of her childish voice and the incoherence of what she was saying. The life in her eyes distracted him altogether from the sense of her words, and he looked into them and marvelled at their depth. What world do they see, he wondered. What heaven lay about her? His silent steady gaze only confused the child and she became more distressed trying to make herself understood. She wanted to make him look at what she was trying to tell him about, not stand there staring at her. He raised his head and looked where she was pointing. He saw three swans glide indolently over the water, and the one in front veered and came near the bank. It came to him she had probably never seen a swan before, and he wanted her to learn words, to be able to put the right name to things.

'A swan,' he said, primly and precisely. 'A swan.'

'A swan,' repeated the child, careful with the sibilant.

She wriggled the hand he was holding and held out both hands towards the water as if she could grasp the swan from a distance.

'A swan is very graceful,' he said, walking after her as she went near the water. 'A swan is lovely.'

'Swan lovely,' the child said.

He looked at her as she clapped her hands at the proud creature. She had a lovely face. For the first time he felt his heart filled with affection for her. From the day she was born until Muriel Marchbanks adopted her she had been a worry and a burden to him. He was too busy fretting about taking care of her ever to feel fond of her. But now she was no longer his responsibility, now she was gone from him, he knew he loved her, just as he knew he loved her mother when she too was gone from him. He had a spasm of longing that the child could have been his. And what difference would that have made to that lovely face, he wondered. Would she have been prettier or uglier, or much the same? But if she were his child she would be another person. The past would have been different, which was impossible. Well, he would do the best he could, and this time things might work out better. The time to hate was gone. There was still a time to love.